MAGIC MADE

ASHLEY HAYES

Copyright © 2019 by Ashley Hayes

Printed in the United States of America.
All rights reserved.

Cover Design: Hampton Lamoureux
Editor/Interior Design: Maribeth Hayes

No part of this book may be reproduced, stored in a retrieval system, or transmitted in any form or by any electronic or mechanical means (including electronic, photocopy, and recording) without written permission from the author. The only exception is brief quotations in printed reviews.

This novel is a work of fiction. Names, characters, places, and events are products of the author's imagination. Any similarity of names to people living or dead is completely coincidental.

ISBN 978-1-09571-580-2

Dedicated to my family, friends, teachers, and classmates who are the inspiration behind the words and ideas in this book.

CHAPTER 1

Cole's shoes kicked up clouds of dust as he walked across the desert sand. The sun was just beginning to rise, but he needed to hurry. He needed to get to the market and then back to the mines before the morning bell rang—before anyone noticed he was missing.

Cole had been working at the mine for five years. If he stayed unnoticed and did his job, things weren't too bad. But if he didn't get back to the mines before the bell rang, Cole was guaranteed trouble.

For a brief second, he debated turning around. He could always try going to the market another day when he had more time, but his hunger was a sharp, familiar pain in his stomach, reminding him why he had decided to take this risk. Cole was given dinner every evening with his rent, but if he wanted any additional food, he had to pay extra. Unfortunately, Cole had already used up most of his money for this week, and he still had a few days left before he got his next paycheck. If he didn't go to the market now, he wouldn't be eating until dinner.

Making up his mind, Cole continued walking, this time at an even faster pace.

About a half mile away from the mine was the Rhomac market, where wealthy people came from Elysia and Nilrith to buy food or handmade items. Even though Cole never had enough money to buy anything at the market, years of hunger had taught him to steal what he needed.

Cole walked through the market quickly. Although it was still early in the morning, the space was already filled with energy. Eager merchants were standing under tents and stands, trying to sell their goods to wealthy visitors browsing the aisles. Cole could hear them calling out sales and prices, trying to entice anyone to buy their products. Everywhere Cole looked, there were delicious smells, music, and excitement. If Cole had more time and money, he would have stopped to enjoy the scene around him. Unfortunately, he didn't have either, and he needed to hurry.

He finally saw what he was looking for. Under one of the tents, a baker was selling a variety of different breads and pastries. Cole's mouth watered just looking at the bread. After a quick glance at the baker, Cole was certain he'd found the right person to steal from.

Since there were no military forces stationed in Rhomac, each person was given the right to carry out punishments themselves. The only requirement was that they catch the thief. Luckily, the baker looked old, and Cole had no doubt that he could outrun him. All he needed was a distraction. He browsed the stands nearby, keeping an eye on the baker's tent and waiting for another shopper to distract the baker.

Finally, another shopper took interest in the baker's tent and looked into purchasing some of the pastries for sale. While the baker and shopper talked, Cole slowly wandered over, waiting for the perfect moment.

The baker handed the woman a bag filled with bread, and she reached into her purse to find her money. At that moment, Cole grabbed a piece of bread off the table and ran.

The baker yelled after him, but Cole was already out of reach. He ran as fast as he could, turning down aisle after aisle at random. Finally, he stopped and looked around. The baker was nowhere near him. He grinned and took a big bite of the bread he had stolen. The outside crust crackled as he bit down on it, and it tasted every bit as good as he had hoped.

Cole took another big bite as he walked. He focused on the ground in front of him, trying not to get distracted by all the sights around him. He knew he didn't have much longer before the mines opened.

When he finally made it to the edge of the market, he froze. The baker he had stolen from was only a few feet away, and he looked furious.

Cole tried to turn back the way he had come, but before he could, the baker moved beside him and grabbed his shoulder. "Oh no, you don't," he said in a low voice. "You're not running away this time."

Cole's breath caught in his throat. He tried to free himself, but the baker was a lot stronger than Cole had first assumed, and his grip didn't loosen.

"If you don't want to get into any more trouble," the baker warned, "I suggest you come with me." Cole nodded, and the baker led him through the market, back toward his tent.

When they got there, the baker stopped and looked at Cole, who looked around quickly, trying to come up with some way to escape.

Finally, the baker said, "I want you to know thievery is something I will not tolerate—ever. Consider this your only warning." Cole relaxed slightly. At least it sounded like the baker would let him off easy. "However, I can understand being a little hungry every once in a while. How old are you?"

Cole answered this question with one of his own. "Why do you want to know?"

The baker watched Cole closely but didn't pressure him to answer his question. Instead, he just asked, "And you work at the mine, I'm guessing?"

Cole nodded.

"Terrible place, that mine. I've never approved of what they do there."

"Yeah, well, there aren't exactly many options around here," Cole said distractedly. "And if I don't get back soon, I'll be in trouble, so—"

"Wait a moment," the baker said quickly. "I wasn't finished yet. Luckily for you, I'm feeling generous today, so I'm prepared to offer you a deal."

That piqued Cole's interest.

"You miners have to sign a contract, right? To work for a certain amount of time?" Cole nodded. "When does your contract expire?"

Cole shrugged. He'd never paid attention to that before since he would just end up re-signing, anyway. "In a few weeks, I think."

The baker nodded. "Okay, here's my deal: You work at the mines until your term expires. During that time, you can visit anytime, and I'll give you some of whatever bread isn't selling. I'll be in town for a month. If your contract expires before I leave, you can come work for me until you pay back everything I've given you." He paused. "What do you think?"

Cole was speechless. He'd never dreamed something like this would end up happening to him. "Yes," he managed to spit out. "Yes, that would be great! Thanks!"

The baker grinned. "Good. That's settled. Here's a piece of bread for today." He handed Cole a roll. "Come back anytime you want."

Cole accepted the bread and grinned back. "Really, thanks so much. I—" Cole could barely hear the morning bell ringing in the distance. Cole's stomach dropped. "I have to go!" he said quickly. "Thanks again." He instantly took off running, shoving the roll of bread in his mouth as he ran.

CHAPTER 2

According to the legends, Lathinium had once been a round world, shaped like a sphere. But as time passed, the wealthier citizens wanted to completely separate themselves from the destitute beggars and thieves roaming the streets. Using new technology and revolutionary thinking, scientists found a way to create large floating disks above the surface world, which could only be accessed by airship.

The wealthy used their riches to build Elysia, a beautiful city on the highest floating disk, far away from the surface world. This city became so popular that two others were created just like it: Ambroise was reserved for military personnel, while Nilrith was for the middle-class citizens. Centuries later, the three cities had become home to almost all of Lathinium's citizens, except for those who were too poor to contribute.

Military patrols circulated throughout Nilrith and Elysia to ensure that any homeless citizens were deported to the surface, where they wouldn't be able to bother the wealthy. Most of those citizens had no choice but to brave the wilderness and create small villages far away from Lathinium. But about twenty years ago, General Sylvester, the head of Lathinium's military, proposed the perfect solution: instead of being left in the wilderness, the poor would be given their own city—Rhomac.

Rhomac was designed to be inescapable. It was a triangle, with two large canyons preventing anyone from leaving. The third side was blocked by a forest inhabited by monsters—and no one was brave enough to venture inside.

Once deported to Rhomac, citizens had two options: work or die.

Therefore, as an inhabitant of Rhomac, Cole had no choice but to work. Completely out of breath, he made it to the mine just as the bell finished ringing. He ran up to the check-in post to clock in and get his supplies for the day. Unfortunately, the mine driver guarding the check-in post today just happened to be Rubert.

When he recognized Cole, Rubert didn't even try to hide his grin. "Well, well, well," he said slowly. "It appears you're just a little too late. I suppose I'm going to have to punish you now. What a pity."

Cole rolled his eyes. "Come on," he protested. "You know it was only a few minutes."

Rubert's smile got even larger. "Talking back! That's another infraction."

Cole didn't argue; instead, he just looked at the ground and waited for Rubert to finish.

"Did you really think you could get away with that little stunt you pulled?" Cole didn't respond. That "stunt" had just been Cole stopping Rubert from beating one of the younger boys. Apparently Rubert still hadn't gotten over it yet. "I told you I'd find some way to make you pay, didn't I?"

"That was over three months ago," Cole pointed out. "Do you really not have anything better to do?"

Rubert laughed. "You have no idea how badly I've wanted this. You know I get to pick any punishment I want for you. But I'll give you a chance. Why don't you beg me to be nice and also apologize for what you did? Maybe I'll reconsider."

Cole ignored him and stared at a half-buried rock in the ground. He knew nothing he did would change Rubert's mind, and he was determined not to let Rubert have the satisfaction of seeing him beg.

Rubert seemed to realize Cole wasn't going to apologize. "Now it's time for your punishment," he said with a grin. He was silent for a while, and Cole figured he was just trying to decide on what punishment would be the most terrible.

Finally, Rubert declared, "I think . . . extra labor today. You will keep working after the bell rings. Continue until I come and get you. Also—" At this point, Rubert broke into another grin. "You will receive a beating after your work is completed."

Cole didn't say anything.

"Not so tough now, are you? Now get down into the mine. You're going to be working until you are begging for mercy."

Cole grabbed a pickaxe and a large bag, and Rubert told him his assigned tunnel.

Then Cole walked down the large, curving ramp, into the depths of the mines. The deeper he went, the darker and colder it was. Everywhere looked exactly the same: tall walls of rock surrounded him on all sides, and threatened to bury him. Cole kept his eyes on the dim lights hanging from the ceiling and used their light to find his assigned tunnel. Once he found it, Cole left the ramp and walked through the tunnel.

Near the end of the tunnel was an open cavern with more lights, and the other six boys in Cole's group who were already working. Cole could see patches of the glowing, white crystal decorating the cave. He found an unoccupied cluster of Anyrite and started working.

His job was simple: he needed to use the pickaxe to break up the rock wall and find as many Anyrite crystals as he could. By the end of the day, his bag needed to be completely full with those crystals.

"There you are. We were starting to wonder if you were gonna show up." Sean walked over to Cole and leaned against the wall. "Why did you get here so late?"

Cole didn't say anything at first. He didn't really want to tell any of the other boys about his encounter with the baker or the deal they had made. It still seemed too good to be true.

Sean, however, was not going to be ignored. "Well?" he prompted after a few seconds of silence.

"I got stuck at check-in," Cole said vaguely. "Rubert was on duty, and you know how he feels about me."

Sean laughed. "So I'm guessing you got a nice, easy punishment?" he asked sarcastically.

"Yeah, something like that."

Sean still leaned against the wall, acting like he didn't have a care in the world. "Don't you have work to do?" Cole asked. The last thing he needed was for Sean to start up a long discussion with him.

Sean shrugged. "I'll get it done later," he said calmly.

Cole tried not to be envious, but it was hard. Even though Sean got the same amount of work as he did, he always managed to finish his work so much earlier and even had time to do extra.

"By the way, I wouldn't worry about Rubert," Sean added. "He's just trying to get at you for that fight you guys had."

Cole snorted. "That's why I'm worried."

Sean shrugged. "Just stop picking fights. And maybe try just minding your own business instead of trying to help everyone. That just makes everyone mad at you."

Cole didn't say anything.

Sean just laughed. "Whatever. You don't need to take my advice. All I know is that I'm doing a lot better than you are, so you might want to eventually listen to me before it's too late." Sean walked off to bother someone else.

Cole just shook his head and kept working. In one more month, it wouldn't matter if he followed Sean's advice or not. He was getting out of here, and he was never coming back.

The bell rang, telling all the miners that the work day was half over. Sean and some of the other boys in Cole's group went to the mess hall for lunch. Cole wanted to join them, but he definitely didn't have enough money to buy anything.

Instead, he just decided to keep working. He heard a loud, raspy cough from behind him. A few minutes later, there was even more coughing, and it lasted even longer. After listening to the coughing for a while, Cole finally glanced behind him with concern.

Leo, another miner in Cole's group, coughed again. As he coughed, his whole body shook. Cole cringed. "You feeling okay?" Cole asked him.

Once Leo finally stopped coughing, he shrugged. "Sure," he said unconvincingly. "I don't know what's going on. It's like this cough just came out of nowhere, and—" He was interrupted by another coughing fit.

"Maybe you should see a doctor," Cole suggested. "That cough doesn't sound good, and it'll probably get worse before it gets better."

Leo laughed. "Sure," he said sarcastically. "Like I have the money for that."

Cole shrugged. "Well, you might not have a choice. If you've got something serious—"

"I'm fine," Leo insisted. "Really." Before Cole could say anything else, Leo turned back toward the wall and started working again.

Finally, the evening bell rang, and all the other miners in Cole's group left. Cole watched them leave, trying to ignore his fear. He knew Rubert was going to be ruthless.

Mise, one of the more even-tempered mine drivers, walked in to supervise him. Cole grabbed his pickaxe and started working. He didn't take any breaks. He couldn't. Rubert had been very clear when he said Cole needed to work for the entire time. If he stopped to take a break, he knew Mise would see, and his punishment time would be extended.

Cole forced himself to keep going, even though his muscles were already screaming for a rest. He worked robotically, too tired to even think.

Time passed slowly, but eventually Cole could hear another person coming down the tunnel. For the first time in his life, Cole was actually grateful when he saw Rubert. Panting heavily, he bent over his knees, trying to catch his breath. Rubert just looked at Cole and laughed. Cole looked over at Mise quickly and noticed that although Mise did nothing to stop Rubert, he also did not join the teasing.

"Are you tired?" Rubert taunted. "Maybe next time you won't be late to work." Once again, Cole stayed silent. "No response? Well, maybe I can force a response out of you."

Cole finally looked up to see that Rubert had brought a whip down with him. That was strange; normally all beatings took place publicly in the mess hall. It was good for "morale" among the miners. The fact that Rubert wanted to beat Cole down here was worrisome. Still, there was nothing Cole could do. He clenched his teeth and tried to prepare for what was going to happen next.

Cole knew Rubert had been waiting for an opportunity to punish him, but he hadn't realized Rubert was this angry.

As the whip made contact, Cole winced at first and clenched his teeth, refusing to cry out. The whip was light, and only stung a little at first. But the longer Cole refused to respond to Rubert's taunting, the harder Rubert swung the whip. Finally, the whip broke Cole's flesh, and he cried out in pain.

Rubert continued to beat Cole angrily. "Did you really think you could be late? Thought what you were doing was too important to come to work on time like the rest of us?" Again, Cole wouldn't respond.

Rubert swung the whip over and over. Cole groaned and arched his back sharply. "Too much of a coward to respond to me?"

Cole still refused to talk. Rubert's whip cut deeper, and Cole could feel his warm blood leaving through his wounds. After a few more minutes, Rubert gave up taunting him, and the beating stopped.

Rubert leaned down and growled in a low voice, "I don't care what kind of an act you are trying to pull here. You are a nobody."

At this point, Rubert grabbed Cole's shirt and held it tightly. "You own nothing. I have complete control over your life." At that moment, Rubert yanked on Cole's shirt and pulled the sleeve completely off.

"You can't do anything to stop me. You have no power. Your very life is dependent on us. You can try to leave," he said with a malicious smile, "but you know there is nothing else. Nowhere else to work, and no other way to survive."

For added measure, Rubert ripped another hole in his shirt. Then he leaned in even closer until Cole could smell his foul breath. "I could kill you right now. The mine doesn't need you," he said in a low voice. "You know there are plenty of other people lined up, desperate to work here. You'd be replaced before you even take your last breath. And if you did die, no one—not a single person here—would mourn for you."

Cole glared at Rubert. He wanted to argue with him and tell him about the baker, but he stayed silent. Rubert shoved Cole again and raised his whip. Cole tried to prepare for another beating, but none came. He looked up in time to see Mise talking quietly to Rubert. Afterwards, Rubert angrily stormed off.

Cole was safe for now. He laid down on the floor, too exhausted and sore to move. He closed his eyes, and his only thought was that he desperately wanted to sleep. Mise, however, had other plans.

He stood over Cole. "You're lucky I was here to stop him," he said finally. "Up. Now," he ordered. Cole moaned, but he did as he was told.

Mise had to practically drag Cole up the ramp and out of the mine. It was past time for the evening meal. Cole didn't even bother asking for dinner. Once out of the mine, Mise looked Cole over, probably assessing the damage Rubert had caused. When his eyes strayed to Cole's right arm, Mise's face suddenly became clouded with an unrecognizable emotion—uncertainty, or possibly fear.

"These the only clothes you have?" he asked gruffly.

"Yes, sir," Cole said quickly.

"Well, I couldn't care less about the state of your shirt—you deserve it. What were you thinking—taking on such a big hot head as Rubert? You must've known he'd have it out with you eventually. I swear you must be the stupidest person I've ever met!"

Cole knew Mise was right, but he was surprised when he continued. "You might wanna cover that marking, though." Mise pointed to the strange mark Cole had on his arm: a half-circle with a cross in the center.

Something in Mise's expression made him nervous. "Why?" Cole asked. "It's just some mark. I don't even know where it's from."

Mise shrugged. "Probably means nothing, but just to be sure. I don't know anything about it, but it's strange, and people don't like strange around here. I'll give you some wrappings to put on your back. Might wanna use them to hide your mark, too."

Mise entered the check-in post and came out with some old cloth strips, which he used to wrap Cole's wounds. Then he gave Cole an extra one for his arm and walked off, leaving Cole to stagger back to his room alone.

CHAPTER 3

Cole left the check-in post and walked back to the barracks. It was dark out, but he knew the way back by memory. He entered the barracks and walked down the long hallway until he found the room he shared with his group.

Cole entered his room quietly, making sure not to wake the other boys. He sat down on the edge of his bed, and stared through the small window. Cole couldn't see much of Rhomac, but what he saw was enough. It all was the same hot, dry desert.

As Cole looked out at his small, boring world, he felt something he hadn't felt in a very long time: hope. He was not going to die here. All he needed was to make it through the month, and then he would be free to do whatever he wanted, to go wherever he wanted.

"It's stunning, isn't it?" Cole heard a voice whisper to him. Gale, one of the miners in Cole's group, nodded toward the window. "There's a blue moon tonight. That doesn't happen very often."

"What are you talking about?" Cole asked, completely caught off guard.

"The moon," Gale said. "At least, I assumed that's what you were looking at."

Cole turned back to the window and looked up. He hadn't noticed the moon at all tonight. "It's huge."

Gale nodded. "Technically, it's the same size as it always is. But because it's closer to the horizon tonight, it creates an optical illusion."

"Oh." Cole wasn't sure how to respond to that. Gale had been working in the mines for less than a month, and this was the longest conversation they'd had to date. "I don't get it," he finally said. "You seem like you know a lot of stuff. How did you end up here?"

Gale shrugged. At first, he didn't say anything, and Cole wasn't sure he was going to answer. Finally, he said, "My parents owned a bookstore in Nilrith. It wasn't huge, but we did all right. I was doing really well in my classes. Actually, in a few years I was going to be accepted into University. Then . . . I don't know. I came home from school one day, and the whole bookstore had burned down. My parents were trapped inside. They didn't make it out in time. Everything was gone. I didn't have any living family to help me out, so I was flown here on an airship and forced to get a job here."

"That's rough," Cole said sympathetically.

Gale laughed. "Yeah, right," he said sarcastically. "I bet you've got a few sad stories of your own."

"None worth sharing," Cole answered vaguely.

"I'm not sure I believe that," Gale admitted. "But whatever. Oh, and before I forget—here." He threw a snack bar and bottled water at Cole.

Cole caught it in surprise. "What's that for?"

"Figured you wouldn't have time to get dinner, so I grabbed you something from the mess hall."

"I mean, why are you giving it to me?" Cole restated. "I know you haven't been here long, but you must have figured out by now that you can only afford to look after yourself."

"Oh, like you?" Gale said sarcastically.

"What's that supposed to mean?"

"You know what I'm talking about. I might have only been here a month, but trust me—it's been long enough to hear plenty of stories about you. You're practically a legend around here."

Cole laughed in disbelief. "For what?"

"Well, people talk about all the fights you get into with the mine drivers. I heard that a few months ago you actually stopped a mine driver from punishing some kid. I also heard it wasn't the first time you'd done something crazy like that. And I heard a rumor that the reason you're so dirt poor all the time is because you keep giving money away to help the kids who can't meet their quotas of Anyrite. And to top it all off, I know for a fact you've tried to help me out a few times, too—so consider this payback."

Cole wasn't sure what to say, mostly because everything Gale had said was accurate. "Thanks then, I guess." He unwrapped the bar, ate it quickly, and then took a long drink of the water.

"I do have to ask you something, though," Gale said a little hesitantly. "Why do you do stuff like that? I mean, pretty much everyone else here sticks to themselves. Like you said, you can only afford to pay for yourself."

Cole didn't say anything, but for a moment, an image flashed in his mind of an older boy screaming. He blinked and looked out the window. "It's none of your business," he said roughly.

He couldn't see the expression on Gale's face, but he assumed his silence meant he was going back to sleep.

After he finished eating, Cole turned his attention to concealing the mark on his upper arm.

"That's strange." Cole jumped, and then looked over at Gale. He was not asleep, but instead he stared at the mark on Cole's arm. "It looks like a burn. Bet there's a good story behind that."

"Not really. I don't remember how I got it," Cole admitted. He looked at it more closely. "I guess it could be a burn. Maybe. But I don't know where I would have gotten it."

"You know, I've seen that symbol before. I read about the written language used by people centuries ago. I'm pretty sure I saw that mark on your arm. The original meaning for the symbol was 'Survivor.'"

Cole fell backward on his bed and stared up at the ceiling. He could feel the springs in his bed poking through his mattress. He tried not to move in order to keep the wounds in his back from hurting any more than necessary.

"Well, I'll see you tomorrow," Cole finally said. "Thanks again for the snack."

"Sure," Gale said. "Thanks for your help at the mines. It's nice to know there's someone looking out for others."

Cole smiled and then felt a twinge of guilt. He considered telling Gale about the baker—and the offer the baker had made—but then he changed his mind. He couldn't feel bad about leaving. He didn't need to stay here. He'd done enough already. It was about time he moved on.

CHAPTER 4

Cole tossed around most of the night. No matter what position he chose, his back hurt terribly. When the sun finally started shining through the windows, Cole jumped out of bed and walked over to the mess hall for breakfast.

Cole joined the long line of miners waiting for their breakfast. When he got to the front of the line, he walked through the row of tables that offered different foods for varying prices. There were fresh fruits and delicious breakfast options, but all of the good food cost too much for Cole to afford.

Cole just decided to grab the cheapest meal offered: a bowl of oatmeal and a bottle of water. When the mine driver gave him the price, Cole reluctantly handed over the money. He took his food over to one of the tables and ate quickly.

Some of the miners sat in groups and talked. Cole noticed Gale sitting with some other boys in his group. Gale waved to him, but Cole just pretended to ignore him, and he sat in the corner by himself. He ate quickly and then hurried to wash his bowl and head to the mines. It was still early, and none of the other boys from his group were there yet, but Cole didn't mind. He walked up to the edge and stared into the huge mine. It was almost a perfect circle, going straight into the ground. As far as Cole knew, there was no bottom. At least, none of the miners had found one yet.

He experimentally moved his shoulders forward and back to see how badly his back still hurt. A sharp jolt of pain answered his question.

"Hey, Cole!" Sean called out from behind him. "Come on! We're heading down now." Cole turned. The rest of his group had already joined Sean, and they were standing near the check-in post. Cole grabbed his supplies and joined them.

After Cole reached the group, Damian told the group, "Today you are mining—"

"You're mining with us, you know." Sean interrupted him, sounding slightly irritated. Damian had been in their group for over a year, but he still managed to always act like he was better than them—something that drove Sean crazy, and he often let his feelings be known.

"Not for long," Damian said smugly.

Sean looked furious. "Oh, really?" he said angrily. "What's that supposed to mean?"

"Well, I'm not supposed to talk about it," Damian said conspiringly. "But I think they're gonna offer me a promotion soon."

That made Sean furious. "Yeah, right," he taunted.

Cole tried to calm Sean down. "Just forget about it."

"No," Sean said under his breath so only Cole could hear. "Look, I know he's just trying to act cool, but he does this all the time, and I'm tired of it."

"He's just trying to make you mad," Cole argued. "And you're falling for it. I mean, seriously—if anyone here would get a promotion, it would be you. And you know they don't give anyone a promotion until they've worked here for at least ten years."

"Tell him that." As Sean spoke his voice got louder. "I'm tired of him pretending to be better than us."

Damian smirked. "Maybe I am. I used to live in Nilrith. Went to school there and everything. Bet I'm smarter than you two combined."

"Well, that's not much of an achievement," Cole muttered.

Sean laughed.

Damian looked flustered, but he wasn't about to give up yet. "Well, at least both of my parents are still alive." For a split second, everyone froze.

Sean was the first to speak. In a low voice, he said, "At least my parents didn't throw me out, like yours."

Before anyone else could speak, Cole stepped between them. "Enough," he said firmly. "You're both being ridiculous. We need to start working." He looked at Damian. "Where are we supposed to be mining today?"

"In Tunnel 5D."

Sean groaned. The lower the level of elevation at the mine, the harder the labor. This was the deepest into the mine their squadron had ever been assigned, and Cole was dreading a day of extremely hard labor.

"I'll lead us there," Damian volunteered quickly.

Sean shook his head. "Maybe I should," he argued, trying to pick another fight.

Cole was getting irritated. "Nobody needs to lead anyone," he said in exasperation. "Everyone here knows where the tunnel is!"

Sean shrugged, "As long as Damian doesn't think that he's in charge."

Cole shook his head in disbelief but didn't comment further. They couldn't keep getting sidetracked. "Okay, since we're already behind schedule, we might as well get started."

The boys walked down the ramp and into the right tunnel. The air was musty and stale, and Cole could hear the mud squishing under his shoes.

Mise was already there, ready to supervise their work. The boys picked a spot in the tunnel and immediately got to work.

They hadn't been working for very long when Cole heard a loud thud. Everyone instantly stopped working. Cole looked around to see what had happened. Ryan was helping Leo stand up again.

"He just fell," Ryan said, with a hint of fear in his voice. "I think he fainted."

"I'm fine now," Leo argued. After he finished speaking, he had another long coughing spell. Cole noticed that this one lasted even longer.

Unfortunately, the commotion had already brought unwanted attention. "Get back to work, all of you," Mise said. "Except you," he added, pointing to Leo.

Leo shook his head. "I'm fine. I can work still. It's—" He was interrupted by another cough.

Mise shook his head. "You're sick," he said quietly. "And probably contagious. You have to go to the doctor or you can't come back to work. The last thing we need is another flu to spread."

"I can't afford to pay for the doctor," Leo said. "I used up my last paycheck, and I'm already in debt."

Mise left for a short while. When he returned, Mise had brought Rubert as well as Drender, the lead mine driver, with him.

"That's him," Mise pointed to Leo.

Rubert was the first to speak. "Maybe he's just being lazy. Kick him out and see if his tune changes."

Mise spoke in a cold, detached voice. "I'm not a doctor, but this boy's not tired; he's sick. He claims he can't pay to see a doctor, either." He looked at Drender. "Not sure what you wanna do."

"Obviously we should get rid of him," Rubert said. "It's not beneficial for us to keep him on if he's sick, and if we pay for his medical bill, we'll have all the miners expecting the same treatment."

"Well, what else do we do?" Mise said. "This boy's sick, and he's not getting better anytime soon."

Drender didn't respond.

"Please let me keep working," Leo begged. "I promise I'm okay. I can still fill my quota."

Drender finally made a decision. "We can't afford to keep you on if you're sick. Disease spreads quickly—the last thing we need is an epidemic. And we cannot afford to get any more behind than we already are."

"What are you saying?" Leo asked.

"You have two options," Drender said calmly. "Pay for the doctor's visit, get a clean bill of health, and come back in time to finish today's quota. If you don't, then you will be escorted off the site."

Cole risked another glance at Leo. There was no way Leo would able to do all that today, and everyone in the room knew it.

Cole tried not to think about it. He hacked at the wall with all his strength, hoping the throbbing pain in his back would distract him from Leo. But no matter how hard he worked, he couldn't stop thinking about it.

"I can't do that," Leo argued. "You know that."

Rubert grinned. "Then allow me to show you the way out."

"No, please," Leo begged. "I don't have anywhere else to work. I'll get better—"

Suddenly, another image flashed in Cole's mind—a memory so strong it made Cole feel actual pain. He worked harder, trying to clear it from his mind.

"Unless you can somehow see a doctor, pay for medicine, and finish your quota for today—"

With a loud, frustrated groan, Cole dropped his pickaxe to the floor and turned around. Before he could stop himself, he quickly blurted out, "I'll do it."

As soon as he said it, Cole realized the mistake he'd just made, but now it was too late. The room went completely silent, and everyone in the room turned to stare at him.

The silence lasted for a minute. "Why are you offering this?" Mise spoke in his usual low voice, but his tone seemed to carry a warning with it.

Cole looked at the ground. "That doesn't matter," he mumbled quickly. Then he looked up at Drender and crossed his arms, doing his best to look braver than he felt. "But if I do it, you give him a few days to get better."

Rubert grinned again. "Fine. But if you don't finish, then his income is cut off, and we get to punish you for being insolent. And if you mess up, even Mise won't be able to stop me this time."

Cole tried to ignore his fear. "Deal."

Drender took a little longer to decide. Finally, he nodded. "Very well." He looked at Rubert. "Get him to a doctor," he said, tilting his head toward Leo. "Give him any of the medicine he needs." He looked at Cole. "I think it's reasonable to assume the money will come from your account?"

Cole nodded, but he felt slightly nauseated thinking about how expensive the medicine would be.

After Leo nodded and thanked Cole, he walked out of the mines with Drender and Rubert. Cole could hear them talking about the deal, making bets on whether or not Cole would be able to win. From what Cole could hear, the bets were not in his favor.

CHAPTER 5

Cole immediately went back to work. He knew Rubert was hoping he would fail, and he was determined not to give him that satisfaction. He already regretted the decision he had made. But now it was too late, and he couldn't afford to fail.

Every time Cole lifted the pickaxe, the wounds on his back would open up slightly. That sharp sting, coupled with the steady throbbing in his muscles, made it nearly impossible for Cole to concentrate.

Sean didn't make it any easier. As soon as the mine drivers left, he stopped working and walked over to Cole. "What were you thinking? You've officially lost your mind," he said with confidence.

Cole laughed. "Did you just figure that out?"

"Seriously," Sean said. "Just yesterday, I told you that you needed to mind your own business, and today you just volunteered to do someone else's work. What is wrong with you?"

Cole didn't have time for this. "I don't know, okay?" he said angrily. As he spoke, he pounded the pickaxe into the wall harder and harder. "You're right—I should have just ignored it, let Leo be kicked out, and not have thought about the fact that he would die. That's what you do, right?"

Sean was speechless.

Cole wasn't done yet. He was tired of being lectured about this. "I should just look after myself and be okay watching the people around me die because that makes sense. Otherwise, I just end up getting beat up, or I get extra work, or who knows? Maybe soon I'll be the one dying. Then you'll just sit there and do nothing, right?"

Cole finally stopped swinging the pickaxe. He was angry with Sean, but mostly he was angry with himself because he knew Sean was right. If he wanted to live, he needed to be silent and just worry about himself. "The truth is, I can't," Cole admitted. "I can't just look the other way and ignore things like that."

"Why not?"

Cole tightened his grip on the pickaxe. "It's none of your business," he muttered, repeating what he had told Gale the day before.

"Whatever," Sean finally said. He walked off and went back to his own work.

Cole worked steadily, using his anger as energy. By the time the bell rang at noon, Cole had only filled half of Leo's bag. He paused and leaned his back against the wall, trying to catch his breath. All the other boys stopped mining and wandered around, enjoying their breaks. Cole wanted to rest, too, but he knew that in order to finish on time, he would need to work through the break. As tired as he was, he forced himself to keep standing.

He picked up his pickaxe and continued to hack away at the wall. The other boys' conversations slowly died down.

A few minutes later, some pieces of Anyrite fell into Cole's bag. He looked up to see Gale working beside him.

Soon after, the other boys in Cole's group joined him.

Sean sat watching them for a short while. "Fine," he finally muttered as he reluctantly got up and joined the others.

By the time the lunch break ended, their combined effort had filled Leo's bag.

"Thank you," Cole said quickly. Then he glanced at the second bag and took a deep breath. He had half a day left, and still one whole bag to fill. He tried to ignore the doubt that threatened to consume him. Somehow, he'd have to finish—he couldn't afford to fail.

Finally, Cole heard the evening bell ring. He sighed and bent over his knees, panting heavily. He looked at the two bags and couldn't help laughing in relief. Both bags were completely full. They had done it.

Cole followed the boys out of the mine, carrying his and Leo's pickaxes in one hand and one bag of Anyrite in the other. Cole handed his bag of Anyrite to the mine driver so the bag could be weighed.

The mine driver paid each boy the amount he had earned. Cole earned a good amount—enough to pay for his room at the barracks and dinner for the next week, with a good amount left over. He stared at the extra money longingly, imagining what he could buy with it. He badly needed a new shirt, and it wouldn't be long before he needed a new pair of shoes, too.

But he had promised to pay for Leo's medicine. The mine driver on duty knew the price for the medicine, and Cole reluctantly handed over all of his extra money. Even after he had given all of the extra money back, he had only paid back half of what the medicine cost.

While all of the other miners went on to eat at the mess hall, Cole trudged back down the ramp to grab Leo's supplies. Without all the usual commotion from the miners, Cole could hear even the faintest noises echoing through the tunnels. He walked quickly, eager to get out of the mines as soon as possible. He hauled Leo's heavy bag back to the mine entrance and put it on the scale. Cole stared at the number, finally allowing himself to relax. Leo's bag weighed enough. He had won the bet.

CHAPTER 6

Cole quickly walked toward the mess hall, eager to tell everyone else the news. He opened the door to the mess hall, expecting everyone to be busy either eating or waiting in line for their food.

Cole stopped and stared at the huge crowd of people standing near the center of the mess hall. That was the first clue something was wrong. No one was sitting, and even more strangely, everyone was whispering. Near the center of the crowd, Cole could hear someone shouting.

Cole noticed Damian, Sean, and Leo standing near the edge of the crowd, so he joined them. "You look better," he said to Leo.

Leo grinned. "I feel better. As long as I stay on the medicine, the doctor said I'm good to start working tomorrow.

Thanks for what you did." He paused for a moment, and his grin was replaced by a look of uncertainty. "I can pay you back for the medicine. I know how expensive it was—"

Cole shook his head. "No, it's fine." He knew Leo had nowhere near enough money to pay him back. Everyone seemed a little on edge. "So, what's going on here?"

"I don't know much, Cole," Sean said hesitantly. "But what I do know isn't good. General Sylvester is here, and he's unhappy with the amount we're mining. When we got here, he was already yelling at everyone else, and I don't think he's going to be done anytime soon."

Cole laughed. "Well, I'm gonna go get a better view of the action," he said. He weaved through the crowd of miners, working his way toward the center.

As he got closer, Cole was able to hear more of their conversation. Sean had been right. General Sylvester angrily claimed the miners were not collecting enough Anyrite to please him.

"I've already told you that I can't do that." This time, Cole recognized Drender's voice in the crowd. "This is a business, and working my miners harder isn't financially beneficial for me. Unless you were willing to pay more," he added quickly.

The general looked at Drender in astonishment. "Our set price stays."

"But the miners—"

"Do you honestly think I care about the lives of these filthy miners? I will sacrifice every miner in this room if that's what it takes! You know there's a surplus of workers lately, and every day more homeless people get deported from Nilrith. Our world is in the midst of a crisis, and my sources believe Anyrite is the key. I'm not asking you; I'm giving a direct order. Bring me more Anyrite, or I will show you the consequences of not meeting my demands."

"Now, that's just not fair," Drender argued. "I've got a business to run here, and you can't come in here and tell me how to do it."

"Really?" General Sylvester replied mockingly. "And what would happen to your so-called business if I stopped making demands?" He faced the crowd of miners and shouted, "What if I just decided not to buy any more Anyrite? What then? Because to me, it seems that you would all be out of a job." He looked back at Drender. "You need my business, and you can't afford to ignore my demands."

The look on Drender's face made it clear that the general was correct.

The general smiled. "Allow me to prove my power to you—to all of you," he said, turning toward the crowd. "You need to know who is really in charge here." He motioned to his guards. They pulled someone into the circle, toward the general. When Cole recognized who it was, he froze.

It was Gale.

"You can't do this," Drender protested. "Until his contract is up, that boy is the property of this mine."

The general laughed. "If you choose to interfere, I will cut all payments to the mine." He stared at Drender. "The choice is yours."

Drender stared back at General Sylvester for a while. Then he slowly nodded his head.

The general smiled. "Pleasure doing business with you," he said. Then he turned to his guards. "Tie him up there," he said as he gestured to the beating post located in the middle of the room.

The general pulled a whip from his belt and wrapped the thick cord around his hand. Then he gave a few quick, experimental flicks with his wrist. Every time the whip snapped, Cole held his breath, waiting for Gale to scream.

The general circled around Gale and addressed his audience. "You all mean nothing to me. You are merely a means to an end—my end. I need more Anyrite, and it is time you understood the cost of failure." He looked over the crowd. "I will never show mercy—never. And just in case any of you doubt me, here is a little *demonstration*." He grinned again.

The general raised his arm and quickly brought the whip down. Gale yelped and arched his back. The general pulled his arm back and prepared to strike again.

Cole watched silently, unable to look away. He saw the flick of the general's wrist, the thick cord rippling through the air and finally making contact with Gale's back. This time, Gale screamed from the pain.

Cole froze. That scream sounded too familiar. For a split second, a memory flashed in his mind of another time when he had seen the general's soldiers—a memory of another boy, screaming for help.

Gale screamed again.

Cole wanted to looked away, to block out the noise and pretend this wasn't happening. He reminded himself that in one month none of this would matter anymore. Besides, he couldn't really do anything—even Drender hadn't been able to stop this.

Despite all his arguments, he couldn't ignore the guilt threatening to consume him. It was too similar, too painful to watch. Gale screamed again, but for a moment, Cole thought he saw someone else instead.

In that instant, Cole knew he could not watch Gale die.

General Sylvester raised his whip. Cole watched the cord move through the air, and he heard Gale scream again as it struck his back.

"Stop!" It sounded more like a desperate plea than a command, but it was enough for the general to pause. The silence that followed was deafening. Cole locked eyes with Gale, but instead of looking grateful, Gale looked scared. Cole knew he shouldn't have said anything, but now it was too late; he had already gotten General Sylvester's attention.

One of the general's soldiers quickly grabbed Cole by the arm and roughly forced him to kneel on the ground.

General Sylvester looked at Cole with contempt. "You have the audacity to tell me to stop this punishment? Why?"

Cole raised his head to look at the general, but he didn't answer the question. Instead, he asked his own. "What has he done to deserve your punishment?"

The general laughed in contempt. "The only reason he is alive—the only reason all of you are alive—is because of me. If it weren't for our constant need for Anyrite, you would all be dead by now. I own your lives, and I have every right to take them away."

Cole stared intently at a smudge on the general's shoe. "If you actually believe you have that right," he said quietly, "then you're a fool."

The words were barely out of Cole's mouth before the general's fist connected with his jaw. Cole's head snapped backward, and his teeth clashed together violently. He gently felt his jaw with his hand, but there didn't seem to be any permanent damage.

"Take note of this," the general shouted at the miners watching. "See what happens when one of your kind decides to insult me." The general pointed to Cole. "For his insolence, this boy will be imprisoned and tortured until he is begging for mercy. And then when he has been broken, I will bring him before you again, and you will be able to watch him die."

Cole felt like the wind had been knocked out of him. He looked around at the audience, but most people avoided eye contact. If it hadn't been so serious, he would have laughed at the irony of it all. He had been so close to freedom a few seconds ago, and now he had never been farther from it.

"Take him," the general ordered his guards.

CHAPTER 7

Four guards surrounded Cole and forced him to his feet. They chained his wrists together with cold iron manacles and then did the same to his ankles. The restraints weren't necessary. Cole had no doubt any of the soldiers could knock him out with just one punch. The guards shoved Cole forward, and he nearly tripped over the heavy chains that bound him. He was led toward the platform where all of the airships going and coming to Rhomac docked.

Cole looked at the long flight of stairs in front of him with dread. The steps were steep, and with the chains on his ankles, he only managed to trip himself and fall. The guards laughed at him and then forced him to his feet again. After a few more painful attempts, Cole learned how to climb the stairs without tripping.

They finally made it to the top, and Cole was led down the long row of docked airships until the soldiers finally stopped. General Sylvester's airship was huge. The outside was decorated with bright green and gold trimmings, and everything about it looked expensive. Cole was forced to board the ship, and then the soldiers led him toward the back, where more stairs led to the hull of the ship. The guards didn't wait for Cole to walk down the stairs; instead, one of them pushed him, and Cole tumbled down the stairs.

Once again, the guards just laughed. Cole moaned and gritted his teeth, trying to ignore the sharp pain in his stomach and arms.

The guards forced Cole to his feet and led him down a narrow hallway. At the end was a large metal door, which one of the guards unlocked. Then someone shoved Cole inside, slamming the door behind him.

The cell had obviously held many prisoners before him. The room was completely dark, and there was a strong smell of decay, which made Cole's stomach queasy. He felt around in the dark, trying to get an idea of what the room looked like. The cell was very small, and the only furniture in the room was a bench along the wall opposite the door.

Cole laid down on the bench, trying to calm himself down. He didn't even allow himself to hope he would survive. The general had been very clear about that. He imagined himself a few days from now, begging the general to save his life but knowing his begging still wouldn't change anything. Just thinking about it made Cole sick.

He couldn't believe this was how he was going to die, especially not now when he had been so close to freedom. He remembered the baker's promise. Just a month more, and Cole would have been free. He was furious with himself. He could have had a chance at a future, and he'd thrown it all away.

Cole had no idea how much time had passed, but by now his hunger was constant. He laid on the bench for most of the time, sleeping whenever he could.

Finally, the door opened, and light filtered into the room. Cole's eyes took a second to adjust. When they did, he saw the general standing in the doorway.

"Stand up," the general ordered harshly. Cole clenched his teeth but did as he was told. The general walked over to him and forced Cole to look into his eyes.

"Tell me, boy. Was playing hero worth this?" Cole looked away, but he didn't answer. He knew his fate was sealed, so there was no point in trying to defend himself. He would not give the general the satisfaction.

The general nodded his head. "I see." He smiled maliciously. "Well, if you aren't willing to talk to me, then there really is no need for me to talk to you." The door opened, and two of the general's soldiers entered the room. They attached the chain on Cole's wrists to a strange contraption hanging from the ceiling.

As the guards wound up the contraption, the chain was slowly lifted into the air, forcing Cole's arms to follow. Eventually, the chain was wound so tight that Cole's arms were stretched straight above his head. Then they took the chain from around Cole's ankles and attached it to a loop anchor that was bolted to the ground, pulling the chain tight.

The contraption had Cole standing straight up, and there was no slack in either of the chains to let him relax. Even if he collapsed and was unable to stand, he would hang there, unable to move.

The general asked his question again, casually grabbing a whip from a nearby guard. "Well? Was playing hero worth it?" Again, Cole didn't respond. This time, though, his silence was met with the stinging pain of being hit by the whip. Cole screamed. His body subconsciously tried to jerk away from the whip, but the chains prevented him from moving.

Another lash from the whip struck him. This time, the wounds he had received yesterday from Rubert burst wide open, cutting even deeper into his back.

Cole couldn't tell how long the beating lasted. When the general finally left the room, Cole was hanging limply from the chains in the ceiling. His back was covered in gashes from the whip, and Cole could feel the warm blood—his blood—trickling down his back. His wrists were raw and bleeding from trying to escape the metal chains that held him in place.

It was pitch black in the cell, and Cole wasn't sure how much time passed. Eventually, a middle-aged woman came to visit him. When she saw Cole, barely conscious and bleeding everywhere, she gasped. She left and quickly returned with some towels and a small flask of water.

"Here," she said as she gently tilted the water flask, allowing him to drink from it. Cole took the water gratefully, gulping down as much of it as he could. Once the water was gone, the woman lifted the back of Cole's shredded shirt and placed the wet towels on his back. She tried her best to clean his wounds gently, but the pressure still stung and made Cole's back hurt even worse.

"Just give him what he wants, dear. You can't win here." She gave him a pitying smile. "You're so young—you have your whole life ahead of you. It would be a shame to waste it."

Cole watched her silently. What she didn't understand was there was nothing Cole could tell the general to make the pain any less.

The woman finished and began picking up her supplies. Cole didn't want her to leave yet. "Do you have anything I can eat?" he asked hoarsely.

Once again, the woman looked at him sadly. "I'm afraid not. The general ordered me not to give you any food. Now, if you'll excuse me, dear, I need to go," she said abruptly, turning away from him and closing the door, leaving Cole in the darkness once again.

CHAPTER 8

The door opened again, and Cole slowly raised his head to see who had entered. This time, it was one of the general's soldiers. Cole studied the man carefully. He was older, but still tall and muscular. If Cole had to guess, he would say the man was around forty. His most noticeable features were the two huge scars that crossed over his right cheek.

The soldier caught him staring. "Do you like these scars?" he said gruffly. "It should serve as a reminder of what can happen to you when you don't follow the general's orders. Although I'm sure you know all about that by now." The soldier leaned in and looked at Cole closely.

"I'll be straight with you: I'm here to talk." He shot Cole a grin. The words sounded a little too threatening, making Cole dread what the soldier had planned.

The soldier walked around Cole until he was directly behind him. Cole struggled to see what the soldier was doing, but the chains holding him in place made it impossible to see behind him.

Cole suddenly heard a loud banging noise. He clenched his teeth, trying his best to prepare himself for whatever was about to happen next.

To his surprise, however, all that followed the loud noise was a low whirring sound, like a chain being unwound. Suddenly, the chains holding Cole's arms loosened, and he immediately fell to the ground.

Cole rubbed his hands and fingers, which were numb from having been held up for so long. Then he gently moved the metal shackles up on his wrist, trying not to wince from the pain it caused his raw wrists. He carefully watched the soldier, who had now walked to the door of the small cell.

"I'm not going to free you, if that's what you're thinking," the soldier said, carefully watching Cole's facial expressions. "I'm here on the general's orders. He seems to think it's important to teach you a lesson." He chuckled to himself. "Can't see why, though. You just seem like a scrawny kid who ended up in a bad situation." He shook his head. "But obviously you can't be sane if you called the general a fool."

Cole's eyes narrowed, but he didn't say anything yet—not until he was sure why the man was here.

The soldier opened his bag and continued to talk. "Like I said, the general thinks it's important to teach you and all those miners a lesson. And I want to keep you alive. Lucky for you, I can be very convincing at times."

As Cole watched, the soldier sat down leisurely, pulled out some food, and began to eat. Cole stared ravenously at the food. He wasn't starving—not yet, anyway. But he was very hungry, and the soldier's simple meal of bread and cheese looked like a banquet to him.

The soldier took notice of Cole's stare and pulled out another loaf of bread, which he threw to Cole. This loaf was smaller and looked overcooked, but Cole was grateful to eat anything right now. He grabbed the food and devoured the loaf of bread as quickly as he could.

The man took longer to finish. When he was finally done eating, he spoke. In his low, gruff voice, he began by saying, "Name's Sarge. You already met my wife, Marylie. She's the one sent down here to clean up your wounds."

Cole nodded, but inwardly he was shocked that someone who seemed so nice would marry a man like him. He seemed just as mean as the other soldiers Cole had encountered.

"Marylie and I have been married for eighteen years now," Sarge continued. "We met at a party, and I fell for her instantly. We were married a few months later." He got a far-off look in his eyes. "That was before I joined the army. Before—" He cut himself off and looked to see if Cole had noticed. Cole had, but he wanted Sarge to continue, so he pretended he hadn't. Sarge didn't seem quite as intimidating now. But Cole still didn't trust him.

The soldier, attempting to change topics, said, "You got any girl special to you?"

Cole laughed in disbelief at that question. He was tempted to ask why any girl would ever show her face at the mine, but he remained silent.

"No, I guess not. Hmm..." Sarge was silent for a while, lost in thought. Cole didn't say anything, either. Noticing Cole's silence, Sarge finally asked, "Not much of a talker, are you?"

At this, Cole's glare returned. "I'm not in the habit of talking to the people who imprison me and torture me."

Sarge laughed. "Well, good to know the general hasn't taken the spunk out of you yet." He paused and stood there, considering Cole. "Although I guess it means you'll be suffering even longer, doesn't it?"

Cole looked away.

"I'm not gonna mess around, boy," Sarge continued in a serious tone. "You've made some dangerous enemies here. You embarrassed the general in front of the lowest men in all of Lathinium. You insulted his pride, and you questioned his courage. There is no reason for the general to keep you alive, and every reason for him to kill you. And he won't just kill you slowly—oh, no." Sarge looked Cole in the eye. "He's going to drag this out as long as possible, until you wish you were dead."

"Thanks for that optimistic outlook," Cole said sarcastically. "Is that all, or is there more you need to tell me?"

Sarge wasn't affected at all by Cole's hostile attitude. "I'm trying to help you, kid."

"Why?" Cole asked suspiciously. "Why do you care about what happens to me?"

"Just because I work for the general doesn't mean I'm evil." Cole snorted in disbelief. "Plus, you remind me of someone I used to know. I couldn't help that person then, but maybe I can help you." Sarge stared at Cole. "Give me one reason—any reason—to keep you alive. Something I can take back to the general and use to convince him to spare your life. Are you smart? Do you have any skills? Anything?"

Sarge looked expectantly at Cole, waiting for a response.

Cole was silent, not because he was trying to be annoying, but because he genuinely couldn't think of anything. He was just a poor miner in a world where wealth meant everything. There was no reason why the general would want to keep him alive. He looked away, acknowledging defeat.

Sarge sighed. "Well then, you really only have one option. You have to beg, apologize, and hope the general decides to spare you."

Cole scowled at the thought. "What's the use?" he said angrily. "The general promised he would bring me back to the mines after I begged for mercy, just so he could kill me in front of the miners."

Sarge nodded. "Sure, he said that, but all he wants is for you to suffer, and once you're dead, the suffering's over. I'll bet instead of killing you at the mines, he'll take you to Nilrith or something and make you his servant—"

"You mean *slave*," Cole argued angrily.

Sarge shrugged. "It's your only option. If you don't, you'll likely be dead in the next few days. And the general will make you suffer—trust me."

Cole glared at Sarge and said decidedly, "I'm never going to do that."

Sarge just stood up and shrugged his shoulders. "It's your life. Waste it if you want. I'm just laying out your options, trying to help you get perspective."

Cole noticed as Sarge looked down at the bandage on Cole's arm. Worried Sarge might somehow see through the wrapping to the symbol underneath, Cole quickly covered it with his hand. Cole knew he couldn't let the general see the mark. He remembered the reactions of both Mise and Gale and felt certain the general would recognize it.

"What happened to your arm?" Sarge narrowed his eyes. "It's wrapped like you injured it, but you use it just fine."

"None of your business," Cole said guardedly.

"You're a prisoner on my commanding general's ship. Of course it's my business," Sarge said sternly as he walked over toward Cole. Cole tried to scoot out of the way, but his ankles were still chained in place. Unable to move out of the way, he continued to shield his arm from Sarge's view.

"Please don't do this," Cole begged.

Sarge shook his head and began reaching into his pocket, looking for something. "I'm awfully sorry about this, kid, but I have to know what you're hiding under there. I wish there were another way—honestly, I do." He paused, trying to reassure Cole. "You seem like a good kid. Maybe I can talk to the general about keeping you alive."

With that, Sarge opened a small box and pulled out a small rag. Before Cole could move away, Sarge placed the rag over Cole's mouth, and Cole inhaled a sickly-sweet smell—it smelled like flowers. He desperately tried to fight Sarge and hold his breath, but it was pointless. Cole eventually had no choice but to breathe in the strange chemicals. It suddenly felt like the world was spinning around him. A few seconds later, Cole fell to the floor unconscious.

CHAPTER 9

"It's just like the drawing." Cole kept his eyes closed, trying to pretend he was still asleep.

"Yes. I can see that. Let me think now."

Cole's muscles tensed when someone suddenly grabbed his arm forcefully.

"We know you're awake. Might as well open your eyes." Cole slowly opened his eyes and looked around. He was still sitting where he had been before he went unconscious. The general held Cole's arm firmly and was staring at the mark, which had been completely uncovered. Cole tried to pull his arm away protectively.

"Oh, please," General Sylvester said with a mocking smile. "I've already seen your brand. There's no point in hiding it now." He studied Cole carefully. "How did you get this mark?"

Cole figured there was a specific answer the general was expecting to hear, but he had no idea what it was. Deciding to just be honest, he said in a hoarse voice, "I don't know. I can't remember anything about it. I've always assumed I was born with it." Cole purposely left out any mention of what Gale had told him.

The general's brow furrowed in confusion. "You don't remember anything about it?"

"No."

"Then why did you feel the need to conceal it?"

Cole amended his previous statement. "Well, I never thought about it until the night before you imprisoned me. Someone at the mines saw it and told me to keep it hidden."

With this admission, the general's interest increased. "What was this person's name? Did he say anything specific about the mark?"

Cole worried General Sylvester would go after Mise next. Cole had no desire to save Mise, or any of the mine drivers, but he also didn't want to cause any unnecessary problems for the only mine driver who had ever shown him a little bit of kindness.

"The mine driver's name was Rubert," he lied. "After he finished punishing me one night, he saw the mark. If he knew anything about it, he didn't tell me. He just said it was strange, and strange was another way of asking for death."

The general nodded to Sarge, who up until then had been standing quietly in the corner. Sarge took a step forward. "Yes, sir?"

"Lead a group of five soldiers to find Rubert. Invite him to stay with us for a while."

"And if he refuses to come?" Sarge asked with a frown.

"Now, I know you know the answer to that," he said in mock disappointment. "I need him alive, but other than that, do whatever you must. It is imperative we discover his role in all this."

Sarge cleared his face of all expression. "Yes, sir. I will begin immediately." With that, he saluted the general and left.

General Sylvester immediately turned his attention back to Cole. "Now then, I'm going to be blunt with you. You pose quite a problem for me. I want to kill you. You deserve to be punished after the disrespect you had for me."

At that moment, the general paused and pulled out his sword. Cole watched the general, beginning to panic. The general raised his sword above his head, and Cole closed his eyes. He held his breath, waiting for the general to use the sword. Instead, he heard the sword slice through the air beside him.

He looked up and saw the general, now pointing the sword at the ground. General Sylvester looked at Cole, seeming to be contemplating something.

Finally, the general said, "But I cannot kill you yet, as much as I would like to."

The general walked behind Cole to reach the crank, which adjusted the length of his chains. He turned it to the right, and the chains slowly tightened. Cole quickly got to his feet and raised his arms before the chain pulled him forcefully.

Once the chains were completely tightened, another soldier shoved a rag into Cole's mouth and tied it behind his head. Cole gagged from the stench. The rag smelled like it had been used on many other prisoners before him.

The soldier who had entered turned to leave, and Cole was once again left alone with the general. General Sylvester polished his sword. "You mean nothing to me. I don't even know your name. You are the lowest person in our world. I am the highest ranking general in Lathinium. Yet for some reason you thought you could challenge me? I obviously have to make you suffer—after all, letting you go could start a rebellion. Mercy is a sign of weakness, and I will not be seen as weak." Cole watched the general carefully, his heart beating frantically. He imagined a variety of different, torturous ways the general could kill him.

"But there is one problem," General Sylvester admitted. "You are much more important than I first thought." Cole looked up quickly in disbelief. He allowed himself to believe he might survive this after all.

"That mark on your arm makes you useful to me, and so I have decided to keep you alive for now." Cole sighed in relief.

The general continued, "Our ship will bring you to Ambroise, where you will be experimented on. You may just be the missing link I need to reach my objective. But to be sure, I will need you to pass one small test."

The general rubbed the broad side of his sword, and Cole held his breath, waiting anxiously. "Oh, don't worry," General Sylvester said, noticing Cole's fear. "I'm not going to stab you. No, this is Rubilac, and it is infused with Anyrite. One side," he said, grasping the hilt, "strengthens the user. The other side, which you will experience soon enough, is what scientists have named 'an Extractor.' It's original purpose was to remove the magic." The general laughed when he saw the look of surprise on Cole's face.

"Oh, yes," he said. "Magic was very real—once upon a time. Now, though, it has completely disappeared." He stared at Cole intently. "Or so we can assume."

He held up his sword. "Rubilac is powerful—too powerful, I'm afraid. Since the magic disappeared, no one has been able to survive an encounter with it."

The general raised the sword and paused momentarily. "I hope, for the sake of my theory, that you will be the exception."

With that, General Sylvester placed the broad side of the sword against Cole's back. At first, the coolness of the metal pressed up against his skin soothed his injuries. But instead of warming up from his body heat, the metal sword became even colder. Soon it was so cold that it actually burned his skin. Cole wanted to scream, but his mouth was moving slowly, and he couldn't get it to open.

The cold spread across Cole's body, taking away any warmth he had left. The coldness paralyzed him, making it harder to concentrate. His eyelids were heavy, and all he wanted to do was sleep. He closed his eyes, but then suddenly opened them back up again. He hadn't been this tired a few moments ago, and he had a feeling this urge to sleep wasn't natural—at least, he thought he hadn't been tired before. It was getting harder for him to remember anything.

Cole tried to fight the tiredness. He couldn't explain why, but he knew he needed to stay awake.

Suddenly, a burning sensation spread through Cole's body, along with a deep, never-ending pain coming from deep inside his heart. He couldn't breathe; he couldn't think. All he could do was scream and thrash as he tried to escape the sword. But the general held the sword firmly, and Cole couldn't escape. Cole let out another scream, and then his world went dark.

CHAPTER 10

Cole opened his eyes quickly. At first, he couldn't remember what had happened. Then memories came rushing back to him: the general, the punishments, and finally that sword. He remembered what the general had said—no one had ever managed to survive it since the magic had disappeared.

For a brief moment, Cole was glad he had survived. Then he remembered the general's plans for him.

There was no way he was going to let the general take him to Ambroise. He angrily remembered how General Sylvester had treated him. He remembered everything that had happened to him, all the pain he'd endured, simply because he'd embarrassed the general—because he stood up to the general and said it was wrong to kill an innocent person.

And now the general didn't even want to kill Cole. He wanted to take him to Ambroise and experiment on him, like an animal. The thought was terrifying. He imagined what Ambroise would look like—the prison, the clean laboratories, the sharp tools and instruments. He hadn't wanted to die, but now that seemed like a better option.

Suddenly, he noticed a strange feeling of warmth near his heart. The warm sensation spread throughout his body, growing in strength as it moved through his body. Cole remembered the burning feeling from the general's sword. This was similar, but gentler. Instead of hurting Cole, this feeling made him feel stronger. The warmth continued to spread. When it reached his feet, the whole room exploded. Pieces of wood flew everywhere, and the chains that bound Cole broke in half.

Cole knew he should have collapsed from exhaustion, but for some reason, he had never felt stronger. He stood there for a second, trying to understand what was happening. Then he heard the sound of footsteps above him and was reminded that he needed to hurry.

He needed to escape—and this might be his only chance.

The explosion had created a gaping hole in the side of the room. Cole moved to the edge and looked through the hole. It was night and the sky was quite dark, but Cole could still see lights shining from the platform.

Cole looked in the direction of the mine. He could see lights shining from the mess hall and guessed it must be around dinner time. Cole then looked past the mess hall, further into the darkness, toward the forest.

Rhomac was bordered on two sides by two large ravines, which were formed after the surface experienced an extremely strong earthquake. At the bottom of both ravines was a rushing river, making it impossible to cross. The third side of Rhomac was bordered by the forest. Everyone in Rhomac knew about the forest and the terrible monsters that lived there. Escaping Rhomac by foot was impossible, and entering the forest was a suicide mission. But waiting for the general to return was an even worse option.

Cole heard shouting and then footsteps stomping down the stairs above him. Suddenly, the prison door opened and the general's guards entered the room.

Cole didn't have time to think. He wasn't sure exactly what was going on, but he thought his sudden burst of energy and the feeling of warmth he had experienced throughout his whole body must have something to do with the magic the general had mentioned. In fact, it felt like the magic was inside of him, pulsing through his veins.

He had no idea where this feeling had come from, how to use it, or if he could rely on it. But for now, he knew it was there and hoped it would be enough to escape.

"Don't move—or we will shoot you!" shouted one of the guards angrily.

Cole froze and stared at the guard.

Suddenly, another soldier shouted from above, "Don't shoot to kill. General's orders."

Cole grinned with relief, and the guard looked nervous. Before the guard could say anything else, Cole jumped out of the airship and onto the supporting bars that held it up. The bars were smoother than he had thought, and he struggled to keep from slipping. His heart was beating frantically, but the magic strengthened him. Cole felt invincible. With a giant burst of strength, he lifted himself up and wrapped his arms and legs around the support beam.

He slid down the beam toward the center frame of the platform. He could hear the guards shouting above him, but knowing they couldn't kill him had taken away most of Cole's fear. He heard the sounds soon after. Bullets aiming for his arms and legs hit the metal frame and bounced off, but he knew one could hit him at any moment. The fear returned, urging Cole on and forcing him to climb even faster.

When he reached the center of the platform, he found a work ladder, which led to the ground. He jumped from the support bar and grabbed the ladder with both hands. He skipped as many rungs as he could, trying to get to the ground as quickly as possible.

Suddenly, there was a sharp burn in his right arm. He cried out in pain, involuntarily letting go of the ladder and falling to the ground. Cole hit the ground hard, banging his head in the process. His vision began to go black, and he blinked quickly, fighting to stay conscious. He forced himself to stand and then staggered toward the forest, moving as quickly as he could.

He could still hear the guards shouting, but he didn't look back to see where they were. He reached the mess hall and leaned against a wall outside while he waited to stop feeling dizzy. Cole could hear the laughter and noise of the miners after a long day of work.

For a split second, Cole actually missed his life at the mines, especially his interaction with the other miners.

As soon as his head had cleared, Cole began sprinting again. His only thought now was to get into the forest as quickly as possible. The pain in his arm was excruciating, but with the rush of adrenaline Cole was experiencing, he was able to ignore the pain enough to keep moving. The guards chasing him were now shining lights in Cole's direction. Cole knew he was running out of time—he had to move quickly.

Finally, Cole made it to the forest line. He glanced back quickly and saw almost twenty soldiers with guns in their hands, running toward him. He assumed the soldiers wouldn't follow him very far inside since the forest was so dangerous—at least, not until they received a direct order from the general.

Cole ran farther into the forest, taking cover within the trees and bushes. Because the forest was dark and eerily quiet, Cole knew any noise he made would be heard. He walked quickly, but with extreme caution, trying his hardest to remain quiet.

He continued on until he could no longer hear the soldiers rushing behind him—and only then did he slow down. The adrenaline was slowly wearing off, along with the extreme energy the magic had given him. He could now feel the pulsing pain in his arm and back, and every step he took was a struggle. He walked for what seemed like hours until he was completely and utterly lost. Even if he wanted to turn himself in, there was no way he could find his way out of the forest now.

Cole continued to walk until he came to a river. He gratefully fell to his knees and drank as much water as he could. It was a running river, and the water was cold and fresh. Now that he had a chance to rest, a wave of exhaustion washed over him.

Cole laid down by the river and looked up at the trees. The branches and leaves were thick, but he knew he could climb to the top and get a good view of his surroundings eventually. He just needed to rest a little first. After a few more seconds of silence, Cole finally allowed himself to close his eyes. Seconds later, he was asleep.

CHAPTER 11

Cole woke up suddenly, completely confused. He couldn't remember where he was or how he had gotten there. As he sat up and looked around, the events of last night came rushing back to him. Cole groaned and reached for his head in an attempt to calm his pounding headache. Upon moving his right arm, Cole experienced a sharp pain and realized the bullet was still embedded in his arm. He figured he'd deal with his arm in a minute; right now, he needed to think.

Cole tried to run through last night's events in more detail. He remembered running frantically, but he hadn't taken the time to keep track of where he was running. He remembered escaping the general's ship, running past the mess hall and into the forest. He remembered the way he had felt with the strange power running through him. Now he was almost certain it was magic, although he still didn't understand how. But the warm feeling of the magic coursing through him was now gone. It had served its purpose and left. Cole hoped it would show up again when he needed help, but honestly, he had no idea how it worked.

Now he was in the middle of the forest, completely lost—but at least he was free.

The first thing Cole needed to do was treat his injuries. He had no idea what lived in this forest, but if the legends regarding the forest were true, he had a feeling he'd need the use of both of his arms. He gently tried moving his arm but was met with a sharp pain. He tried again, but no matter what he did, he could not move it.

Cole curiously lifted his arm with his other hand. Upon letting go, he watched his arm drop to his side. His arm was completely limp.

Cole looked at the wound closely. He had been shot about two inches below the strange mark on his arm, and the bullet was lodged almost an inch into his arm.

Unsure of the best way to get the bullet out, he had no choice but to keep it in his arm for now. He hoped it could heal on its own as long as he managed to keep it clean.

Cole got up and walked back over to the river he had found last night. Then he kneeled down so that his right arm was nearest to the water and gently cleaned his arm with his other hand. The pain was excruciating and made Cole instantly feel nauseated. He clenched his teeth and tried to clean the wound as best as he could.

Once the blood on his arm was mostly gone, he ripped off a strip of his t-shirt to protect the injury. The wrapping was dirty, but Cole figured it was better than nothing. He used his teeth and other hand to wrap the strip around his wound and tie it in place.

Then Cole quickly cleaned his wrists, hands, and face. When he was calm enough to think, he looked at his arm once more.

With his injuries taken care of, Cole decided to assess his situation better. His wrists and ankles were still cuffed with the metal, but most of the chain part had broken off, allowing Cole to use his arms and legs freely. He briefly attempted to break the cuffs off, but whatever power he had used last night was completely gone.

He carefully looked around the forest. The trees were tall and formed a thick canopy above him that allowed some sunlight through, but not much. Cole guessed it was about noon. He had already wasted half the day.

He considered climbing one of the trees to get his bearings, but with his arm injured, climbing anything would be nearly impossible. Cole's stomach growled, and he briefly wondered how long it had been since his last meal. He tried to ignore his hunger and to think about something else. He'd never been in any forest before, so he wasn't really sure what to do. He decided it would be safer to just follow the river and hope he was going in the right direction. Hopefully, if he stayed near the river, he'd be able to eventually find something edible.

As he walked along the river, Cole listened carefully for any signs of danger, but the forest seemed completely peaceful, which was strange. Cole was certain the howling sounds he'd heard while sleeping in the barracks originated from the forest. He was convinced they were the sounds of dangerous animals. But now that he was in the forest, it seemed like paradise. The howls he'd heard at night had been replaced with the sounds of birds calling to each other.

Cole continued to wander along the river, noticing various berries and fruits on the bushes as he walked. Unsure if they were safe to eat, he just kept walking. It was humid out, and occasionally Cole would stop to cool his face with water from the river.

Eventually, he found a large bush with some fruits he remembered having seen at the market—a cluster of tiny, round, dark purple and blackish berries.

He'd never tried them before, but he had seen many other people eating them, so he figured they were safe. Cole carefully used his left hand to pick one of the berries, and he hesitantly tasted it. The berries were delicious, and Cole shoveled as many mouthfuls as he could into his mouth.

Once he was full, Cole continued walking through the forest. It was getting darker out, which made it difficult for him to see where he was going. Cole eventually just stopped and sat down against a nearby tree. He closed his eyes and listened to the sounds around him. The river gurgled as it flowed past, and in the treetops, he could hear the birds still singing. Cole actually smiled.

As he drifted off to sleep, he reminded himself that he was almost out of the general's reach for good. Once he was far enough away, everything would be perfect.

Cole abruptly woke to the feeling of water on his face. He was soaked and shivering from the cold wind. He groggily glanced around. It was still dark out, but rain was falling down on his face, making it impossible for Cole to fall back asleep. At first, Cole refused to move, hoping he would be able to ignore the rain enough to go back to sleep, but the rain was starting to fall even harder.

Cole finally got to his feet and began to look around for shelter. There were trees nearby, but despite the leaves above him, the ground below was soaking wet.

He stumbled around with only the light of the moon to see by. Even though there was a full moon tonight, the canopy of the trees only allowed a small amount of light through. The further Cole went from the river, the darker the forest seemed to get.

Unable to see clearly in the darkness, Cole unexpectedly stumbled over a tree root and rolled painfully down a hill. Cole sat up quickly and struggled to see his new surroundings in the dark. The rain was falling faster, and Cole was shivering.

Finally, Cole saw it: not too far away from where he had fallen was a tree hollow.

Cole made his way to the tree, stumbling over multiple tree roots along the way. When he reached the tree, he could tell it was large enough for him to fit inside. Cole stood outside for a few more seconds. He assumed the feeling was because it was late at night and he was tired, but he couldn't shake his uneasiness.

"It's nothing." Cole spoke out loud for the first time since he'd entered the forest, hoping the noise would calm him. He had seen no dangers in the forest thus far, and he didn't see how this tree would be any different.

Angry at himself for being paranoid, Cole decided there was nothing to worry about. Still, he paused briefly before entering the tree hollow. By this time, Cole was soaking wet, and the rain was coming down faster by the minute.

Before Cole could second guess himself, he forced himself to enter the tree.

Once inside, Cole didn't see anything unusual, and he couldn't help laughing at himself. He had no idea why he had been so worried. The tree itself was small, only about three feet in diameter. Cole sat down, leaning against the side of the tree opposite the entrance. The tree was warm inside and sheltered Cole from the wind. He watched the rain falling outside his tree until he finally fell asleep.

CHAPTER 12

When Cole woke up the next morning, the rain had slowed to a light drizzle, so he decided to start journeying again. As he took in his surroundings, he began to realized that he had no idea where he was.

His first priority was to find the river. He needed a water source—and soon. Not only that, but his arm was beginning to hurt again. He quickly peeked under his makeshift bandages and saw his bullet wound was already starting to look infected. He put the bandages back and tried to ignore the pain in his arm. If the wound was infected, there was nothing he would be able to do for it.

Cole wandered around the forest, trying to get his bearings. After a few hours of wandering, Cole realized how strange this part of the forest was. The trees were thicker and blocked out more of the sun, and it was completely silent. Cole suddenly realized he hadn't heard or seen a single bird or animal since he had left his tree that morning. He wandered on, completely directionless.

Cole was sure his infected arm was getting worse, and he knew he probably had a slight fever as well. His only goal was to find water. By now he was drenched in sweat, although Cole wasn't sure if that was from the weather or his fever.

His only thought was to keep walking. Then he saw a thick, steady fog moving toward him. When the fog reached him, it made his feet feel very cold and wet. Cole watched the fog around him grow until it was too thick for him to see through.

Cole tried to turn around and go back the way he had come, but he could no longer see where he was going. He stumbled along blindly for a time. Suddenly, he walked into something large and sticky. Cole's arms and legs were covered in silky, sticky strings. Cole struggled, trying to free himself, but every movement he made only entangled him more.

At that moment, Cole began to hear strange noises. The sounds were faint, but it sounded like multiple small feet walking toward him. With a sickening feeling, Cole suddenly realized what he was stuck to. He had seen a few small spiders in Rhomac, but he had heard legends of larger spiders created by scientists and placed in the forest. He thought they were only stories meant to scare children. Besides, it had seemed impossible to him that any living creature could be created by scientists. But now it seemed that this "story" was going to eat him alive.

Cole struggled even harder to free himself from the giant spider web. The sound of the feet was getting louder as the spider drew closer. There was no way Cole could escape. Just as the spider was about to reach him, Cole was suddenly grabbed at the waist and pulled out of the web. Cole tried to focus on the new threat he was facing. Although it was still dark and foggy, he was able to see well enough to be able to tell what was carrying him.

Cole immediately wished that he had never seen the frightening sight that met his eyes.

He was being carried sideways in the jaws of a giant ant that was at least three times his size. He wriggled and tried to escape the ant's grasp, but that just made its hold tighten. He assumed the ant and spider had been created the same way. In fact, he assumed that they had been part of the same science experiment. But he still didn't understand why they were in the forest or why they had been created in the first place. Not that it mattered—Cole had no doubt these giant creatures intended to eat him.

Cole watched as the ant carried him forward and then down into a tunnel. At first, Cole tried his best to keep track of all the twists and turns, but there were so many that he quickly gave up. The tunnel walls were smooth and almost perfectly round. The only thing he could hear was the thousands of feet scurrying around.

The longer Cole was in the cave, the more ants he saw scurrying around—and the more impossible escaping seemed.

Suddenly, Cole had an idea: the magic. It had saved Cole the last time he was in trouble.

The only problem was that Cole had no idea how to call on the magic. He tried to summon the strange warm feeling the magic had given him before, but all he felt was a distinct emptiness the magic should have filled.

Cole knew he was running out of time. "Come on," he muttered to himself. An explosion would be nice right about now—or anything other than being eaten.

Eventually, the ant dropped Cole in a large cave. By now Cole had lost any sense of direction. He looked around the cave in awe as the other ants quickly surrounded him. The ant had dropped him in a large cavern. The floor was covered in piles of jewels, other treasures, and more gold than Cole had known existed in the whole world.

His eyes swept across the scene, landing finally on a huge ant lying near the back of the room. She was almost twice the size of the ant that had carried Cole. He knew instantly that she must be their queen. All the ants stopped moving.

He couldn't help but feel as though they were waiting to see what Cole did.

He took a step back in fear and heard a sickening crunch under his shoes. Cole's looked down and realized the cave floor was littered with bones. They looked like they had been there for a while, and Cole feared it wouldn't be long before his bones joined the ones below him.

The ants moved closer to Cole, forcing him to back up. He tried to stay where he was, but one of the broken chains on his ankles got caught on something and he stumbled, falling right on top of a pile of bones. He quickly got to his feet, but in the process he noticed a sword lying nearby.

It was beautiful and still looked brand new. Cole quickly grabbed the sword with his left hand, silently hoping the sword would serve him better than it had served its previous owner. Cole had never used a sword before, and without his right arm to help him, he knew it wouldn't be easy, but the weapon gave him a little more confidence.

Cole was now only a few feet away from the queen ant. He tried to summon the magic one more time, but it was useless. The magic wasn't coming to his rescue.

Determined to go down bravely, Cole lashed out with his sword. He managed to scrape one of the ants, causing it to jump back in shock. With a cry, the ants advanced and made a tighter circle around him.

Cole was now beside the queen. He again raised the sword, but this time he faced the queen. Using all his strength, he speared the queen, pushing on the sword until part of the sword showed through to the other side. The queen made an ear-piercing shriek, forcing Cole to cover his ears quickly.

The queen's shriek caused the tunnel walls to weaken and begin to collapse. Cole pulled the sword out of the queen ant's body and ran as fast as he could through the tunnels. Once the other ants realized what had happened, they angrily chased him, desperate to defend their fallen leader.

Cole sprinted as fast as he could, dodging falling rocks as he ran. He didn't know the way out, but when he came to a turn, he always chose the path that led uphill. He kept running, and he finally saw the way out. The ants were still close behind him, but their large size made it harder for them to dodge the falling rocks, and many of them were crushed. Cole jumped at the last second and barely made it through the exit. He lay on the ground, gasping for air as he watched the rest of the tunnel fall around him.

Cole wanted nothing more than to just lie there and take a nap. His arm was throbbing, his mind was clouded and disoriented, and he was freezing—even though it was hot outside and he had just finished running.

But before he could even catch his breath, the ants burst through the ruins of their cave. With the queen dead, all the ants were angry and confused. When they saw Cole, they charged at him, moving as fast as they were able.

Cole quickly got to his feet and began running as fast as he could. As he ran, he noticed his vision beginning to blur. It was subtle, and hard to notice at first, but Cole was certain. The fever and the infection were seriously affecting him, and he didn't know how much longer he could keep going. He only had two coherent thoughts: to keep his grip on his sword and to get away from the ants.

Cole was running out of energy and time. Suddenly, he saw a hill. As much as Cole dreaded the idea of climbing it, he remembered he had fallen down a similar hill the night before. Cole hoped that by climbing this hill, he would find the river again and find a way to escape the ants. The hill was steep, and covered in wet leaves and dirt. He struggled up the hill as fast as he could without slipping in the mud. The ants were much faster and quickly gained on Cole. Finally, Cole made it to the top. The other side was almost completely flat, and Cole was able to move much faster.

He glanced behind him and watched one of the ants make it to the top. Then the ant was suddenly repelled backward by an invisible force. The ant angrily shrieked and tried to attack Cole again, but no matter how much the ants tried, they were unable to move any closer to him. Cole watched, transfixed and unable to comprehend what was going on.

The ants piled up on top of each other and swarmed in front of Cole, desperately trying to reach him, but after a few minutes, they started to give up. Soon, the pile had been reduced to a few frustrated stragglers.

Cole was safe.

Cole sighed in relief and wiped the sweat off his forehead. As his breathing returned to normal, he listened to the birds chirping around him. Once he was certain he was in no immediate danger, he laid down on the grass floor.

Suddenly overcome by a wave of exhaustion, he involuntarily closed his eyes. Before he even realized what was happening, he was asleep.

CHAPTER 13

Cole's body jerked as he became conscious again. He opened his eyes and looked around, taking in his new surroundings. He was lying on a sleeper sofa inside a small house, which was much cooler than the weather outside.

His bed was in the living room, which was adjoined to a small, orderly kitchen. Right now, it looked like the house was empty. Cole attempted to sit up, but he didn't have enough strength. His arm was still pulsing with pain, and he couldn't move himself without sending a wave of pain through his body.

Giving up on trying to move, Cole stared up at the ceiling, trying to stay as still as possible. He was exhausted, but his fear of the unknown was keeping him awake. He wasn't sure where he was, and he worried the general would find him. To make matters worse, Cole's mind was clouded, and he could still feel the effects of his fever.

Eventually, the front door opened, and Cole saw a tall, slim girl who looked to be about his age. She was wearing a loose, white tank top and jean shorts and had a light green button-up shirt tied at her waist. Her hair was tied back in a messy bun, with a few strands of hair resting in front of her eyes.

Cole stared at her, trying to figure out whether or not she was a threat. He had never interacted with a girl his age before. All of the miners were men, and although he had seen some girls at the market, he had never actually had a conversation with one.

The girl looked over at Cole. When she noticed he was awake, she looked relieved. She smiled at him, but that made Cole even more nervous.

"Oh, good! You're awake," she said excitedly. "For a while I was worried you wouldn't make it. That infection you had in your arm was terrible, and without treatment it would have spread. I don't think you would have lasted more than another day on your own."

Cole was still guarded. This girl seemed too good to be true. And it was too convenient that she'd shown up just in time to help him.

"Where am I?" he managed to croak. He hadn't realized how dry and sore his voice was, and he angrily thought about how weak he must look to this girl. He tried again to sit up, but he just ended up wincing and falling back down. He was so tired, and he struggled to even keep his eyes open.

"Be quiet," she ordered. She seemed to know what she was doing, but Cole was still annoyed that she was so comfortable ordering him around. The girl propped up some pillows behind him and helped him sit up. She then grabbed a bowl from the kitchen and sat down beside him on the bed so that she could spoon-feed him some soup.

Cole was frustrated this girl didn't think he could feed himself. She didn't even let him try. At first, he considered resisting the food, just to prove a point, but as soon as he tasted the stew, he realized how hungry he really was. He continued to allow her to feed him, eating as much of the stew as he could.

After eating, Cole looked down at his arm and grimaced. The wound was now the size of his fist. It was red and obviously still infected. Just looking at it made Cole pale.

The girl, however, didn't seem very bothered by the sight. She stayed calm, and when she noticed Cole looking at his arm, she said, "Don't worry about it. I can fix your arm. Soon you won't even be able to tell you were hurt. My name's Aria, by the way. I was outside when I saw you on the other side of the river, and I brought you here. That was two days ago, though." She paused, waiting for his reaction.

Cole was shocked. He struggled to remember any sense of time passing, but he couldn't remember anything after he had escaped the giant ants.

Aria continued, "You were just lying there, so I came over to see if you were okay, but then I saw the blood and realized you were injured." She grimaced slightly. "I managed to drag you here, but you were really heavy."

Cole was skeptical. "How did you get me across the river by yourself?"

"I'm stronger than I look," Aria said. Then she admitted with a laugh, "There's a point not too far from where you were lying, where the river becomes really shallow and slow. I got you onto a sled and dragged you across. That was the easy part. Then I had to get you inside, unfold the bed from the couch, and get you onto it. I found some old metal clippers from our barn and cut the chains off of your wrists and ankles. Then I got that bullet out of your arm." She waited, looking at Cole.

It was obvious Aria wanted some kind of thanks, but Cole pretended to ignore her. He shifted in the bed, accidentally moving his right arm. Suddenly, he felt a wave of pain so strong that he thought he was going to be sick.

Instead of feeling sorry for him, Aria just rolled her eyes. "I already told you not to move," she reminded him.

Aria got up and quickly rinsed the bowl out in the sink. After she had finished, she looked over at him.

"What's your name?"

"Cole."

"Okay, Cole," Aria said. "I'll be right back. Don't move—I mean it."

With one final glare, she walked down a hallway. She returned a few seconds later with a handful of cloths and a bottle filled with some clear liquid.

"I need to clean and dress your wound. The infection was really bad, but I tried to do what I could while you were sleeping. At least you already look a lot better than you did the other day."

Cole looked at his arm again. "If this is better, I don't want to know how bad it looked yesterday."

Aria laughed. "No, you don't," she agreed. Then she began laying out the things she had brought into the room. "You will need to stay still for this," she warned, looking down at Cole. "It's really going to hurt, but I promise I know what I'm doing."

Cole watched as Aria expertly took one of the cloths and soaked it in water. "Okay," Aria said, folding up the wet rag. "Now, open your mouth."

Instead of listening, Cole skeptically asked, "Do you know what you're doing?"

Aria laughed. "Oh, sure," she said sarcastically. "I take care of injured strangers practically every other week."

"That's not comforting."

Aria shrugged. "My dad used to be a doctor, and I've read about stuff like this before, so it should be fine. Besides, you don't really have any other options."

Cole didn't say anything, but he knew she was right.

"Now, open your mouth."

Finally, Cole agreed, and Aria quickly shoved the wet cloth in his mouth.

"If the pain gets unbearable, just bite down on that rag. It will keep you from biting off your tongue." When Cole looked at her nervously, she smirked. "Don't worry—this needs to be done. Your arm is still infected. So far, I've only been able to keep the infection from spreading. This should help get rid of the infection completely."

Aria then grabbed another cloth and poured a strange liquid onto it. The smell was very strong, and Cole instantly knew it wasn't water. When Aria noticed his curious expression, she explained, "This is an antibacterial liquid that's used a lot in Nilrith. It'll eliminate the infection and help your wound to heal, but it's also going to burn," she warned. With that, Aria gently lifted his limp arm and wrapped it with the soaked cloth.

Cole was glad for the rag in his mouth. Without it, he would have screamed. His arm felt like it was burning—he tried to jerk it away, but Aria held the rag firmly. "This will hurt less if you stay still. Stop moving!" Cole forced himself to stop moving, trying his best to ignore the pain. He bit on the rag as hard as he could until the intense pain subsided to a dull burning sensation.

After a few minutes of torture, Aria gently removed the rag from his arm. She went to the kitchen and returned with yet another bottle. This bottle contained a strange, gel-like substance. Aria squeezed the bottle and carefully applied the gel to Cole's wound.

She then picked up another cloth and tore it into strips, which she then used to wrap Cole's arm. "There!" she said triumphantly.

Coal moaned. Aria reached over to feel Cole's forehead with one hand, while nervously rubbing her necklace with the other.

She frowned. "You still have a fever, but it seems much lower than it was earlier. It should be completely gone by tomorrow. You'll feel better then, but it may still take days for your arm to completely heal from the infection. You will need to rest as much as possible. You are more than welcome to stay here as long as you need, but I do have one request."

Aria grimaced slightly, looking down at Cole's clothes. "You've got to change into some clean clothes right away."

Cole attempted to disagree with her—his clothes were fine—but he still had the rag in his mouth. All his arguing just ended up being grunting noises. Aria laughed again and removed the rag from his mouth. "Maybe I should leave it there. You are much more enjoyable when you aren't talking, you know."

Cole scowled at her. "What else am I gonna wear?" he argued. "I don't exactly fit in your clothes."

"Really?" she asked in mock surprise. More seriously, she added, "My dad probably has an extra shirt that will work. I'll go grab that now. Don't move," she ordered.

When she came back, she held up the shirt for Cole to see. It looked too big, but at least it was better than what he had on right now. He reached out with his good hand for the shirt, but Aria held it captive. "No way," she said. "Your arm is still way too sore. I'm gonna have to help you."

Cole wasn't too happy about that idea. "I can do it myself." He tried to move his arm, but the pain was so bad that his vision went slightly black, and he gritted his teeth together.

Aria looked furious. "What's your problem?" she asked furiously. "Your arm is injured. You can't move it, so stop trying to and just listen to me."

Cole stared at her, surprised she was getting so upset.

Aria wasn't done yet. "Stop trying to act tough—trust me, I'm not impressed. Just get over yourself and let me help you!" She paused for a breath. "Are we clear?"

Cole just nodded.

"Good," Aria said, calming back down. She grabbed a small knife from the belt at her waist. "Now, don't move." In a few quick motions, she cut off the remainder of his shirt. When the shirt fell off Cole's back, she stiffened, and Cole suddenly remembered all the cuts and scars on his back.

He winced, but not from pain. He could only imagine all of the questions Aria was going to ask him. Cole tensed as her fingers gently traced his most recent cuts—the ones General Sylvester had given him.

"Who did this to you?" Aria's asked, her voice barely above a whisper.

Cole shrugged. "It's nothing. I just got those earlier."

"Okay, but how and who—"

"I told you, it's nothing!" Cole couldn't think of any way to explain them without causing even more questions, and he was worried Aria would stop helping him if she knew he was running from the general. "I don't want to talk about it. Just help me get a new shirt on."

Aria bit her lip and nodded slightly. "I won't ask you about it if you don't want me to, but at least let me put some medicine on those cuts."

Cole rolled his eyes irritably. "Do whatever you need to do. Just don't ask me about it again."

Aria nodded and quietly cleaned his back with water. Then she applied the gel and cloth strips to his back.

After she finished, Aria picked out a clean shirt and helped Cole put it on.

"What time is it?" Cole asked.

Aria looked behind him and then answered, "Around noon." She glanced at Cole. "You look completely exhausted, though. Maybe you should take a nap."

Cole shook his head stubbornly. "I'm fine," he said.

Aria just smiled. "All right," she said, but she clearly didn't believe him.

"Do you live out here alone?" Cole asked suspiciously. "How do you get food? Water? Do you have electricity?"

"That's a lot of questions," Aria laughed. "Especially from someone who won't answer any." Cole glared at her, and she just smiled. "I live here with my dad, but he's in Rhomac right now. He sells stuff there, makes money, and then buys what we need from Nilrith. He's still gonna be gone for a few weeks this trip," she added. "And we have running water and electricity, too. My dad was a scientist, so he knows a lot about Anyrite. We use it to power the house." She looked at Cole. "Any more questions?"

Cole shook his head and yawned. He suddenly realized he was tired after all.

Instead of sleeping, Cole watched Aria work. She seemed to always be doing something, and Cole noticed that she spent a lot of time playing with the necklace she wore. It was a simple silver chain, with a blue gem hanging from it. It was beautiful and looked like it had cost a small fortune.

Aria continued cleaning the house, although there was never a thing out of place. She arranged and rearranged things so many times that Cole lost count.

When the sun set, Aria checked on Cole's injuries again. She poured more of the soup into a bowl and fed him dinner. Once Cole was finished, Aria stood up.

"I'm going to bed now," she declared as she dimmed the lights in the room. "The fire won't burn out for a while, but you should get some rest—you look absolutely terrible." She smiled at him.

Cole just nodded and obediently closed his eyes, only opening them briefly to watch the lights in the hallway go out as Aria walked to her room. Then he closed his eyes and peacefully drifted off to sleep.

Chapter 14

Cole awoke the next morning to the sound of humming. He opened his eyes and watched as Aria put a pan in the oven. When she noticed him, Aria smiled. "Good morning! Did you sleep well?"

"I slept as well as I could with you singing," he said, trying to sound irritated.

"How are you feeling today?" Aria asked. Without waiting for a response, she walked over to Cole and put her hand to his forehead. "You still have a pretty high fever. How do your arm and back feel?"

"Much better," Cole lied. He hoped he could convince Aria he was better and get out of here before she asked any more questions. "My arm still hurts, but at least the lashes don't hurt anymore."

Cole realized his mistake too late. He waited for Aria to say something about it, but all she said was, "Honestly, you don't *look* much better. Are you sure you're feeling okay?"

"Sure," Cole said. "I feel amazing."

"Well, why don't you try standing up then?" Aria offered. "Just to see how you're doing."

Cole nodded. Using his good arm, he was able to get into a sitting position, and then he stood up. As soon as he stood up, he felt lightheaded. He staggered to the side slightly and tried to hold himself up with the couch arm.

"See? I'm fine."

"Um . . . no. I don't think you are." Aria looked worried. "Try taking a few steps toward me."

Cole took a step forward, but his vision wobbled back and forth as if the world were tilting. He took a few more steps, hoping his head would clear once he started moving.

"Cole!"

When Cole opened his eyes again, he was on the ground, with Aria leaning over him. His head felt like it had just been hit with a hammer. "What happened?"

"I decided that you are definitely not okay and that you're not leaving your bed without help until further notice."

"What?" Cole protested. "I'm fine—really."

"Oh, is that why you just decided to take a nap on the kitchen floor?"

"Well—"

Aria was quickly losing patience. "You fainted, Cole. You have a high fever. You look terrible. You still can't even use one arm. Exactly how does any of that make you fine?" She stood up and reached out her hand. "Come on, let's get you back to your bed."

Cole scowled, but he took her hand. Aria helped him stand up and walk back to his bed. Once he was sitting down again, Aria went back to the kitchen and didn't say anything else to him.

The smell from the oven filled the house.

"That smells good," Cole offered, trying to break the tension. "What is it?"

"I'm making a breakfast casserole with eggs, sausage, potatoes, and cheese."

When the casserole was finished cooking, Aria took it out of the oven and brought a small slice over to Cole's bed. "Can you feed yourself today?" she asked teasingly.

Cole scowled at her. "Of course I can," he said confidently. He tried to lift his right arm, but the movement brought more pain than he had expected.

Aria noticed him wince and shook her head. "You probably shouldn't use that arm yet."

"I can use my left hand," Cole offered.

Aria thought for a moment before replying. "No, I don't think that's a good idea. You'll end up knocking the food off your plate. I'll just go ahead and feed you again," she decided.

"That's not necessary," Cole said adamantly. "I can just feed myself."

"You can't use your arm," she argued.

"Well, I can try."

"No," Aria said firmly. "Either let me help you or you're not eating."

"Then I won't eat," Cole said stubbornly.

"Fine." Aria walked over to one of the kitchen chairs and took a seat. Then she picked up a fork and began eating the meal she had originally offered Cole.

Cole tried to ignore her, but the food smelled so good, and his stomach was growling loudly.

"This is really good food," Aria said dramatically. "So delicious. Are you hungry yet?"

Cole glared at her. She just smiled back sweetly.

"Okay, fine," Cole finally consented. "You can help me today. But tomorrow I want to do it on my own."

Aria grinned. "Great!" she said. She cut him a new slice of the casserole and walked over to Cole. Then she sat down on the side of Cole's bed and began feeding him. Cole took the food, even though he was furious about the whole thing.

Aria seemed to enjoy feeding him, which only made Cole more upset about it. Once the food was finished, Aria put the plate down, but she didn't leave yet.

"So... I don't really know anything about you," Aria stated, trying to sound casual.

Cole tried to brush off her probing with a laugh. "There's really not much to tell."

"Well, for one thing, what are you doing in the forest with a bullet in your arm? Did someone shoot you? And you came from the south, too. You must have gone through the dark woods, but how did you survive?"

Cole tried to avoid her questions. "The dark woods? Is that the place with all the crazy bugs?"

Aria nodded. "Years ago, some scientists created the monsters. They genetically modified the insects to make them giant killers. I think they were planning to use them in wars, but the bugs were uncontrollable, so they trapped them in that part of the woods with an electrical barrier to keep them from invading the mines." Cole realized the barrier must have been what had prevented the ants from following him up the hill.

"But what were you doing in there?" Aria asked him after a few seconds of silence. "Why did you go there in the first place? Don't you know you aren't supposed to be here?"

Cole shrugged. "I don't want to talk about it."

Aria was far from finished. "Don't make this harder than it has to be. When I found you, there were broken shackles attached to your wrists and ankles. And there are lashing scars on your back. Right now, it looks like you're an escaped criminal, and if you are, then I could be in danger. So I need you to tell me the truth: What are you doing here?"

Cole hesitated. "The truth?" Aria nodded. "The truth is that I'm not a criminal," Cole said. "And I won't hurt you—I promise."

Aria wasn't satisfied. "So what are the chains from? And the bullet wound?"

Cole wasn't sure how to answer her. "I don't want to talk about it," he finally said. "But none of that was my fault."

CHAPTER 15

The next few days passed slowly for Cole. His injuries had healed enough to move around, but Aria continued to clean and change the bandages on his arm twice a day. She insisted he keep his arm in a sling as often as possible to ensure he didn't overuse it.

Aria's house was located in a large clearing, surrounded by trees. Behind the house was a garden and large barn. After the first few days, Aria relaxed and allowed Cole to wander around freely.

Sometimes Aria would finish her work early, and then they would have nothing to do. On one of these afternoons, Aria asked Cole, "Do you know how to play chess?"

Cole shook his head, and Aria grinned. "Then let's do that." She grabbed a chess board and the pieces off of a nearby bookshelf and started setting it up on the kitchen table. "You sit there," she said, pointing to the side opposite her. Then she held up some chess pieces. "These are the pawns, and that's a bishop." She went through each of the pieces, patiently explaining the function of each piece, but Cole felt completely lost.

Aria finally finished the long list of rules, and then they played. Cole lost in five turns.

"Seriously?"

Aria laughed. "Sorry, I had to do that," she said. "That's one of the tricks my dad taught me. It's the fastest way to win." She reset the board. "Let's try again, but this time I'll go easy on you."

Aria guided him through the first few moves, and soon Cole was getting the hang of it. They played five games total, and Cole lost every one of them, but he had to admit that it was fun.

After they finished the last game, Aria went to the refrigerator and pulled out a strawberry pie that she had made earlier. She served them both a piece, and Cole ate his as quickly as possible.

Aria laughed. "You know it's not going to disappear off your plate, right?" she teased.

"It's just so good," Cole said, trying to slow down.

"So, where are you from?" Aria asked in a casual tone.

Cole could tell the mystery was driving her crazy, but he shook his head. "It doesn't matter," he said, trying to avoid her question. "I'm not going back." Changing topics, he asked, "Do you think I can have another piece of pie?"

Aria was kind, but she was curious and was always trying to figure out where Cole had come from. Because of this, Cole was always forced to stay on his guard around her.

Cole had no idea if General Sylvester was still looking for him, and he worried Aria would stop helping him if she figured out that he was being hunted.

Cole was even more worried at night, and his sleep was restless. Any noise the house made woke him up in a panic. Even after Cole realized there wasn't any danger, he had a hard time getting back to sleep. The restless nights were affecting his ability to concentrate, and every day Cole felt more exhausted.

"Is it uncomfortable?" Aria asked suddenly while they were making dinner one night.

Cole looked up at her in confusion. "What?"

"Is your bed uncomfortable? You seem really tired all the time, so I was wondering if you needed a softer bed—"

"No," Cole said, shaking his head. "The bed is great—it's really soft."

"Oh," Aria said, lost in thought. "What about the blankets? Is it too light out here? I can move you to a back bedroom if you want—"

"No. It's fine." All Aria's questions were overwhelming Cole's mind. "Really, everything's fine."

Aria obviously didn't believe him. "Then what's wrong with you?" she asked. "You're so jumpy all the time."

"I said it was nothing," Cole said. He hadn't meant to sound angry, but the words came out a lot harsher than he had intended.

Aria pointed at him dramatically, as if he'd just proved her argument. "See? You're jumpy."

Cole shook his head. "I'm fine," he repeated.

They ate their dinner in silence, and as soon as they had finished the dishes, Aria looked over at him. "I'm going to bed now," she announced. "You should, too. You look exhausted. See you tomorrow."

Cole nodded. "Good night."

"Wake up!" someone shouted. Cole sat up and opened his eyes quickly, feeling slightly sick. Even though it was dark out, all the lights in the house were turned on, and Aria was standing over his bed.

She looked worried.

"What's wrong?" he asked in confusion. "I was finally getting a good night's sleep."

"A good night's sleep?" Aria asked, looking even more worried than before. "You don't remember what you were dreaming about?"

"No," Cole said slowly. He couldn't remember anything. Suddenly, he realized why Aria looked so worried. "I had a nightmare." It wasn't even a question.

Aria nodded slightly.

"Did I say anything out loud? Anything strange?" Cole needed to know how much he had said.

Aria hesitated. She reached for her necklace slowly and gently twisted it around her fingers. "It doesn't matter," she finally said quietly. "You were just having a bad dream—that's all."

Cole wasn't satisfied with that answer. "How bad? What did I say?"

"It's . . . it's fine," she said with a fake a smile, but she still looked worried. "You were just shouting 'No!' repeatedly, and I came out here to make sure you were okay." She paused but then changed the subject. "Well, try to get back to sleep."

Cole yawned. Even though he wanted to figure out what he had given away in his sleep, his eyes had a mind of their own. It wasn't long before Cole fell asleep again.

When he woke up the next morning, he noticed Aria asleep on a couch nearby. He tried to sit up on his own, but his arm buckled out from under him, and he fell back onto the bed. Cole frowned. He was able to sit up on his own yesterday. He tried again, and this time he winced from the pain. Cole grabbed his arm protectively and groaned—it felt like his arm was burning.

His groan must have woken Aria up. She opened her eyes quickly and looked at him with concern. "Are you okay?" she asked worriedly.

"I'm fine," Cole said quickly, trying to hide his pain. "Did you sleep out here all night?"

Aria nodded slightly. "I was worried," she said awkwardly. "After your nightmare last night . . . I just decided to stay out here in case you needed anything." She blushed slightly.

Cole tried to act casual. "So . . . what did I say?" He forced a laugh. "It must have been bad if you decided to sleep out here."

Aria laughed as well, but she didn't answer him. "Your arm looks like it's hurting you again." She got up and walked over to Cole. "How's it doing?"

Cole shrugged, continuing to hold his arm protectively. "It's fine," he lied. He didn't want her to know it actually hurt worse than before.

Aria didn't look convinced. She gently reached for Cole's arm and unwrapped the bandages. When she saw his wound, she frowned slightly, shaking her head. "It doesn't look fine to me," she said slowly.

Cole looked down at his arm immediately. The wound, which had been healing steadily, had completely reopened. Cole's bandages were covered in blood, and the injury looked almost as bad as it had when Cole first arrived at Aria's house.

"Great," Cole said sarcastically. "Now what am I supposed to do?"

Aria frowned and shook her head. "I don't understand," she said. "You've been resting and not using it. It should be practically healed by now." She examined the wound more closely. "At least it doesn't look infected," she said. "But the wound definitely reopened."

She thought for a moment and then looked at Cole curiously. "I wonder if it has anything to do with last night. You were moving around a lot in your sleep. Maybe you were moving your arm around too much and injured it again, but that still shouldn't have happened."

Cole didn't say anything.

"Well, whatever the reason, I don't think you should go anywhere until that arm is completely healed," Aria said as she wrapped up his arm again. Cole wasn't too upset about that—he didn't have anywhere else to go, anyway—but he still didn't like not being able to use his arm. If the general did find him here, he'd be completely helpless.

Aria seemed determined to keep him from being worried. They played every board game she could think of, but the hot weather kept them from spending too much time outside.

"I have an idea," Aria announced one day. She grinned at him—the grin she always had whenever she was planning something fun. She got up and grabbed some bread and chips and started making two peanut butter and jelly sandwiches. Then she looked at Cole. "Can you grab two towels? They're in the closet across from the bathroom."

Cole did what she asked. When he got back, Aria had packed the sandwiches, chips, and some drinks into a bag.

"What are you doing?"

Aria grinned. "Well, since it's so hot outside, we're going to the river!" she announced. "For lunch. It's not too far from where we are right now, and I know a spot where the water gets pretty shallow."

Cole nodded. It was better than anything they would be doing here. Aria finished packing everything up, and then they started walking.

"It's only about fifteen minutes from here," Aria said. Neither one of them said anything for a while, and Aria started humming quietly to herself. The forest was calm and peaceful. Cole heard a few birds singing, and with the sun shining down through the trees, the place looked almost magical.

"It's nice here," Cole said offhandedly.

Aria nodded. "Yeah, I like it," she said, "but it's still all the same." Cole noticed that her hand strayed to her necklace again. "I'd really love to go to Rhomac again—the market there is amazing, and there's always so much excitement!"

Cole snorted. "A little too much excitement at times," he muttered, remembering the last time he'd been there.

"That's the best part," Aria said. Then she looked back at him. "Also, I know that's where you're from," she added. "I'm guessing you worked at the mines?" Before Cole could say anything else, she said, "Don't worry—you can still stay here as long as you like. I was just wondering why you left."

Cole shrugged. Since Aria had already guessed most of it, he decided to stay as close to the truth as possible. "I couldn't stay there anymore," he said. "I was tired of it, plus the mine was getting too dangerous." He didn't say why, and Aria didn't ask. "How did you figure it out?"

Aria rolled her eyes. "Well, for one, you're a terrible secret keeper." Cole smiled at the irony of that comment. "And there aren't many places around here. My dad has told me all about the mines, and it was pretty easy to figure out where you got all the scars on your back. But why didn't you just tell me in the first place?"

Cole didn't know what to say. Luckily, he could see the river straight ahead and hastily changed the subject. "Is that where we're going?" he asked.

"Yep."

"Great," Cole said. "Race you there."

Before Aria could say anything, Cole was sprinting toward the river—and away from more of Aria's questions.

"Watch out for your arm!" Aria said, chasing after him.

Cole ignored her. When he finally made it to the river, he stopped. The long, snake-like river he had followed before flowed out into the small, calm lake in front of him. The water was so clear that Cole could see the sand under it.

"Isn't it nice?" Aria said. She put the towels and lunch on the ground and then jumped into the water with all her clothes on. She made such a big splash that the water hit Cole where he was standing.

"Hey!" Cole said, jumping back quickly.

Aria laughed. "Come on!" she said. "It's fun."

Cole looked at the water hesitantly. "I thought we were going here to eat," Cole said. "Not get soaking wet."

"We came here to have fun," Aria reminded him. "And getting soaking wet is fun!"

It was pretty hot out. The lake they were at was out of the cover of the trees, and the sun was beating straight down on them. The water did look pretty nice.

"Fine," Cole agreed. He slowly entered the lake until the water was almost reaching the bandage on his arm, but he didn't go any farther.

"Come on!" Aria was floating on her back nearby.

Cole shook his head. He'd never gone swimming before and didn't want to completely humiliate himself by trying. Instead of telling Aria that, though, he just said, "I can't—my arm, remember? You said I still have to take it easy."

Aria seemed to accept the excuse, and she went back to floating. "Watch this," she said. Then she took a deep breath, bent backward, and did three somersaults in a row. When she came up for air, her hair was plastered in front of her face. She pushed it back and grinned.

"Bet you can't do that," she teased.

Cole was sure she was right, but he wasn't about to admit it. "Of course, I could. Just not right now," he lied, moving his sore arm slightly.

"Sure," Aria said sarcastically. Then she kicked the water, splashing Cole in the face.

"Hey!" he shouted as he reached up to wipe the water out of his eyes.

"Oops."

Cole glared at Aria, who didn't look the least bit apologetic. "What about my arm?" he asked.

Aria shrugged. "Don't know," she said, "but I'm guessing you'll survive. It's just water." She splashed him again. This time, Cole tried to retaliate, but Aria just ducked under the water again.

"No fair," he complained.

They swam for about an hour and then decided to stop for lunch. When Cole got out, his clothes were soaking wet. "You know, it's gonna take forever to dry," he complained.

Aria dried her hair with a towel and then wrung out her clothes as best as she could. "Oh well," she shrugged. "It's not like it matters, right?" She reached into the bag and pulled out their lunches.

"Here," she said as she handed him his food. Until that moment, Cole hadn't realized how hungry he was and hastily took a big bite of his sandwich.

Once they finished eating, Aria laid down on her towel and closed her eyes. Cole looked at the lake again and sighed with contentment. It was so peaceful here. As he looked more closely at his surroundings, he suddenly noticed a strange boulder off to one side, with some scratch marks on it. He nudged Aria's arm. "Hey, what's with that rock over there?"

Aria looked where Cole was pointing and then smiled. "That's a rock my dad carved for me a while ago. When he used to tell me stories about the magic."

Cole froze. "What kind of stories?"

"I can tell it to you if you want," Aria offered. Cole nodded, and Aria began to tell the story. "Long ago, the world was at war. There was beauty and chaos, growth and destruction, life and death. And at the center of it all: the magic. It flowed through the earth, just as common as the sky and water, but it was just as dangerous as fire. Everyone knew it was there, but only a few could control it.

"These people were special. Sometimes they were adored and loved, other times they were hunted and killed. Over time, they learned to avoid other people, to mostly keep to themselves. Most people were content to leave the magic and the wielders alone, but there were some who were jealous and searched for a way to harness the magic. They wanted to use it for their own purposes.

"These people hunted down and imprisoned the wielders. They tried to take the magic from them, but what they didn't realize was that not everyone could control the magic. They were able to take the magic, but they weren't able to control it or use it. Chaos ensued. Without the wielders to keep the magic at bay, it became an uncontrolled, deadly force that destroyed towns and turned cities into dust.

"However, there was one wielder who hadn't been taken: a young girl. She had watched as her family and friends were captured. She had watched as her village burned to the ground. Her life had been ruined by the jealousy and corruption of mankind. But instead of letting them get the punishment they deserved, she pitied them.

"This girl brought a special sword to a circle of giant stone arches surrounding a large anvil, which many believe is the heart of the world—the Center Stones. Using the magic, the girl pierced the anvil with the sword. She harnessed all the magic in the world, took it all into herself, and channeled it directly into the anvil. The magic was stored in the anvil, and the sword was unable to be harnessed by anyone. That single act of selflessness saved the world, but it also cost that girl her life.

"The sword remained in the anvil for some time. Inscribed into the anvil's side were the words, 'The Sword of the King.'"

At this point, Aria broke off for a moment. "Actually, many people differ on what the inscription technically said. Most historians believe the sword was merely a symbol of hope, but my dad says the sword was actually capable of controlling the magic. When I was little, I begged him to show me what the anvil looked like, and he made that rock."

"What else happened in the story?" Cole asked.

Aria smiled and continued speaking. "Although many tried to pull out the sword, none were able. Over time, the story was forgotten. Even without magic, the destruction and chaos only worsened. The dark ages of mankind continued without end, and it seemed the girl's sacrifice was in vain. Then years later, a young boy came to the Center Stones. He was a poor servant boy who worked for a cruel master. After a particularly rough day, the boy had run to the circle to escape. He had heard about the sword—everyone had. But he had never tried to pull it out before. That day, though, he approached the sword and wondered what it would be like to pull it out.

"Just once, he decided to try. He bent down and pulled on the sword. Without any struggle, the boy was able to pull the sword out of the anvil.

"With the sword in his hand, this young boy became a hero—and the first person in over a century to control the magic. The boy became a king, and he used the magic in the sword to destroy the cruel leaders who tormented the weak and poor. This boy brought with him an age of reason and truth. A great kingdom was formed, ruled by both kindness and justice.

"However, even the noblest of hearts can't live on forever. The king eventually grew old and weak. Many began to covet the sword and its renowned power. One man in particular desired the king's sword and wanted to use its power for his own. One night, this man brutally killed the king and stole his sword. What this heinous man didn't know is that the magic chose who could harness it. And the magic didn't accept this evil man.

"Without the magic, the people suffered again. Corruption once again took over the kingdom, leaving it in complete ruin. All that remained was grief and despair.

"But the magic is still in the sword, waiting. And one day, a new hero—brave, strong, and true—will find it. The magic will then be restored and happiness will return once again."

Aria was silent for a short while, lost in thought. "That story is important, Cole. It's true—I just know it!"

Cole looked at Aria and laughed, trying not to show how interested he'd been in her story. "I don't know. It sounds like a ton of nonsense to me! And besides, everyone knows magic isn't real, right?" Cole wanted to see if she knew anything about what he had discovered.

"Well, just because magic doesn't exist now doesn't mean it didn't exist back then."

"Maybe," Cole said, trying to hide his relief. Aria didn't know he had the magic—at least, he hoped he still had it. He hadn't been able to summon it again since the day he had escaped the general, but he figured it must still be a part of him. He just had to learn how to use it.

Cole forced himself to focus on the conversation again. He laid down on his back and stared up at the sky. "What I really don't understand is why people make stories sound so crazy." He shook his head in disbelief.

Aria looked confused. Her tone was guarded. "What do you mean?"

Cole tried to find the right words to explain it. "It's just so . . . fake. I mean, you might think it's true, and maybe some parts of it are, but the whole 'hero risks his life to save the day' part is really unbelievable."

Aria frowned. "What's so unbelievable about the story?" she asked slowly.

Cole laughed. "Seriously? It's just too easy. The heroes are unnaturally brave. They save the day without any problems. They don't have any fear. That girl in the story died to protect people who killed her family. Those things just don't happen in real life. And that boy, the one who was a servant, what happened to him? Why would he go back and save everyone? Why didn't he get revenge? They just aren't believable people."

Aria was definitely upset now. "What makes you think there is no one good enough to stand up to the villains? The hero saves the day because his courage is greater than his fear. And there are problems in the story, but you don't focus on those. What matters is that the hero overcomes them. The pain the hero faces hurts, but it doesn't defeat him. Pain is hard, but anybody can overcome it with enough courage."

Cole looked at Aria, unsure if he had heard her right. He had experienced pain his entire life—the emotional pain of feeling alone, the physical pain from working the mines, not to mention the pain Cole experienced when he was tortured by General Sylvester.

Aria had spent her whole life in this perfect forest, oblivious to the pain of everyone else in Rhomac. She sat at home, reading stories about kings and heroes all day, and yet she acted like she knew everything.

Cole shook his head and asked, "Aria, what do you know about pain?"

Aria shrugged. "I don't know anything about it," she admitted. "But I'm betting you do." Cole flinched slightly, wondering how much she actually knew. "What are you doing here, Cole?" she asked slowly, drawing out each syllable. "If you're from Rhomac, you must have been working at the mines for a while. But why did you leave now? And what are you hiding?"

Cole stared at the trees, refusing to look at Aria. "It's none of your business," he said angrily. "I'm not obligated to tell you my entire life story."

"I want to help you," Aria said.

"But I don't need your help!"

"I think you do," Aria said quietly. Cole looked back at Aria in confusion. "You want to know what I saw that night you had your nightmare? I saw through the wall you keep up. You were begging something to stop, screaming for help."

Cole froze. He didn't understand what Aria was saying. "I don't know what you're talking about."

"You may not remember anything from your dream," Aria said firmly, "but I don't think I'll ever be able to forget it. I've never seen someone so terrified. I know you—"

"You don't know anything about me," Cole interrupted, looking away and focusing on a blade of grass in front of him. He wanted a way out of this conversation.

"But I want to." Aria looked at him with a sincere expression on her face. "I want to know why you're here, why you had a bullet wound in your shoulder, and why you always seem so tense and worried all the time. I want to help you."

Cole wanted to believe her. He wanted to tell her everything and ask for her help, but he couldn't risk it. "I don't want your help," Cole lied. "I'm fine. I've made it this far on my own, and I don't need anyone's help now. I got here on my own—"

"You would have died if I hadn't saved you," Aria reminded him quickly.

"And I appreciate you saving me," Cole said truthfully. "I appreciate all of the help you've given me—really, I do. But my life isn't some problem you need to fix."

Aria seemed upset, but she didn't say anything. "Fine," she conceded. "If you won't tell me, I can't force you. But I do want you to know you can trust me." She looked him straight in the eyes. "If you ever do want to tell me what's bothering you, I'll listen."

Cole looked away.

"Well," Aria said, sounding disappointed. "We should probably head back to the house. It's getting late."

Cole nodded and helped Aria gather everything up. They walked back to the house in silence. When they got there, Aria made dinner. Normally, Cole would offer to help, but tonight he just sat down on the couch, lost in thought.

He couldn't make sense of what Aria had been talking about, and that worried him. His stomach tightened as he remembered everything she had said. He had obviously exposed some of his fear to Aria, and it frightened him not to know how much he'd revealed.

He just hoped Aria would never find out the truth about the magic.

Suddenly, Cole heard a low rumbling noise above the house. He looked out the window and saw a small airship sinking toward the house.

Immediately, Cole felt like he couldn't breathe. The general had found him, and he had no way to escape in time. Before he could decided whether running or hiding would be more successful, Aria ran to the door and said, "It's my dad! He's home!"

CHAPTER 16

It took a moment for Cole to realize what Aria had just said. "Wait—your dad owns an airship?" he asked.

"It's just a small one," Aria said quickly. "We have to get food somehow, don't we?"

Cole hadn't thought about that.

"Anyway, I should go help him unpack."

"I can help," Cole offered. He wanted to get a closer look at that airship.

Aria shook her head. "You should probably stay here until I can explain you." She cringed. "My dad might not be crazy about the fact that a strange guy has been staying in our house the whole time he's been gone."

"Fine," Cole told her. He watched through the window as Aria ran outside. As the airship got closer to the ground,

Cole realized it was different from the big ones he'd seen in Rhomac. This airship looked like a small flying box.

The box landed, and a man exited through a door in the side. Aria ran up to him and gave him a big hug. Then she walked to the back of the airship, opened the door to what appeared to be a small storage area, and pulled out several bags. Her father hurried over to help her, and together they carried the bags through the living room and to the kitchen.

Cole stood awkwardly by the living room window, completely unnoticed.

"So," Aria said slowly. "Dad, there's someone I want you to meet." She walked over to Cole, and her father turned.

Cole froze. Aria's father was the baker who'd tried to offer him a job in Rhomac.

"I found him not too long ago. He was pretty much dead." Aria laughed. "Not to brag, but I think I've done a pretty good job helping him."

It was obvious from the expression on his face that Aria's father recognized Cole, too.

Cole wasn't sure what to do, so he just nodded and said, "Hi. I'm Cole." He waited for Aria's father to show some reaction, but his face remained completely emotionless.

He finally said, "I suppose you can call me Ulrik—since you're here." He studied Cole for a moment before adding, "I must admit, I didn't expect to see you again."

It was obvious Ulrik was looking for an explanation.

Instead, Cole forced a laugh and vaguely said, "Things got pretty crazy, and I ended up here." He hoped Ulrik hadn't heard anything about his escape. Suddenly, he had an idea. "You wouldn't still be offering a job, would you? Since I'm already here—"

Before anyone else could say anything, Aria interrupted. "Hold on. You two know each other? How?"

"I caught him stealing from me, realized he was broke, and then offered him a job—which he didn't take," Ulrik said as he looked at Cole.

"Oh," Aria said teasingly. "That explains everything."

Cole looked away. She had no idea how much more there was to the story than that. "I just stole some bread," he mumbled quickly, trying to defend himself. "I was hungry."

Aria laughed. "Well, that hasn't changed much." She looked at her father. "So can he stay? Please?"

Cole held his breath.

Her father looked at Cole. "Do you want to stay here?"

The question was so blunt that it caught Cole off guard, especially since he didn't know the answer. "For now, at least," Cole said hesitantly. He didn't know how long it would be safe here with the general searching for him.

Ulrik glanced at Aria quickly and then back to Cole with a frown. His eyes strayed to his injured arm.

"What happened?"

Cole shrugged. "Nothing really," he said quickly. The last thing he needed was more questions.

Unfortunately, Aria dove into the entire story just as quickly. "He was shot. I tried to clean up the wound, but it's taking a while to heal properly."

"Shot?" Suddenly Ulrik looked much more interested in Cole. "May I see your injury?" Before Cole could respond, Ulrik grabbed his arm and unwrapped the bandages.

"It doesn't look terrible," he said, looking the injury over. "Aria did a good job. I'd say you'll be completely healed in a week, maybe a little bit longer. You're lucky. An injury like that could have—" He broke off suddenly.

Cole noticed Ulrik's gaze had strayed to the mark on his arm. Ulrik's grip on Cole's arm tightened. "So this is why he's after you," Ulrik said quietly. "After all this time, he finally found you again."

"What are you talking about?" Aria asked. "Who?"

Cole was frozen to the ground. "What do you mean, after all this time?"

Ulrik ignored his question. "This mark—do you remember how you got it?" Ulrik's voice was barely above a whisper.

"No."

For a second, it almost looked like Ulrik was relieved about something. "But he has seen the mark, hasn't he? That's why he's searching for you." There was no doubt Ulrik was talking about General Sylvester.

Cole nodded.

Ulrik's eyes were wild. "You can't let him find you here—you must stay hidden!" he whispered. He looked like he knew much more than he was saying.

Cole couldn't help smirking. "That's kinda the plan," he pointed out.

"What are you guys talking about?" Aria was getting frustrated. "Hello? Anyone?"

"And the general? Did he get it to work?"

So Ulrik knew about the magic. Cole nodded.

For a second, Ulrik's eyes gleamed. "I knew it would work!" he said excitedly. His expression suddenly shifted, and he looked terrified. "But if General Sylvester succeeded, you're in grave danger. You're proof—"

"Okay, stop!" Aria shouted suddenly. Both Cole and Ulrik stared at her. Once she was sure they were listening, Aria said, "Tell me what is going on. Now!" She crossed her arms and waited.

Cole took a deep breath. As much as he was dreading it, he knew there was no way around telling Aria the truth. He kept his eyes fixed on the floor so he couldn't see the look on Aria's face as he quickly explained how Mise had first noticed the mark in the mine, how Cole had stepped in to save

Gale, how the general had taken Cole captive and had discovered the mark on Cole's arm, and how Cole himself had discovered the magic and had escaped to the forest.

"So you have magic? Real magic? And you never told me?" Aria asked, sounding very annoyed.

"I wasn't going to tell anyone," Cole pointed out. "I just wanted to forget about it and live a normal life."

"But it's *magic*," Aria said, as if that were all that mattered.

"It's dangerous," Ulrik said, regaining control of the conversation. "Cole, did the general follow you into the forest?"

"I don't know," Cole said. "I mean, the soldiers know I went into the forest, but I lost them pretty quickly. And then there were the giant bugs—"

"Bugs?"

"Yes. He ended up wandering into the dark forest," Aria explained quickly.

Ulrik nodded. "Good. Then they might have lost your trail." He looked at Cole. "I cannot express this enough: you must not let the general find you. If he does—" For a second, it looked like Ulrik was scared. "If he finds you, we will all be in trouble."

Cole nodded. "What if I leave? You could use your airship and fly me—"

"No," Ulrik said quickly. "You can't leave." Cole felt a little uneasy about how harshly Ulrik said that. "I can help you,"

Ulrik added in a friendlier voice. "I can teach you about the magic and help you use it."

Cole wasn't so sure. "I don't want to know how to use it," he told him. "I want to get rid of it."

"That can be arranged."

Suddenly, Cole was a lot more interested. "Seriously?"

Ulrik nodded. "But I won't tell you until you help me," he continued, deflating Cole's excitement. "Stay here, let me do some research and teach you about the magic. Then I'll tell you how to get rid of it, and we can part ways."

Cole wasn't happy about it, but it didn't look like he had much of a choice. "Fine," he said.

Ulrik nodded. "Now, if you'll excuse me, there's something I need to find." He looked at Aria. "Will you two be okay alone?"

Aria rolled her eyes. "Dad, Cole's been here for over a week now. I think we'll be fine."

Ulrik nodded, but the corners of his lips started to twitch into a smile.

"Ugh, just go!" Aria said. "Go do your research stuff."

Ulrik walked down the hallway and into one of the back rooms. Aria turned back toward Cole. For a second, it looked like she was blushing. Then she cringed and said, "Sorry."

Cole shrugged but couldn't help laughing at the look on Aria's face.

Aria glared at him. "Since you're staying here now, you can unpack all the groceries," she said bossily.

"What will you be doing?" Cole protested.

Aria grinned. "Supervising." When Cole glared at her, she laughed and added, "I'm going to make something for dinner since I don't think dad will be back out here anytime soon."

Aria was right—Ulrik didn't come out of his study, even after Aria had finished preparing their dinner. She and Cole each served themselves a plate and sat down at the kitchen table to eat. For the first few minutes, neither one of them said anything.

"So . . . you have magic," Aria finally said.

Cole shook his head. "Let's talk about something else." He didn't want to think about the magic right now.

"Why? I mean, no one's had magic in centuries! If I were you, I'd be thrilled."

Cole frowned. "Well, you're not me," he said, "All I want is for the magic to go away."

"But why?"

"Because," Cole argued. "What good is it? It's not like I have cool powers. And it's put a huge target on my back." He shook his head. "You don't get it: before I had the magic—in Rhomac—I figured I didn't stand a chance of ever getting out. It was like I could see my future self doing the same thing every day for the rest of my life until I finally died."

"That sounds horrible."

Cole shrugged. "You get used to it, and then you don't really think about it." He looked up at her. "And then I met your dad at the market, and everything changed for me. I let myself imagine a new future—a better one, where I'd eventually have a good job and lots of money and a nice house in Nilrith. Now I'll never even be able to go to Nilrith—I couldn't even get a job in Rhomac anymore. I'll always be on the run, hiding from the general. All because of the magic." His voice was now full of anger.

"You don't have to run," Aria said quietly. "You know that, don't you? You could stay here."

Cole didn't say anything. He knew Aria was just trying to help, but it didn't change the fact that he was stuck here—just like he'd been stuck in Rhomac. "All I want is to be free," he finally said.

"Then learn to use the magic," Aria said. "With that much power, who'd be able to stop you? You could do anything you wanted and go anywhere."

Cole hadn't thought about it that way. "You think so?"

Aria grinned. "Of course!" she said. "There's a reason you've got the magic, Cole. It's a gift—not a curse. And I know you'll figure out the right thing to do with it."

Cole wanted to say more, but at that moment they were interrupted by Ulrik, who had finally left his study and had come into the kitchen. Aria stood up quickly and washed her plate in the sink.

Ulrik walked over to Cole and held up a book. "I've found it!" he said excitedly. "This book should have everything you need to know about the magic. You can start by reading this tonight, and then tomorrow we can start trying to figure out the basics."

Ulrik handed the book to him, and Cole thumbed through the pages quickly. He hesitated. "One problem," he said slowly. "I can't read it."

Aria turned off the sink and turned to stare at him. "You can't read?" The way she said it made Cole feel as if he'd just admitted to murdering someone.

"Well, I didn't exactly have time for school when I was growing up," Cole said defensively. "I learned some important words. But this book—" he pointed to an open page of the book Ulrik had given him. "This book is full of huge words I've never seen before."

"I can teach you," Aria offered.

Ulrik looked at her quickly and then shook his head. "No, that would take too long. I'll just summarize it for him." He looked at Cole again. "You should get some sleep. We start training tomorrow morning."

Cole nodded.

Then Ulrik looked at Aria. "You should rest, too," he told her. "I have a feeling you'll want to be there tomorrow morning when we start training."

Aria grinned and nodded. "Good night," she said, waving to Cole. Then she headed down the hallway to her room.

Ulrik looked at Cole for a little longer. He shook his head in disbelief. "After all this time!"

Cole was suddenly uneasy again. "How do you know so much about the magic?" he asked suspiciously.

"That doesn't matter—"

"It kinda does," Cole said. "How am I supposed to know if I can trust you?"

Ulrik laughed, which just confused Cole even more. "You don't need to trust me. You need my help, and for now that's good enough. When you need to know more than that, I'll tell you."

Before Cole could say anything else, Ulrik turned and headed back down the hallway. "See you tomorrow," he called back over his shoulder.

CHAPTER 17

"Wake up!" Cole opened his eyes to see Aria standing over him with a huge grin on her face. "Come on," she said eagerly. "It's time."

Cole yawned and slowly sat up.

"Let's go," Aria said persistently.

Cole made a special effort to take as long as possible to stand up.

Aria rolled her eyes. "Okay, I get your point," she said. "I'm just excited to see what you can do." She started to walk away but then paused to add, "Dad's in the barn. We're supposed to meet him there. I'm going now." Aria then went outside.

Once Cole was ready, he walked over to the barn. As Aria had said, Ulrik was already there. "Welcome. Have a seat." Ulrik pointed to the three chairs that had been set up in a circle. Aria was already sitting. Cole sat down next to her, and Ulrik took the last chair.

"So, let's start with some basics," Ulrik suggested. "Magic, at its simplest form, is the ability to control the flow of energy. Energy has many definitions, but the most useful one for our purposes is the ability to do work. Theoretically, then, the magic will allow you to adjust the work output of any given object."

Cole stared at Ulrik blankly. "Can you put that in English?" he asked.

Ulrik sighed impatiently. "The magic should be able to do six things: explode or combine objects, move or stop them, and heat or cool them. These tasks can be divided into three groups: separatory, kinetic, which refers to motion, and thermal, which refers to heat."

Cole was still processing what Ulrik had said, but Aria nodded and Ulrik continued quickly. "So . . . we're going to teach you to control each of those categories at will." Ulrik walked over to the side of the barn and pulled out the sword Cole had found in the dark woods. "Here," he said, handing it to him.

"I don't know how to use this," Cole argued.

"You won't be using it as a weapon," Ulrik said. "You'll be using it to control the magic. Just like Anyrite, the metal acts as a conductor."

Ulrik grabbed a small wooden box and set it down in the middle of the room. Then he motioned for Cole to come over to the box. "Point the sword at the box," he directed. "And imagine all of your energy moving through the sword to the box—so much energy that it will explode from all of the pressure."

Cole tried it.

Nothing happened.

"Maybe try closing your eyes?" Aria suggested.

Cole closed his eyes, waited a little longer, and then opened his eyes again. "I feel ridiculous," he complained.

"You need to keep trying," Ulrik encouraged.

Cole shook his head. "This isn't working," he said in frustration. Suddenly, one of the chairs next to Aria exploded. Aria screamed and jumped up quickly.

"Did you just do that?" she asked angrily.

Ulrik nodded. "Right now, the magic only feeds off Cole's emotions. You need to control it or the magic will control you. Go again."

Cole spent the next few hours practicing, but by lunch time he'd only managed to explode five boxes—plus the chair he'd accidentally exploded earlier.

The lack of progress was beginning to discourage everyone, even Aria. They headed to the house to eat lunch. After they finished eating, Ulrik and Cole went back to the barn.

"This time, try visualizing the magic," Ulrik suggested. "Feel it running through you to the object."

Cole closed his eyes. Just like before, the warmth of the magic rushed through him. This time, though, he mentally pushed the magic through the sword. The box in front of him instantly exploded.

"Again," Ulrik ordered.

Cole instantly exploded the second box.

"I think I'm getting it," he said excitedly. The more times he did it, the easier it was for him to visualize. It was almost like he could see the magic moving where he wanted it to go.

Ulrik forced him to practice a few more times, but the force was making Cole tired. Finally, Cole dropped his sword. "I need a break," he said.

"A break?" Ulrik almost sounded angry. "Do you think the general will give you a break when you fight him?"

"I'm not going to be fighting him," Cole pointed out. "I'm hiding from him, remember? And I need a break. Using the magic makes me exhausted."

Ulrik's expression changed. "Interesting," he said. "So using the magic depletes your energy supply, does it?" Cole nodded. Ulrik appeared to be lost in thought. After a moment, he looked at Cole and nodded. "Fine, you can have your break. We're done for the night. Let's start back up first thing tomorrow."

They headed back to the house. This time, Ulrik cooked dinner, and Aria continued her chess lessons.

"Checkmate!" Aria exclaimed. Cole watched as she took his queen with her knight. She laughed. "Don't forget—you have to always anticipate my next move and act first," she reminded him. "When you just react to my moves, you're letting me control you."

Cole stared at the game board. "Sometimes I feel like you just enjoy beating me," he said.

Aria laughed. "Well, I do enjoy that, too," she admitted. "Let's play again."

Before Cole could answer, Ulrik told them, "Maybe a different night. Dinner is ready now."

Aria looked disappointed, but she nodded. Immediately after dinner, Ulrik tried to send Aria to bed.

"But why?" Aria asked. "It's still early."

"Cole's tired," Ulrik said. "And he has to keep working tomorrow. He needs to get plenty of sleep."

Aria didn't look happy, but she nodded and headed down the hallway to her room. Ulrik left soon after, and then Cole got into bed.

For once, Cole didn't have a hard time falling asleep. He felt safe. Ulrik would teach him to use the magic and then tell him how to get away from the general for good. Then everything would be perfect.

CHAPTER 18

Cole was awakened sometime later by someone shaking him. He felt disoriented and unable to comprehend what was going on.

"Cole!" Aria whispered.

Cole groaned and rolled over toward the noise. Without opening his eyes, he asked, "What time is it?"

Aria was silent for several minutes. Finally, she said, "This was a bad idea. Sorry—you can go back to sleep."

"Wait!" Cole sat up and opened his eyes. It was dark out, and the only light in the room came from a flashlight Aria was holding. "What did you want?"

Aria fidgeted with her flashlight, and for a second Cole thought she was blushing. "I couldn't sleep," she admitted. "I was wondering if you were awake, but obviously you weren't."

Cole laughed. "Well, I'm up now," he offered. "What's up? Is something wrong?"

Aria shrugged. "I couldn't sleep," she repeated. "Sometimes I get so excited—it's like I can't stop thinking."

"Excited about what?"

Aria didn't answer.

"Aria?"

Finally, Aria said, "My dad was talking to me about the magic. About what you have to do with it."

"What are you talking about?" Ulrik had never told him that he had to do something.

"He said he's preparing you," Aria admitted. "He thinks you'll be strong enough to defeat the general by yourself."

Cole couldn't help himself. He laughed.

Aria frowned. "What's so funny?"

"You two," Cole said, trying to explain his frustration. "It's like you're writing a story, and I'm the 'chosen hero.' Except you never bothered to check and make sure I actually wanted to be in the story."

"That's why he told me not to tell you," Aria said. "My dad says you don't believe in yourself enough."

That stung. "I believe in myself," Cole argued. "I just don't want to be a hero."

Aria shrugged. "He'll convince you," she said confidently. "Once you understand what's at stake."

Cole didn't respond. He didn't feel like arguing with her over it. His eyes strayed to the window. "There's a full moon tonight," he finally said. Cole remembered the last full moon he'd seen, back in Rhomac.

Aria smiled. Suddenly, she looked at him excitedly. "I know where we can get a better view," she said, standing up. "Come on!"

She quietly opened the front door and started running toward the barn. Cole followed her, although a little more hesitantly. "Aria!" he whispered. "What are you doing?"

"Come on," she called back. She opened the barn door and walked over to a tall ladder in the corner. "Up here." Aria began climbing higher and higher.

The hayloft platform stretched across to both sides of the barn. One of the walls had a large window cut out of it, which was covered by a gray and white patterned curtain. Directly in front of the window was a huge pile of straw covered with blankets. In the corner was a bookshelf that held some lanterns, more blankets, and a few other items.

Aria walked over to the bookshelf, grabbed two of the blankets, and handed one to Cole. Wrapping the other one around her shoulders, she then walked over to the pile of hay and sat down near the window.

"Over here," she said to Cole, motioning for him to sit next to her. When he had sat down, she looked at him and grinned.

She pulled the curtains to the side. "Look at this," she whispered, looking up at the sky. "The best view in the world."

Cole couldn't help agreeing with her. From the barn, Cole was able to see high above the trees. The moon was in full view, and there were more stars in the sky than he'd ever seen.

Aria leaned her elbows on the windowsill. "This is my favorite spot," she admitted, looking up at the sky.

Cole looked back anxiously. "Won't your dad be mad if he wakes up and sees us out here?"

Aria shrugged. "Let him get mad," she said casually. "I don't care. It's not like we're doing anything wrong. Besides," she said with a grin, "he's so busy teaching you that we barely have time to talk anymore."

Cole was pretty certain that was intentional, but he didn't tell Aria that. Instead, he just yawned. "There isn't much to talk about," he said. "You already know about the magic."

Aria shook her head. "But there's a lot more I don't know. What's your favorite color?" she asked suddenly.

Cole was shocked by the randomness of that question, but it didn't take him long to answer. "Green. What about you?"

"Purple. What about your favorite type of weather?"

"Cloudy, but not when it's windy."

Aria nodded. "I like that, too, but my favorite days are rainy days because the air smells nice, and everything looks so much brighter."

Cole nodded.

"When's your birthday?"

"Hold on," Cole said instead of answering. "Is this just gonna be an interrogation?"

Aria smiled. "Sorry," she said. "I'm just curious. You can ask some questions, too."

Cole wasn't sure he wanted Aria to ask any questions, but he couldn't think of a way to get out of this game. Plus, she seemed so eager to talk. Cole looked at Aria. For some reason, he didn't want to disappoint her.

"Um . . . sure," he said. "When's your birthday?"

"October 21st. You?"

Cole wasn't sure whether to give Aria the long answer or not. Finally, he said, "It's sort of January 5th."

"Sort of?"

Cole tried to think of a good way to explain. "I don't really know when I was born," he admitted. He drummed his fingers on the window sill nervously. "The earliest memory I have was being on the streets in Nilrith. I didn't know anything about who I was—my name, birthday, parents . . ." He shrugged. "You get the idea."

"That's why you never went to school," Aria said.

Cole laughed. Aria's priorities seemed a little misplaced. "I didn't get to do a lot of things," he admitted.

"It must have been hard."

Cole shrugged. He was uncomfortable talking about it. "You just kinda accept the cards you were dealt and move on with life. I don't really think about it." He needed to switch topics. "What's your biggest fear?"

"Probably not doing anything special with my life," Aria said. "That's why you're so lucky. You can do something so special—something I'd give anything to be a part of."

Cole didn't answer.

"How did you survive in Nilrith?" Aria asked.

Cole cringed and immediately regretted telling her about it at all. "I'd rather not talk about it."

"Please?" Aria begged. "You can trust me. I just wanna know what it was like."

Cole looked at the moon. "At first, it was all luck. Some shop owners would take pity on me and help out when they could. And when that didn't work, there was always stealing." When he saw the look on Aria's face, he shrugged defensively and added, "It was that or not eating some days. Still, I probably wouldn't have lasted through winter if it hadn't been for another boy who helped me. His name was Rex. He was like an older brother—" His voice cracked, and Cole stopped for a second.

Then he smiled. "He led a group of kids—homeless boys and girls who were hiding from the patrols. Called them the 'lost kids.'"

Aria smiled. "He sounds great."

"Yeah," Cole agreed. "He was smart, too. He was hung up on this dream of helping us have a future. He started his own school for the kids to teach us the basics. He always said an education was the only way to get anywhere in life. He's probably the only reason I can read anything at all," Cole admitted. "But I never got to finish."

"What happened?"

Cole tried to fight it, but it was too late. The memories resurfaced like a tidal wave, threatening to wash Cole away. He remembered that day perfectly—the day that changed everything. "He was killed—murdered." Cole remembered the soldiers surrounding him, Rex, and the other boys. "The soldiers in Nilrith found us one day. They were supposed to take us to Rhomac," Cole said angrily, clenching his fist. "That was their job."

He looked out the window quickly, trying to hide how much pain the memories caused him. "I was still a kid when they came. None of us even stood a chance against them."

"What did they do?" Aria said hesitantly.

"They didn't want to take us to Rhomac—they wanted to terrify us." He remembered the soldiers grabbing him, holding him still. "They made an example out of Rex," Cole said, his voice barely above a whisper. "They killed him and forced us to watch, promising that we would be next."

He remembered Rex's cries for help. Some of the boys tried to fight back, but Cole just stood there, too terrified to move. He had done nothing. He remembered the screams, the struggling, the fear, and finally the silence that had followed. And he remembered the moment when he realized Rex was truly gone, that he was never coming back.

Cole looked at Aria, his eyes burning with anger. "They killed him," he repeated. "They stood there and beat him to death, and there was nothing we could do to stop them."

Aria closed her eyes. "I'm so sorry," she whispered. "I can't imagine what that must have been like."

Cole shrugged his shoulders. "You wanted to know more about me," he said quietly. "There's the truth. I'm a coward." He looked Aria in the eyes. "Everything I do is either out of fear or guilt, and I'm tired of living that way. I have to be free."

Aria put her hand over Cole's and he jumped slightly. She didn't move. "Listen to me," she said firmly. "You can't judge yourself for what you did—or didn't do—as a kid. Everything was different back then. You were different. The younger you wouldn't have stood a chance against those soldiers. Now, though, with the magic, you really have a chance to do something." She smiled. "You know, I really think Rex would be proud of the person you've become."

Cole smiled. He wanted to believe her. They stayed like that for a moment longer, and then Cole moved his hand.

He had shared more than he had planned. Changing topics, he said, "So what about you? What's the story behind that necklace you always wear?"

Aria sighed and unclasped the necklace, holding it out for Cole to examine. It was made from a sapphire that had been cut into the shape of a heart. A thin, silver strand looped around it, holding the sapphire in place and connecting it to the necklace.

As he looked at it, Aria began speaking. "Ulrik's not my real dad. He adopted me when I was just three years old. I was too young to remember anything before him. He said he found me wandering around the Rhomac market by myself. This necklace hung from my neck with a note, asking whoever found me to take me in because my real parents couldn't take care of me."

Cole didn't know what to say. "I'm sorry."

Aria shrugged. "It's not your fault. It's not like I remember them, anyway. I always hope I will suddenly remember something about them, but I never can." She smiled. "I know it's silly, but I keep hoping that if I do something great—like, really famous—that they'll find me, and we can be a family again."

Cole shook his head. "There's nothing silly about that," he said.

Aria smiled. "Okay, my question. What are your goals for the future?"

"I'd love to know the answer to that question, too." Cole laughed. "I just want a normal life—like what you have."

"But not here?"

Cole nodded. "I need to be free, and I feel like I'll always be scared of the general if I stay here. I'm hoping that once your dad finishes teaching me, he'll tell me how to get rid of the magic for good. Then everything will be better."

Aria didn't look so sure. "Just make sure that's what you want," she warned.

Cole stared out the window, lost in thought. Finally, he said, "Don't you think it's strange that Ulrik knows so much about the magic?"

Aria shrugged. "I never really thought about it, but I guess. Does it matter, though?"

"No," Cole admitted. "I guess not. It's just strange. And when I asked him how he knew, he just said I didn't need to know and that he'd tell me when I did. I just can't help feeling like he's hiding something important."

"I know how we can find out," Aria said conspiratorially. "I bet there are notes in his office somewhere. I'll look tomorrow while you're training, although I don't think we'll find anything."

Aria yawned, and Cole was reminded of how late it was. "We should be getting back," he suggested. "Before we're too tired to walk."

Aria nodded and climbed down from the ladder. Cole followed behind her. When they got back to the house, he opened the door for her, and they entered.

"That was fun," Aria whispered.

The moment the door closed, the lights turned on. Ulrik was glaring at them. "I hope you had fun," he told Aria, "because you're grounded until further notice."

Aria groaned. "But we were just looking at the stars."

"You both snuck out of the house at night without permission. You know that's not allowed. Now go to your room," he said firmly.

Aria didn't look happy, but she walked off without arguing anymore. As soon as she was gone, Ulrik turned to Cole. "I'm letting you stay in my home and eat my food, and I'm keeping you safe from the general. The least you could do is respect my orders."

Cole nodded. "I'm sorry," he said. "Aria just woke me up, and the next thing I knew we were outside. But all we did was talk—honest."

"I'm not interested in what happened," Ulrik said. "But since you obviously aren't tired, I'll expect you to be up with the sun tomorrow for training. No more breaks."

Cole nodded, eager to appease Ulrik's anger. Satisfied, Ulrik turned around and headed to Aria's room. Cole heard them talking for a little while longer—and then only silence.

Cole tried to be angry with Aria for getting them in trouble, but the truth was he didn't mind. It had been worth it.

Shaking his head, he tried to rationalize his thoughts. Cole couldn't stay here. Eventually, Ulrik would tell him how to get rid of the magic, and he would leave. He'd be free, just like he'd always wanted, and nothing would hold him back.

He eventually fell asleep, but not before wondering if he would ever be able to move on completely.

CHAPTER 19

Morning came too quickly. "Wake up," Ulrik ordered, turning on every light in both the kitchen and the living room.

Cole groaned and covered his head with a blanket. He was so tired that he felt nauseated.

Ulrik just pulled the blanket off. "I said to wake up. We've got more training to do, and it's not my fault you decided to stay up all night."

Cole finally sat up and opened his eyes. Aria was nowhere to be found. Ulrik had obviously been very serious last night.

"Let's go," Ulrik said. "The sun's up, so you need to be up, too. Meet me in the barn."

Cole forced himself out of bed and quickly got ready. The barn looked the same as yesterday, with the chairs still set up to the side. Ulrik was standing in the center. In front of him were two buckets full of water.

"What are we doing?" Cole asked, looking at the buckets in confusion.

Ulrik handed Cole the sword. "Today you'll be learning to control thermal energy. In order to make this water hot, you'll need to transfer more energy into it, just like yesterday. This time, though, you need to keep the water compressed. If you do it right, the water will boil in the bucket."

Cole pointed his sword at the bucket. The energy pulsed through him, and he channeled it through the sword toward the water in front of him. Suddenly, the water flew out of the bucket, soaking Cole in the process.

Cole wiped the water off his face.

"You didn't keep the water contained," Ulrik said. "When you added the energy, you just forced it to explode." He grabbed a hose and refilled the bucket. "Try again."

Cole did it five more times. Each time, he ended up covering himself in water so that hardly any water was left in the bucket after his fifth attempt.

On his seventh try, the bucket didn't explode, but Cole did notice little bubbles rising from the water. "Good," Ulrik said. "Very good. Keep the energy flowing into the water."

Suddenly, the water flew out like a geyser. Cole jumped back, but the boiling water still splashed his arms.

"Ow!" he shouted. "That hurt."

"That was pretty good," Ulrik called out encouragingly. "Try again."

By the end of the day, Cole could successfully freeze and boil a small bucket of water. Ulrik seemed ecstatic with their progress and ran to his room to record the details in his notes.

Cole hadn't seen Aria all day, and he still didn't see her for dinner. With Ulrik in his room, Cole had nothing to do but sit. He picked up the chess game Aria and Cole had finished yesterday and rearranged the pieces.

"Checkmate," he said quietly, knocking the black king over.

"Maybe you should play against a real opponent."

Cole looked up quickly. Aria was standing in the doorway. "What are you doing out of your room?" he asked. "I thought you were grounded forever."

"Shh!" Aria whispered. "I am. And I'm not supposed to be out right now. I just thought you'd be interested in what I found." The look on Aria's face changed—she looked guilty. She held up a small black notebook. On the front was an image of the exact mark on Cole's arm.

"What is it?" Cole asked.

"I think we need to talk to my dad," Aria said. "If this is accurate—"

"What?" Cole asked. "What's in there?"

"You are—I think."

At that moment, Ulrik walked down the hallway. When he saw Aria, he looked furious. Then he saw the book in her hand, and his expression changed. "I guess you want answers?" he asked calmly.

Aria nodded. "This isn't right, is it?" She looked upset. "I mean, it can't be—" She broke off suddenly.

"What are you guys talking about?" Cole looked at Aria, but she just shook her head. Cole turned to Ulrik. "Well?"

Ulrik sighed in defeat and slowly sat down on a couch opposite to Cole. He was silent for a while, and when he spoke, he looked pained. "Let me preface this by saying that fear can be a powerful motivator. None know that better than General Sylvester. I used to work for him, but I regret every second of it, and now I'm hoping to use the knowledge I discovered for good."

Ulrik was silent for almost a minute. "I suppose I should start at the beginning. I grew up in Elysia and eventually went to the university, where I studied the magic and its properties. I graduated at the top of my class, and soon after college I was recruited to work on a highly classified project in Ambroise, the general's own private city."

"Ambroise? But no one ever goes there!" Aria exclaimed.

Ulrik shook his head. "No. Many people go, but few are ever lucky enough to leave. When I was recruited, the general was pushing a project involving Anyrite. At the time I was recruited, the lead scientist had suddenly refused to continue her work. From what I heard, she just snapped, snuck into her lab in the middle of the night, and tried to destroy all of her work. By the time they had discovered the damage, she had already escaped, and only a portion of her notes remained. The general hired me to replace her and complete the project." He paused and shook his head. "I should have taken that scientist's sudden desertion as a warning, but I was young, prideful, and eager to show off my knowledge.

"The goal of the project was to recreate the power of the magic using Anyrite. The general gave me all the notes his former scientist failed to destroy, which wasn't much. However, the notes I was given listed some of the differences between Anyrite and the magic. The notes also outlined the original scientist's plan to make Anyrite more like the magic. It was ingenious!"

Ulrik seemed to be lost in thought as he recalled these memories. "Since I only had a rough outline, I had to practically start at the beginning. At first, it was simple—all theory. Then the general wanted to turn those theories into reality." Ulrik paused. "That process was much more painful."

Ulrik's face darkened. "With the general's urging, I used the Anyrite to create fifty artificial hearts. It was almost too easy to find test subjects. There are safety and cruelty laws preventing the use of humans in experiments, but working for the general allowed me to 'overlook' those roadblocks. I was taken to the poorest parts of Rhomac, escorted by a small group of the general's soldiers."

Ulrik's voice caught, and he continued quietly, his shame showing on his face. "The general offered families a large amount of money for any young children they would allow to participate in our study. I was forced to buy children—young children. The families were more than happy to comply. In all, I returned to Ambroise with fifty children, ranging in ages from three to seven."

Ulrik paused again. "In short, I gave each child a heart transplant, replacing their previous heart with one of my Anyrite creations. To me, it seemed necessary. The general had made it clear that I would not be allowed to leave Ambroise until I had succeeded."

Cole's voice was barely audible. "What happened to all of the kids?"

Ulrik didn't respond.

It was Aria who finally answered. "Only one of them survived." She looked at Cole. "And it was Cole, wasn't it?"

When Ulrik nodded, Cole felt his entire body go numb. Ulrik continued the story, even though he was clearly upset. "You were very young—about five years old. For a while, I thought I was going to lose you, too. But somehow you pulled through. It was a miracle."

Cole snorted. "Some miracle," he muttered.

Ulrik cringed. It was obvious he didn't want to continue, but he said, "When you were stable, the general burned that mark into your arm so we'd be sure to never lose you. I moved you to Nilrith. My plan was to keep you safe and train you to reach your full potential with the magic. Then once you were strong enough, I was supposed to steal your power and give it to the general." Ulrik looked at Cole. "But you had no magic."

"So what did you do?" Aria asked. Cole was grateful that Aria had enough courage to ask the question.

Ulrik's face was grim. "I tried to stimulate a reaction." He looked at Cole again. "At first, I experimented slowly. I carefully monitored you for any adverse reactions and made sure to limit the pain. I didn't want to hurt you. But then the general became impatient. He demanded progress, and I was forced to do harder and more painful experiments."

Ulrik laughed darkly. "Naturally, this made you even more eager to escape."

Cole didn't say anything.

"One evening, I left the door to you room unlocked. You were gone by the morning, and I never saw you again. When the general found out, he was furious. I was terrified, so I ran. I left everything behind and moved to Rhomac, hoping to leave the general and my past behind me."

He looked at Cole for the first time since he had begun. "And then you arrived, and brought it all back to me."

Cole was speechless.

"So that's why you're so interested in Cole," Aria said, sounding angry. "After all that, you're still trying to use him?"

"No," Ulrik argued. "I'm trying to help. I know more about this than anyone else. I can help him reach his full potential—"

"Just like you wanted to do before," Aria accused.

"I did what I had to do back then," Ulrik said. "I'm not proud of it, but I had no choice."

"You always have a choice," Aria said stubbornly. She rubbed her temples, as if this discussion had given her a headache. "I can't believe this!" she said angrily.

Cole was still struggling to comprehend everything Ulrik had just confessed to. He felt like he should be devastated, but for some reason, knowing the truth didn't bother him. In a lot of ways, it didn't matter at all.

Ulrik looked at the clock on the wall. "We'll talk more tomorrow," he promised. "But now it's late, and we should all be getting to bed." He glanced at Aria. "For real this time."

Aria rolled her eyes. "I'm not tired," she argued.

"You're grounded," Ulrik reminded her.

"And apparently you're a murderer," Aria spat back. Ulrik flinched, and the room was deathly silent. Aria's glare was so fierce that Cole was just grateful it wasn't directed at him.

Then Aria quickly turned around. "I'm going to bed," she mumbled. She walked down the hall to her room and then slammed her door.

Ulrik looked at Cole. "I'm sorry," he said. "And I want to make this right. Let me train you. I'll teach you to use the magic. You'll become powerful enough to defeat even the general. No one in Lathinium will be able to stop you."

Cole didn't say anything for a while. Finally, he asked, "Why do you want to train me so badly? What do you get from it?"

Ulrik's eyes flashed. "I want the same thing you want," he said. "Freedom. The general has complete power, and I hate that as much as everyone else. No one here stands a chance against him—except you." Ulrik spoke with both passion and anger. "He needs to be destroyed, and you're the person to do it! If you can learn to use the magic to its potential, you could go to Ambroise and defeat the general single handedly."

"And then what?" Cole asked.

"Then you're done." Ulrik made it sound so simple. "You can leave—go anywhere you like. I don't care. Without the general, who'd stop you?"

Ulrik was too desperate to see the thousands of flaws in his plan. Cole shook his head. "You're crazy."

"I'm right," Ulrik said. "You've got enough power running through your veins to level a city—if you learn to control it."

"I don't want to control it," Cole argued. "I want you to tell me how I can get rid of it—like you promised."

Ulrik nodded. He walked over to the bookshelf and pulled out a rolled-up map. Cole recognized Rhomac in the center. Ulrik pointed to one of Rhomac's three corners. "This is a special location called the Center Stones. If you get here, there should be a way for you to release the magic—"

"*Should*?"

"Well, all of this is theoretical," Ulrik admitted. "But since all the other theories have worked, I don't see why this one would be any different. I can fly you there in a day, and you can get rid of the magic for good."

Cole looked at Ulrik suspiciously. Like everything else with him, this offer seemed too good to be true. "That sounds too easy. What's the catch?"

"Let me finish training you." Before Cole could object, Ulrik added, "Just for posterity's sake. When you do release the magic, it should go back into the world as it was before. A lot of people are going to have questions, and it's important that we figure out as many of the answers as we can."

Cole wasn't sure he agreed. "How long would that take?"

"Two days," Ulrik said. "It would take you at least four to get to the Center Stones on foot—and that's assuming you walked nearly all day. Even with my research, you'll get rid of the magic faster by helping me."

"Fine," Cole agreed. "But after two days, you'll take me there—no matter what."

Ulrik was unable to hide his happiness. "I promise," he said. "Now get some rest. We have another big day tomorrow." He walked back to his room.

CHAPTER 20

The next morning, Cole woke up without anyone having to wake him up. He'd barely slept at all last night, and the morning sun was a welcomed relief. Ulrik met him in the front of the house, and they walked to the barn together. While they walked, Ulrik quickly reviewed the skills Cole had learned the past few days.

"Time for the most challenging skill yet," Ulrik said when they reached the barn. "Movement. At its core, movement is simply pure energy—and you can control any amount of energy." When Cole didn't respond, Ulrik sighed and said simply, "You're going to try to freeze objects in motion."

"How am I supposed to do that?"

Ulrik held up a small ball that he'd been carrying. "You need to direct the magic at the ball and mentally push it away from you." Ulrik pointed to the center of the room. "Stand over there." Cole did what he was told, and then Ulrik threw the ball at Cole.

Cole caught it with his hands.

"Don't catch it!" Ulrik sounded frustrated. "Use the sword to control the magic." This time when he threw the ball, Cole hit it with the sword, as if it were a baseball.

"No," Ulrik said. He sounded even more frustrated than before. Cole grinned, which just made Ulrik look even more frustrated. "You need to push with the magic. Imagine the ball moving away from you."

This time, Cole actually tried. He felt the magic coursing through him. Then he imagined the ball moving toward him. At the last second, he moved his hand, as if he were throwing something.

The magic shot through the sword and blasted everything in front of him. Ulrik doubled over, as if he'd been punched in the gut.

"Good," Ulrik managed to say through gritted teeth. "But this time, try aiming."

They practiced a few more times, but no matter what Cole tried, he could not direct the magic where he wanted it to go.

Finally, Ulrik dropped the ball onto the ground. "This isn't working." He sounded extremely frustrated.

"I'm trying everything you told me," Cole argued.

Ulrik nodded. "Let's stop for a while," he suggested. "I need to make some quick notes while everything is still fresh in my mind, and you look like you could use a break. I'll come get you when I'm ready."

Cole didn't argue. Using the magic was draining, even if he used it only for a moment. By now, they'd been going for a few hours.

They entered the house, and Ulrik went to his study. Cole sat down on the couch and closed his eyes.

"Everything all right?"

Cole opened his eyes. "Yeah. Why?"

Aria shrugged. She moved to the couch next to him and sat down. "I just saw my dad go to his room and wondered how training went today."

"Fine," Cole said. "I just can't seem to get the magic to work right."

They were both silent for a while. From the look on Aria's face, Cole figured there was something specific she wanted to talk about.

After a few more minutes, Aria couldn't seem to remain quiet any longer. "Okay . . . I'm tired of sitting here pretending everything is fine. Can we talk about last night?"

Cole shrugged and tried to play innocent. "What's there to talk about?"

"How about the fact that my dad is a deranged mad scientist? Or that your parents sold you for an experiment?"

Cole was shocked by Aria's abruptness. "Does it matter?"

Aria wasn't fazed. "You tell me," she said.

"No," Cole decided. "It doesn't matter."

"Aren't you upset?" Aria persisted. "At least, a little?"

"Not really," Cole admitted. "I mean, it makes sense with what little I do remember, and—"

"I mean, knowing the truth," Aria persisted. "Didn't you ever—you know, make up stories to explain everything?"

Cole stared at her for a second and then laughed.

"What's so funny?" Aria asked defensively.

"Sorry," Cole said, trying to hide his smile. "It's funny because I never really thought about it like that." He shrugged. "I mean, I never knew what happened, but I also never tried to explain it. Honestly, it never mattered to me one way or the other where I came from."

Aria didn't look convinced. "So you aren't upset?"

"Well, I don't like it," Cole said. "And I don't trust your dad—no offense—but I'm also not devastated. Knowing all of that doesn't change anything."

Aria didn't look happy. "Well, I'm upset," she said. "I can't believe he'd do that!"

Cole glanced at her in surprise. "You're more upset about this than I am," he said dryly.

Aria laughed. "Apparently," she said. "It just makes me so mad to know he'd do something so wrong!" She scowled. "How can he even live with that guilt? And how can you not be furious with him?" Cole thought that Aria's sense of justice was so black and white that it was nearly comical.

"Well, he said the general forced him," Cole pointed out.

"Yeah, right." Aria glared at the ground. "That doesn't excuse what he did—"

"I'm not saying it does," Cole interrupted. "I'm just saying that he wasn't evil."

"He might as well be," Aria said. "Doing wrong is wrong—no matter what."

Cole didn't answer. He was pretty sure it wasn't that simple, but Aria seemed too angry to argue with her anymore. "Have you talked to him?"

Aria laughed. "No. How can I?"

Cole shook his head. "Are you always like this?"

"Like what?"

"I don't know." Cole tried to find the right word. "Idealistic? Extreme? You're acting like the judge, jury, and executioner—all in one!"

Aria frowned, looking offended. "Don't you think what he did was wrong?"

"Yes, I do," Cole admitted. "But I also don't really care. I know I should," he added quickly, before Aria could object.

"Especially since I was affected by it. But I don't—not really. It's just how life is. People do wrong stuff all the time." He shrugged. "It just happens."

Aria glared. "It shouldn't."

Cole laughed. "When you find a way to change the entire world, let me know," he said. "Until then, though, I think you have to get over it."

Aria gave him an even angrier look while shaking her head stubbornly. "It's still wrong," she said.

Cole smiled, realizing that this conversation wasn't going anywhere. For better or worse, he knew Aria's opinion would never change.

"So you're going to the Center Stones?" Aria finally said.

Cole nodded. "Ulrik said I can get rid of the magic there, so that's the plan."

"That's it?" Aria asked.

Cole was confused. "Is there more?"

"Releasing the magic." Aria spoke as if Cole were a child. "It's going to end years of misery. Imagine people—ordinary people—being able to do what you can do. Imagine people using their powers like they did in the ancient times to achieve remarkable feats. You're literally going to change the world, and you're acting like it's as ordinary as eating dinner."

"I just want my life back to normal," Cole said. "The rest of that's great, I guess, but it's not why I'm doing this."

Aria shook her head in disbelief. "You and I are very different people," she muttered.

Cole couldn't agree more.

CHAPTER 21

Ulrik came back a few minutes later, and then they went back to the barn to work again.

"I'm going to try something new," Ulrik warned. "This might hurt a little, so let me know how you feel."

Ulrik pulled out a thin metal band and handed it to Cole. "Try holding this."

Cole slowly grabbed the band. The instant he touched it, the magic reacted, and he felt slightly nauseated. He dropped the band quickly.

"How did it feel?" Ulrik asked.

"It's hard to explain," Cole said slowly. "It's like the metal is taking the magic away."

"That's what I was afraid of," Ulrik said grimly. He took the band away from Cole, and the feeling instantly vanished.

"This metal is infused with Anyrite, which is the direct opposite of the magic. The magic gives energy, while Anyrite absorbs it. When the two meet, the Anyrite starts to draw the magic out of you."

"It made me feel tired," Cole added, suddenly realizing how drained he had felt. Now that the band was no longer touching him, he was already starting to feel better.

Ulrik nodded. "The magic is a part of your energy. The two cannot be separated without harming you, so naturally the magic took your energy with it."

"Wait," Cole said, realizing what Ulrik had just said. "If the magic can't leave without harming me, how can I get rid of it?"

The look on Ulrik's face proved that he'd said something he hadn't meant to say. "Don't worry about that," he said quickly. "Releasing the magic is different."

Cole didn't believe him. "If the magic and I are linked," he said, thinking quickly, "then getting rid of the magic would kill me, right?"

He looked at Ulrik, waiting for him to correct him. Ulrik looked at the ground. Suddenly, Cole felt sick to his stomach.

"It *will* kill me?" he asked in disbelief. "You knew it was going to kill me, and you were still going to take me there?" Cole knew he probably shouldn't be surprised, but he had never expected something like this.

"It wouldn't kill you," Ulrik said assuredly. "The magic would leave, yes. But your heart was originally made of Anyrite, so it probably would compensate for the lack of magic."

"Probably?" Cole repeated. He laughed sarcastically and shook his head. "I can't believe this. So there's no way to get rid of the magic, is there?" Before Ulrik could answer, Cole added, "Don't bother trying to answer that question—I'm not going to believe anything you say, anyway."

At that moment, Cole heard a loud noise from outside. A second later, Aria ran into the barn and shut the door behind her. "The general!" she said frantically, out of breath. "He's here—his airship is landing in front of our house."

Cole froze. It was all over now. With the general this close, there was no way he could run without being seen. He was trapped.

Aria looked at Ulrik accusingly. "Did you call them?"

Ulrik had gone pale. "N—no," he stuttered. He took a deep breath and then looked at Cole. "He's probably just looking for you. I'll go tell him you aren't here."

Aria nodded. "I'll go with you," she offered.

Ulrik shook his head. "No, stay with Cole," he said. "I know how to handle the general, but you could potentially complicate things."

Aria looked like she was going to argue more, but then she glanced at Cole and stopped. "Fine," she agreed reluctantly.

Ulrik smiled. "Thank you." He looked at Cole. "I'll be back soon. Don't leave the barn. As soon as I finish talking to the general, I'll come get the two of you. Understand?"

Aria and Cole both nodded. "Okay," Aria said.

CHAPTER 22

Ulrik left the barn and shut the door behind him. Cole tried to stay calm. Ulrik had promised to keep him hidden, and they'd probably search the house, not the barn.

This thought would have assured Cole if it weren't for the fact that Cole already didn't trust Ulrik, and there was no way they could see if Ulrik was keeping his word.

Aria didn't give him any more time to worry. She looked over at Cole and said, "Come on. We need to follow him."

"That's a terrible idea," Cole protested. "The general's out there, remember?"

Aria just glared at him and rolled her eyes, which made Cole even more irritated. He opened his mouth to argue with her, but before he could, something in her expression changed. Cole wasn't sure what to make of it.

Cole waited for a few minutes, but Aria seemed to have completely become lost in her own thoughts. "Aria?" he finally prompted her.

Aria blinked and looked back at Cole. "Sorry," she said quickly, looking away distractedly. "I was just thinking."

Cole shook his head. "Your dad told us both to stay here," he reminded her.

"Technically, he only *suggested* you stay in the barn, and he told me to stay with you," Aria argued. If you come with me, then I won't be disobeying. Plus, you can make sure to keep us from getting caught."

She paused for a moment, and then begged, "Come on! You know I'm right."

Cole didn't want to go anywhere near the general, but he also didn't want Aria going alone. "What if I say no?"

"I'll go, anyway," Aria said with her arms crossed. "I really don't need you to come. Although if you don't come, you won't know whether I got caught or not. Your choice."

Cole didn't like either option. "Why do you want to go so badly?"

"Aren't you curious?" Aria asked.

Cole was curious, but only because he wasn't sure he trusted Ulrik to keep him hidden. "Fine," he finally spat out. "I'll go with you. But we need to stay out of the way—no matter what. Promise?"

Aria acted like she didn't hear him. She grabbed his sword and sheath from nearby and handed it to him. "Here," she said. "Just in case we need to use the magic." She helped him strap it to his back and then turned toward the door. "Come on! Let's hurry," she called over her shoulder.

Before Aria had even taken a step, Cole quickly grabbed her shoulder. "Wait," he said. Aria turned around and glared at him angrily. "I'm not going anywhere until you promise to stay quiet."

"Okay," Aria said. "Can we go now?" She opened the door and said, "If you're too scared, stay here." Then she shut the door behind her.

Cole opened the door, only to see Aria walking calmly toward the house. Cole was angry at her now. She wasn't even trying to be discreet, and her reckless actions were going to get them both killed.

He sprinted after her, grabbed her shoulder, and spun her around. She instinctively pulled her knife out of her pocket. Aria's reflexes were so instantaneous that Cole barely had time to notice the knife coming at him. It was only a few inches from his face when he quickly grabbed Aria's wrist and forcibly held it away from his face.

"Aria, it's me," he said urgently.

When she finally realized what she was doing, Aria unclenched her fist and lowered the knife. "Sorry about that," she said, laughing nervously. "I thought you were one of the general's soldiers."

When Cole didn't release his grip, her eyebrows creased together in anger as she struggled to free herself.

"Let me go!" she demanded, glaring at Cole.

"No," Cole argued, pulling her back toward the barn. Aria was stronger than he'd expected, but Cole was able to keep his hold.

When they were inside the barn again, Cole relaxed his grip a little. Aria glared at him, completely furious. "What was that for?" she demanded. "You said we could go!"

Cole returned her glare this time. "If you run out there like that again, you'll likely get us both killed!" he yelled at her. "You've never interacted with the general or his soldiers before. You have no idea who these men are or what they're capable of. I need you to listen to me." He waited until Aria finally nodded her head in silent agreement.

Cole released her arm, and Aria immediately rubbed where he had grabbed her. When she noticed Cole watching her, she glared at him. "What?" she asked. "Do you feel bad now?"

Cole laughed. "Actually, no," he lied. Trying to justify himself, he added, "That's nothing compared to what the general would do to us if we were caught."

Aria smiled. "Sure," she said sarcastically. When Cole didn't respond, she asked, "So . . . what's the plan?"

"If these men are after me, then everything will be fine as long as we stay hidden. We can listen and watch, but we can't be seen. Just one of these men could easily kill us. I need you to promise me you will not get involved." Cole looked at Aria, making sure to emphasize this last part. "No matter what, you can't draw attention to us. Do you promise?"

"Fine," Aria snapped, glaring at him again. "But can we go now?"

"Yes, I guess so," Cole said reluctantly. When Aria jumped up again, he quickly added, "But we need to be smart about this. Is there anywhere we can hide and still hear them without being seen?"

Aria rolled her eyes. "I'm smarter than that, you know. I've already got a perfect hiding spot: a shed that's connected to the house. You can only get into it from outside, but my dad never really used it, so it's kind of run-down now. It's hard to see it from a distance because it's hidden by weeds and plants." Aria grinned. "The best part is that there's a crack in the wall that lets you see what's going on inside the house."

Cole nodded. "That sounds great."

They quickly crossed the short distance from the barn to the house, being careful to stay low to the ground so that they wouldn't be seen. Cole motioned for Aria to be quiet as they crept along the outside of the house until they were one corner away from the front door.

"Hold on," Cole whispered. "I'm gonna see where the soldiers are." Then he crouched down even closer to the ground.

His heart was beating rapidly. Cole tried not to think about what would happen if he were caught—every part of him wanted to run away now, before it was too late. But Aria was determined to know what was happening, and if he didn't help her, then she would only make things worse for the both of them. Cole took a breath and quickly peeked around the corner to the front of the house.

He was able to see the front porch. Ulrik was by the front door, talking to General Sylvester, who was backed by a group of armed soldiers. Cole wasn't able to hear their conversation from this distance, but he was able to see Ulrik motion to invite General Sylvester inside.

The general went inside with three of the guards, leaving the remaining guards to watch outside. Cole's stomach sank. The general and his guards definitely had Ulrik surrounded. Cole ducked around the corner of the house and headed to the back of the house, motioning for Aria to follow him. They slowly crept to the back of the house.

Cole whispered to Aria, "The general just went inside with Ulrik. There are some guards near the front door, and three more inside the house."

Aria nodded and then whispered back, "The entrance to the shed is this way. Follow me." She quietly led him around the house. Just like Aria had said, the ground was overrun with weeds and other plants. The shed looked like it hadn't been used in over a decade.

Cole started to open the door, but Aria quickly grabbed his hand and shook her head. She bent down near the ground and picked up a small, ornate key. Something on it glimmered in the sunlight, and as Aria brought it closer, Cole noticed the handle had small pieces of Anyrite embedded in it.

Thankfully, when Aria opened the door, it didn't creak. The inside of the shed had been empty for a long time. Cole could see a thick layer of dust coating the wooden floor, and there was a large spider web in the corner.

Aria sat down first. She pushed herself into the corner farthest from the door. Cole sat down diagonal to her and quickly closed the door. It was a tight fit, and the sword on Cole's back pushed up against the wall oddly. The closeness made Cole uncomfortable, and he hunched his shoulders to give Aria as much space as possible.

Aria didn't even seem to notice his discomfort. She was already staring into the living room, completely absorbed in General Sylvester's conversation with Ulrik. The crack Aria had mentioned was larger than Cole had expected, and it was easy to see what was going on in the living room.

General Sylvester was seated on one chair in the living room, and Ulrik was seated directly across from him. They talked for a while about how things had been since Ulrik left. Ulrik looked worried, and his voice stuttered whenever he talked.

"How did you find me here?" he finally asked.

General Sylvester laughed. "Oh, I always knew where you were. But after you let that boy escape, I didn't really have a use for you." He paused and then added, "It's really such a shame he escaped. We were making so much progress with him."

Ulrik looked at General Sylvester quickly. But then he seemed to relax and replied, "Yes. It was a huge misfortune. I was so close to success."

General Sylvester leaned in, an intense expression on his face. "Then you miss it? You miss the work you were doing for your fellow citizens?"

Ulrik looked unsure. He hesitated before finally answering, "Yes. I do wish I had been successful."

General Sylvester spoke quietly to avoid being heard by the guards in the room. "Not all hope is lost. My men recently imprisoned a miner. He was a young boy—probably fifteen or sixteen years old. He had a mark on his arm you might recognize."

The general showed Ulrik a picture. Ulrik did his best to appear surprised. "Is this the runaway I've heard so much about? I heard he caused a great deal of trouble for you and your men."

General Sylvester growled. "Yes. He was far more powerful than we ever thought. It appears your experiment has worked. I used Rubilac on him, and it was just as you had hypothesized. The extractor reacted perfectly with the metal and the Anyrite, and . . . well, you have already heard how that ended."

Ulrik listened to all of this quietly before finally asking, "So . . . why are you here? I haven't seen the boy, if that's what you're asking."

The general gave Ulrik an impatient look, as though the answer were obvious. "I need you to come to Ambroise and continue your experiments. We will catch the boy—there is no question of that. I have my soldiers looking for him day and night. And when we do find him, I will need you at the forefront of our research. Your expertise and experience makes you the ideal man for this job."

Aria tensed, and Cole was afraid that she was about to say something.

General Sylvester got to his feet and continued, "I had no doubt you would agree with me on this matter, so I already took the liberty of ordering your supplies. I already have a state-of-the-art facility ready for you in Ambroise, and I also have an airship with a private laboratory below deck." The general moved toward the door, but when he looked back, he noticed Ulrik wasn't following. "Aren't you coming?"

Ulrik nodded his head in silent agreement, but he didn't move yet. He looked scared, but when he spoke, his voice was firm. "What if you don't find the boy?"

General Sylvester just smiled. "Then we'll do it again. We'll perform the experiment again and again—as many times as it takes until we succeed."

Ulrik paled. "I can't go through that again," he argued. "There were too many casualties."

"You will do it as many times as I need," the general said calmly. "I will not take no for an answer."

Ulrik shook his head. "If I'm coming back, then I have some conditions."

The general looked up in mock amusement. "You are making conditions now, Professor? What can you possibly offer me that is of any value?"

Ulrik looked at General Sylvester confidently. "First, my conditions. No matter how the experiments end, you will not hold the results against me. When you do catch the boy, there's a chance the experiment will fail. Whether I succeed or not, you'll let me leave at the end."

The general smiled slightly. "Whatever you have to offer, it must be priceless."

Ulrik nodded confidently. "I know where the boy is."

Cole froze. The general's eyes lit up. "The boy? You have him here? Where?"

Ulrik shook his head. "First, our deal."

The general waved his hand impatiently. "Yes, yes. You can have anything you want. Now, where is the boy?"

Aria looked at Cole nervously. Cole could barely breathe, and when Ulrik spoke his next words, Cole felt nauseated. "He's in the barn with my daughter. I told them I would protect him. They won't be expecting you."

General Sylvester smiled. He looked at one of the guards in the room. "Take half of the soldiers to get the boy."

Cole was frozen in fear. The general knew he was here, and they wouldn't stop searching until they'd found him. He knew he needed to escape now, while he still had time, but he couldn't move.

"And you'll keep your promise?" Ulrik had a hopeful look on his face. Cole was tempted to laugh despite the tense situation. He couldn't believe how naive Ulrik was—the general couldn't be trusted to keep any promises.

Sure enough, the general's next words confirmed Cole's opinion. "Oh, Professor, you should know better than that." Ulrik's face paled. "Your reward will be determined by your success. I cannot afford to have another failure."

With that, the general nodded to the remaining soldiers holding Ulrik, and before Cole could blink, Ulrik fell to the ground unconscious.

CHAPTER 23

Aria gasped loudly. "No!" she shouted in horror. Cole jumped and quickly covered her mouth, but it was already too late. Aria pulled Cole's hand away from her face. "Sorry," she mouthed silently.

The general had heard Aria's shout and motioned for the guards to search the house. When the guards returned to the living room empty-handed, General Sylvester was furious. "Gather the rest of the guards," he ordered. "Two of you will return with me to Ambroise to help the professor settle in. The rest of you will search the entire property. Find the boy." The guards saluted before quickly exiting the living room.

Cole knew he needed to act quickly if they were going to escape. He quietly whispered in Aria's ear, "We need to leave now. When I tell you, we need to run toward the forest. I need you to hurry, Aria. Run like your life depends on it—because it does. If they catch us, there's no telling what they will do to us. Do you understand?" He worried that Aria would be too upset to listen, but she just nodded.

Cole slowly opened the shed door, and they both got to their feet. He motioned for Aria to follow him. When he looked around the corner of the house, he could see some of the soldiers making their way to the barn. Cole panicked. Once the soldiers realized he wasn't there, they would search the rest of the property.

Cole looked at Aria. "There are guards headed to the barn right now." He paused for a moment. Aria was barely registering what he was saying. Cole tried to remain calm. "We have to get into the forest as quickly as possible. Follow me."

He peeked around the opposite corner and watched two soldiers as they carried Ulrik onto a small airship. General Sylvester followed behind them.

The distance to the forest wasn't very far, but they would have to make it past General Sylvester and the soldiers undetected. Cole hesitated.

"Why have you stopped?" Aria whispered impatiently.

Cole didn't answer her. He couldn't move. His mouth was dry and his heart was pounding frantically. More than anything, he wanted to stay put against the wall and wait for the general to leave.

Unfortunately, Aria was tired of waiting. "This way," she said quickly. Before Cole could stop her, she grabbed Cole's wrist and started dragging him toward the trees.

When they had made it safely to the forest, they crouched as low to the ground as they could. Cole turned back to get one last look at the general. The airship was still on the ground, and the general was pacing in front of it quickly. One of the soldiers ran over to him—Cole guessed it was probably to tell General Sylvester that Cole was already gone. The general looked furious, and he shouted at the guard angrily. Then the soldier nodded, and a group of them headed into the forest, opposite from where Cole and Aria were hiding.

This meant they needed to go in the opposite direction from where the soldiers were headed.

"Let's go," Aria said quickly as she marched ahead of him. She was completely silent, and Cole wondered what was going through her mind. She didn't seem as sad or scared as Cole had expected.

He finally decided to voice his thoughts to her. "Aren't you upset? I mean, we just left your dad with the general, and you're acting like it was nothing."

Aria shrugged. "He made his choice," she said coldly. "It's not my fault it didn't work out."

Cole couldn't help laughing. Aria's sense of justice was as strong as ever. He looked above them. It was already well into the afternoon, so he knew it wouldn't be long before it was evening—and then it would be too dark to see. The obvious question was what to do now.

Aria still walked calmly in front of him. Once they seemed far enough away from the general, Cole stopped.

Aria didn't.

"Where are you going?" Cole finally asked.

Aria looked back impatiently, but she didn't slow down. "We have to go somewhere, don't we? And I know the perfect spot: a tree house not far from here that I built with my dad—I mean, *Ulrik*." She sounded disgusted as she said his name. "It's far enough away from the house, and I don't think anyone will find it—and definitely not at night."

Cole wasn't convinced. "Are you sure you can find it?"

Aria rolled her eyes. "Seriously?" Cole immediately regretted saying anything about it. "I've been exploring this forest my entire life," Aria said. "I know every square inch of this place."

"Fine," Cole said quickly, trying to appease her anger. "Lead the way."

Aria began walking quickly, and Cole hurried to keep pace with her. He listened to the pine needles crushing under their feet with every step they took.

Aria didn't let the silence last very long. "So . . . do you have a plan?" she asked.

Cole laughed. "Escape the general?"

"After that," Aria clarified. "I mean, we obviously have to release the magic, but after that—"

"Actually, I'm not going to release the magic," Cole said hesitantly, afraid of how Aria would respond.

Aria stopped walking. "You have to," she insisted.

Cole shook his head and kept going forward. "No, I don't," he argued. "If I release the magic, it'll kill me."

"How do you know that?" Aria asked. "Did my dad tell you that?"

"Well, not exactly," Cole admitted. "He said it might not, but I know it would. Ulrik said the magic and I are connected. If I lose one, I lose both."

Aria didn't say anything for a while. When she did speak, she sounded slightly annoyed. "I'm not going to tell you what to do, but I really think you should release the magic."

Cole laughed. Of course, Aria thought that he should release the magic.

"You heard the general: if they don't catch you, they'll just do this again to another boy," Aria argued. "You've got the chance to do something amazing!"

"Something that will kill me."

"You don't know that," Aria reminded him. "And imagine all the people you'll help. Releasing the magic will change everything. It's like a dream come true."

"Not the dying part."

Aria shrugged. "You'll be fine," she said. "I know you'll make the right decision."

Cole tried to suppress his frustration. "You aren't listening," he said. "I'm not doing it."

"Let's just wait and see," Aria said. "You might change your mind."

Cole laughed. "Not likely." Before Aria could say more, he changed the subject. "So you really aren't upset about leaving your dad? Not at all?"

"I'm not heartless," Aria said. "Of course, I'm upset. I wish things had gone differently, and I'm scared something bad will happen." She was silent for a while before saying with a sarcastic smile, "But I guess the general still needs him, right? So he'll be fine."

Cole nodded. "Yeah." He looked around the forest. All the trees and bushes looked the same to him, but Aria seemed to know where they were going. "Do you really know this whole area?"

"Yep," Aria said proudly. "It's not too hard, once you know what to look for. Ulrik was gone a lot, even when I was younger, and I had loads of free time. Sometimes I'd pack myself some camping stuff and just walk as far away as possible. Then I'd spend the night somewhere and try to find my way back the next day."

"You're crazy," Cole said. "Why would you do that? Weren't you scared you would get lost?"

Aria shrugged. "What's the point of living if you're always too afraid to do things?" she asked. "I love being outdoors, and you only get lost if you don't pay attention."

The sun was beginning to set when Cole finally spotted the tree Aria had mentioned. It was easy to find. The trunk was very wide—it was probably at least twice the length of Cole's arm span. Huge, thick branches spread out from the trunk, and some of them were so heavy that they touched the ground. Wooden planks were nailed across the branches to make a large, flat platform, walls, and ceiling. Several long, sturdy tarps were hanging from the tallest branches as an extra precaution against rain. Off to the side of the tree trunk was a ladder, which led up through a hole in the center of the platform.

Cole stopped and stared at the tree house. "It's huge," he said in shock.

Aria quickly climbed up the ladder and looked down from the top. "Come on," she called down to Cole. "It looks a lot better from the inside."

When Cole saw the inside, he definitely agreed. Aria had clearly made this tree into a second home. Wooden planks formed a wall around the platform. In the center of each wall, a window had been cut and was covered with blue curtains. In addition, there was a large rug covering the floor.

Aria even had furniture inside her tree house. She had a bed, nightstand, dresser, desk, bookshelf, and even a small bean-bag chair. Everything was clean and perfectly organized, just like her house. She had paintings and pictures hanging from the walls, and Cole noticed other decorations placed strategically inside the tree house.

Aria watched Cole examine his surroundings. "Nice, isn't it?" she finally asked him.

Cole nodded in agreement, trying his best not to feel jealous. "You even have a bed in here?" he asked in disbelief.

Aria grinned. "It was ridiculously hard to convince my dad, but he finally said yes." She walked over to the dresser and opened one of the drawers. "I even keep a ton of supplies in here." She began rummaging through the drawers, pulling out a sleeping bag and other sacks full of items. "Just in case I ever decide to have a spontaneous campout."

Then Aria handed Cole a few boxes. "There are some snacks in there: dried fruits and meat, snack bars, and I think some trail mix."

It was getting increasingly harder to see inside the tree house now. Cole set the boxes on the floor, walked over to a window, and pulled the curtain aside so that he could see out the window. It was almost completely dark outside. "I don't suppose you have any lights in here?" Cole asked sarcastically.

"Actually, yes." Aria went over to the bookshelf and grabbed two lanterns. "Here," Aria said. "They're powered by Anyrite, so they'll never run out of power," she added as she turned one on and handed it to Cole. Then she grinned. "The perks of having a mad scientist for a dad."

Cole set the lantern down on the desk and walked back to where he had left the boxes of food. He picked up one box and dumped the food out, immediately noticing that there wasn't anywhere near enough food. Like Aria had said, all of the things in the boxes were just snacks—nothing substantial. The snack bars would probably be the most useful, but there weren't that many of them. Divided between the two of them, Cole guessed the snacks would only last them two or three days.

He looked up to see what Aria was doing. By now she had turned on the other lantern and was constructing a makeshift bed on top of the rug.

Cole grabbed two snack bars and one of the bags of trail mix and took them over to her. Aria took one of the bars and then glared at the makeshift bed in frustration. "I only have one sleeping bag and some extra blankets."

Cole shrugged. "I'll just use the blankets—you're gonna need the sleeping bag once we start moving." He looked at the bed and laughed. "There's no way we're taking your mattress with us."

Aria just rolled her eyes. "Very funny," she said dryly. Then she unwrapped her snack bar and started eating. Cole did his best to pace himself as he ate, trying to make the snack bar seem like more than it actually was.

Aria obviously didn't have the same strategy. She devoured the bar quickly and then moved on to the bag of trail mix.

Cole looked over at Aria, trying not to laugh. When she noticed, she blushed and forced herself to eat more slowly.

Cole couldn't keep himself from laughing. Aria glared at him. "I'm hungry!" she protested.

Cole shrugged. "I didn't say anything."

Aria rolled her eyes. "Here," she said as she handed him a plastic water bottle. "Try not to drink it all, though. We only have two bottles each, and we can't refill until we get to the river."

Cole took a big gulp of water and then yawned. "It's getting late. We should go to bed now and get an early start in the morning."

"We still need to decide what we're doing," Aria reminded him.

Cole ignored her and just turned off the lantern he had been using. He layed down under the blankets, but he instantly remembered he still had the sword attached to his back. Sighing, he unfastened it and put the sword nearby. Then he laid down and pulled one of the blankets over him.

Aria was still sitting next to him and didn't seem like she was moving any time soon. She stared at the lantern, looking completely lost in thought.

"You okay?" Cole finally asked her.

"Yes," Aria said abruptly. "Actually, no," she admitted more quietly. "It just feels so real, you know?" She grabbed her necklace and started twisting it through her fingers. Then she looked at Cole and grinned. "We're runaways. Wanted criminals, trying desperately to evade capture."

The way she said it sounded way too heroic.

"*I'm* a runaway who's trying to sleep," Cole clarified. "And you're being way too dramatic."

Aria didn't seem to care. "I still can't believe him!" she said angrily. "My dad—I mean, Ulrik." She scowled. "I can't even call him my dad anymore. After everything he did to you, and then raising me like nothing happened? And then, after everything, he just betrayed us again!"

Trying to make light of the situation, Cole said, "At least Ulrik took care of you, and your parents didn't sell you to a deranged scientist."

Aria snorted. "I guess I do have that to be thankful for," she said sarcastically. She looked over at him. "But now that you have the magic, what are you going to do with it?"

Cole looked away. "It's getting late," he said. "I'll see you in the morning."

Aria was silent for a few minutes. Finally, she just whispered, "Good night." Then she picked up the other lantern, which she had left on the floor earlier, and walked over to her bed. She placed the lantern on her nightstand, climbed into her bed, and after a few more seconds, reached out and turned out the light.

Cole rolled onto his back and looked up at the wooden ceiling. He'd wanted to sleep, but it seemed impossible with everything else he had to think about. He knew Aria wanted him to release the magic, but he didn't want to risk it. He thought back to his conversation with Aria's dad. Ulrik had been almost completely certain releasing the magic wouldn't hurt him, or at least that's what he'd said. And Cole was sure the general would never stop looking for him as long as he still had the magic.

Cole knew Aria just wanted him to be a hero—she had said so multiple times—but he'd already told her the truth: he wasn't a hero, he didn't want to be a hero, and he wasn't going to risk his life for anyone.

CHAPTER 24

Cole only managed to sleep for a few hours when he was woken up by sunlight shining in his eyes. He sat up, yawned, and glanced around. He saw that Aria had already finished packing a backpack with food and her sleeping bag, and she was now tying her hair back in a messy bun. When she saw that he was awake, she dramatically said, "Finally! I've been up for an hour already."

Cole stood up and began fastening the sword onto his back. "Sorry, but I was exhausted after having to drag you out of danger yesterday," he replied sarcastically.

Aria snorted. "That's not how I remember it," she teased. "Weren't you the one frozen in fear?"

"I was not!" Cole protested. He turned away when his face warmed—the last thing he needed was for Aria to see him embarrassed. To keep himself busy, he started folding the blankets he'd used last night.

Luckily, Aria didn't say anything else about yesterday. "Here," she said, throwing a gray backpack at him. Then she stood up and said, "I'll be right back."

While she was gone, Cole put the folded blankets into the backpack Aria handed him. Then he looked at his half of the food. It wasn't much, and Cole knew it definitely wouldn't last him more than a couple of days. He considered skipping breakfast, but he also knew he needed to eat something. He finally grabbed one of the bars and unwrapped it.

Once he'd finished eating, he put the rest of the food and the water bottles into the backpack.

"Are you ready yet?" Aria asked impatiently.

Cole looked up from his backpack to see that Aria had changed into a white shirt and black leggings, a dark green jacket tied around her waist.

Cole tried not to laugh. "You have a change of clothes up here, too?"

Aria shrugged. "I told you—this place is like a second home for me. And I never knew when I might end up needing it. Just being prepared."

Cole shoved the last bite of the bar in his mouth. "I'm ready when you are," he said, picking up the backpack and swinging it over his shoulder.

Aria smirked. "Sorry, but I don't have any extra clothes for you."

Cole looked down. "What's wrong with these?" The clothes Aria had given him were still fairly nice.

Aria just shook her head. "Never mind," she said. "It doesn't matter." She rocked on her feet excitedly. "Come on, let's go!"

"Just one problem," Cole said. "Where are we going?"

Aria laughed. "The Center Stones, obviously," she said. "So you can release the magic!"

Cole was so shocked that he wasn't even sure how to argue with her. It was as if she hadn't heard anything he had said yesterday.

Aria kept talking excitedly. "I can't believe we're doing this! I've always wanted to do something like this—"

"Wait a minute," Cole interrupted. "Slow down. I never agreed to do that." He was starting to get extremely irritated with Aria's persistence.

"The Center Stones are at the edge of Lathinium. So I figured we'd release the magic, and then you can leave. Once you're not in Lathinium, the general can't find you, right? And by releasing the magic, he wouldn't have any reason to find you, anyway."

"Aria, I don't want to release the magic!" Cole said angrily. "Why can't you just listen to me?"

"Because we have to release the magic!" Aria said adamantly. "That's the whole point of this."

"No," Cole argued. "The point was to survive—for me to live and have a nice, long, happy life."

"You can have a happy life *after*." Aria spoke as if it were the most obvious thing in the world. "Releasing the magic is not going to kill you. You're being paranoid."

Cole didn't answer. He was tired of arguing with her about this. Aria didn't know what she was talking about, and he knew she'd never agree with him.

Then he remembered what she had just said. "If I make it out of Lathinium, the general wouldn't find me—right?" he asked.

Aria shrugged. "How could he? If we get out there, he won't even know where to start looking. And when we release the magic, he won't have any reason to find you," she reminded him.

Except that Cole wasn't going to release the magic. But he still nodded. "Fine," he lied. "I'll release the magic."

Aria looked ecstatic. "Really?" she asked. "You promise?"

As Cole nodded, he tried to ignore the sick feeling in his stomach. "How do we get to the Center Stones?"

"Over here." Aria went over to the desk and began drawing a triangle on a sheet of paper. "Ulrik showed me a map of Lathinium a while back. Rhomac is shaped like a triangle, bordered on two sides by a deep canyon and this forest on the third side. The Center Stones is here," she said, pointing to where the two canyons intersected.

Then she drew a squiggly line. "This is the river you were at when I first found you. We need to cross it and get through the remainder of the forest to get to the desert, and then we can follow the canyon."

"And that's the edge of Lathinium?" Cole asked, pointing to the Center Stones.

Aria nodded. "Yes. Then you can release the magic."

Cole didn't answer her. "Lead the way," he said.

They walked for hours, traveling at a fast pace and only stopping a few times to rest. There was no actual path through the forest, leaving Cole to wonder if Aria actually knew where they were going.

When they stopped for lunch, Cole handed Aria a snack bar. "We need to watch for soldiers, too. The general knows we're around here, and he'll be sending guards out after us."

A while later, Cole was starting to get tired. He asked her if she wanted to take a break, but she just shook her head. "We have to keep going," she insisted. "This is important. The whole world is relying on us getting to the Center Stones so that we can give back the magic."

Cole laughed. "Aria, no one knows where we're going, and releasing the magic won't do anything for anyone."

"You don't know that," Aria argued. "And when it's back, everyone will be grateful. We're going to change the world—you'll see."

Cole smile faltered. "I wish I believed you," he said honestly.

CHAPTER 25

They arrived at the river a while later. The thought of crossing it made Cole's stomach drop. "We aren't swimming across *that*." The river was only twenty feet wide, but the water was moving fast.

Aria looked at Cole in surprise. "What do you mean? Can't you swim?" she asked.

"I live in a desert." Cole laughed nervously and shook his head. "I've never tried."

"What about the lake? You were swimming then."

Cole looked at the rushing river in front of him and shook his head. "I was just standing in the lake—not swimming," he clarified. "But this water's moving pretty fast. Isn't there another way across?"

Aria looked at the river. "Not that I know of."

The water was clear and seemed safe to drink. Cole knelt down and began refilling the water bottles. When he looked up at Aria, she was staring at the water.

"Aria?" Cole called, trying to get her attention. "What are you doing? We need to find a way to cross." He laughed and said, "It's not gonna move by you staring at it."

With those words, Aria spun around to face him. Looking at Cole with unrestrained excitement, she exclaimed, "That's it! You can move the water!"

Cole faltered. "I can *what*?"

"You can use the magic to move the water, and then we can walk across." Aria acted like it was the simplest idea in the world.

"No way," Cole said in disbelief.

"Why not? You practiced it with Ulrik."

"And I failed miserably." Cole thought of all the times he'd attempted unsuccessfully to stop the ball in midair.

"Well, if you have a better idea, I'd love to hear it," Aria told him.

Cole was silent. The truth was they didn't have any other options. He just rolled his eyes, pulled out the sword, and concentrated. He walked up to the edge of the river and looked across.

"There's no way this is going to work," he said negatively.

"Just try," Aria pleaded.

Cole held the sword out in front of him and waited. "Nothing's happening," he whispered.

"Really?" Aria's voice was full of sarcasm. "I hadn't noticed. Just try again."

Cole glared at her. "This is ridiculous," he protested, trying to hide his embarrassment at not being able to control the magic. Still, he did as Aria suggested, trying even harder to focus on moving the water.

At that moment, he felt the warm, familiar feeling spread from his chest to the rest of his body. The magic was ready. Now he just needed to find a way to direct it. Cole closed his eyes, mentally willing the magic to travel through the sword and toward the water in front of them. Cole could feel the energy coursing through his veins.

Suddenly, Aria gasped.

Cole opened his eyes quickly. The water directly in front of Cole was beginning to move on its own. They watched as the water continued to clear away. Once the water had receded the whole way back to be about a couple feet from where they were standing, it stopped.

Aria smiled at Cole. "I told you it would work," she teased. Cole shook his head. The sword felt like it was getting heavier. He was able to hold the water for now, but he could feel the pressure of the rushing water, and somehow he knew he wouldn't be able to hold it forever.

"If we're going to cross, we need to do it now. I don't know how long I can control the magic," he warned. When he'd practiced with Ulrik before, it had always been with smaller amounts. Holding the full force of the river back was already tiring him.

Aria hesitantly stepped out onto the dry sand, which had been covered by water just a few moment ago. The water moved with Cole's every step, always clearing a couple feet in front of them.

Aria looked around in amazement. "This is the strangest thing I've ever seen," she said quietly. Cole silently agreed, but he remained focused on the magic. The only thing he wanted to think about was getting across safely. If he lost control now, the water would fall down around them and sweep them downriver.

Once they were safely across the river, Cole lowered the sword. As the sword descended, the circle of dry land shrunk until the river looked exactly as it had before. Cole dropped the sword and bent over his knees, gasping for breath.

"Ugh," he grimaced, wiping the sweat off his forehead. "I feel like I just ran a marathon."

Aria looked around. "Well, it's getting late," she said. "I guess this is as good a place as any to stop."

Cole nodded and sat down. Aria sat down next to him. They both remained silent for a short while, lost in their own thoughts. "That was . . . amazing," Aria said eventually. "I didn't actually think that would work."

Cole couldn't help grinning. "I definitely didn't think it would work," he replied between breaths. He thought for a moment and continued, "It's strange. This time, I actually had control over the magic. I was able to feel it and control the amount of energy I used—like Ulrik kept talking about."

"You would have probably gotten a lot better with practice. And stronger, too—no offense," Aria added quickly. "It's too bad you won't have enough time to see everything the magic can do."

Cole didn't say anything.

Aria grabbed her backpack and started digging through it. "Well," she said slowly, "It looks like we have snack bars . . . or snack bars." She laughed. "Which would you like for dinner?"

Cole grinned. "I guess a bar?"

Aria nodded. "Here." She handed one to Cole.

He eagerly unwrapped it and started eating.

Aria still managed to finish eating first. She climbed into her sleeping bag and stared up at the sky. After Cole finished eating, he pulled the folded blankets out of his bag, settled himself on the ground, and closed his eyes.

"I wonder what will happen when you release the magic," Aria said, ignoring the fact that Cole had his eyes closed. "Will it go everywhere?" She grinned. "Do you think I'll get some of it? Just kidding," she said quickly with a laugh, but Cole could see how badly she wanted it to be true.

"It's not fair," she added enviously. "I would have given anything to have the magic. You're literally so lucky!"

Cole couldn't believe what he was hearing. "Lucky? Exactly which part are you jealous of?" he asked in disbelief, with a hint of sarcasm. "The awesome parents I grew up with? Or my amazing, fun childhood? Or maybe," he added, "it was the great job I had in Rhomac before I became a wanted criminal?"

Aria laughed. "You know what I mean."

Cole had no idea what she was talking about. "You're the lucky one," he said. "I would give anything in the world to live a normal life—like you! You have no idea how great you've had it. Growing up here, having Ulrik to take care of you, learning to read and write, having time to play games and relax."

"But you have magic!" Aria argued. "You get to be a hero."

Cole shook his head. "But I don't want to be a hero. I just want a nice, calm life—not working in the mines, not tortured by the general, not chained up, and definitely not being hunted like a criminal."

"Well, you'll get all that," Aria reminded him. "As soon as you release the magic." She smiled. "I know you didn't ask to be a hero, but you'll do a great job at it."

Luckily, it was too dark for Aria to see the look on Cole's face. She yawned and stopped speaking, leaving Cole to his own thoughts. In just a few minutes, he heard the sounds of Aria's deep breathing, and he knew she was asleep.

Cole stared up at the sky, looking at each individual star.

He remembered what Ulrik said about releasing the magic, but he also couldn't shake the fear that releasing the magic would kill him. What bothered him more than his fear was that Aria was okay—actually eager—for him to willingly sacrifice his life.

She expected him to do it.

But even though Cole knew he was making the right decision, he couldn't stop feeling guilty about lying to Aria. He looked over to where she was sleeping. He wanted to tell her the truth, but he knew he couldn't.

They were too different. She would never understand.

CHAPTER 26

Cole was the first one awake the next morning. He had barely slept all night. No matter how hard he tried, he hadn't been able to stop thinking about how he needed to tell Aria the truth.

He looked over at her. She was still sleeping, with a faint smile on her face.

More than anything, Cole hoped she would forgive him for running away. He wanted her to understand why he couldn't do what she wanted. But truthfully, he didn't think Aria would ever forgive him. And that was the worst part. He didn't know why, but Aria's opinion of him mattered.

Cole laughed to himself. He couldn't believe how his opinion of Aria had changed. She still annoyed him at times, and her naive opinion of the world angered him, but the longer he was with her, the more he began to understand her—and like her.

At that exact moment, Aria opened her eyes. "Why are you staring at me?" she asked defensively. "Was I snoring?"

"No." Cole looked away, but he could already feel his face flush. "It was nothing," he said. "I was just thinking."

He tried to distract himself by attaching his sword to his back. Aria looked like she expected more of an explanation, but Cole stubbornly refused to even look at her.

Finally, she gave up and began digging through her backpack. "I'm going to eat something. Did you eat yet?"

Cole hesitated for a second. "No," he finally said. "I'm not really hungry." Cole had looked at the food this morning, and he knew that their snack bars would run out by the end of day. "I'll just eat later."

"You're not really hungry?" she asked. Cole could tell she didn't believe him.

Cole grinned. "Well, I'm a little hungry," he admitted unabashedly. At that moment, his stomach growled loudly, and Aria started laughing.

"Not hungry at all?" she teased. Then her face became serious, and she added, "I know we're almost out of food—I'm not blind."

"So if I don't eat now, then we can preserve our food for at least a little longer."

"Well, then I won't eat, either," Aria decided. She put the bar back in the backpack and stood up. She turned and looked over at Cole. "You ready to go yet?"

They started traveling as soon as possible. As usual, Aria led the way and Cole just followed silently. After a few minutes, Aria slowed down until she was walking beside Cole.

"So, you did great yesterday," she began after a while. "With the magic, I mean. How did you do it?"

Cole shrugged. "I'm still not sure. Even with all those tips Ulrik gave me, it's like the magic has a mind of its own. Usually it's a lot more out of control than it was yesterday."

"Like blowing up the general's ship?" Aria said.

Cole laughed. "Pretty much."

"I still can't believe what you can do with the magic." Aria looked at Cole with curiosity. "What's it feel like—to have that much raw power inside of you?"

Cole stared in front of him and tried to find the right words to describe it. "It's like a warm, comforting feeling rushing through me." He paused for a moment before continuing. "It feels like a part of me—like it's the blood flowing through my veins. I've only known of it for a short while, and I already can't imagine going on without it."

Aria looked at him with sympathy. "Well, I guess you're going to have to get used to not having it since we're almost to the Center Stones."

Cole sighed. He knew he needed to tell her the truth. "Aria, listen," he began. "I need—"

"Quiet!" Aria whispered suddenly. She grabbed Cole's hand and pulled him down with her behind a bush.

Cole was confused until he heard the voices. The general's ground patrols must have caught up with them somehow. He looked at Aria. Her eyes were filled with fear.

A group of seven men stood in the clearing, directly in front of them.

One of the men, who appeared to be their leader, asked, "Are you sure you heard something, Sarge?"

Cole inhaled quickly. Aria looked at him, worried. She looked like she wanted to ask a million questions, but Cole shook his head. Not now.

He looked closely at the men, and sure enough, he recognized one of the soldiers. Cole had hoped he would never have to see that face again.

He watched Sarge walk around the clearing. He still couldn't understand Sarge's motives. When Cole had first met him, Sarge had seemed as mean as all the other soldiers Cole had encountered. But once Cole had started talking to him, Sarge had seemed much nicer. And Cole hadn't forgotten that Sarge had given Cole food and had said that he wanted to help Cole. But then Sarge had told the general about Cole's arm, and that mark was the reason the general was looking for him now. In that moment, Cole wondered if it would be such a terrible thing to kill these men. They would kill him in a heartbeat—or worse, they would take him back to the general alive.

Cole slowly drew his sword and imagined taking revenge on these men—the men who had caused him so much pain. He looked at the clearing. Sarge was so close. It would only take a few seconds to stab him with the sword. Then he could use the magic to take the rest of them down. As his frustration rose, so did the pull of the magic. He knew the magic could do it, too. It would be so easy.

Sarge was five steps away.

Three.

Two.

At the last moment, Cole dropped his sword to the ground. He couldn't do it. He looked at Aria and shook his head. Her eyes filled with relief. They stayed there hidden behind the shrubs, completely silent, waiting for the men to either find them or leave.

The leader ordered the men to spread out and search. Cole waited breathlessly. Suddenly, Sarge looked right at Cole.

There was no mistake. Cole knew they had been seen. Sarge stared at Cole for a minute. Cole's heart was racing as he returned Sarge's gaze. But then Sarge turned away and continued to search the nearby bushes.

Cole sat completely still, afraid to even breathe. He wasn't sure why Sarge hadn't turned him in yet, but he knew he would eventually. Suddenly, it occurred to him that Sarge was dragging this out to make his capture even more enjoyable.

Once again, he considered fighting them, but he couldn't. Just the thought of killing them made his hand shake. All of the sudden, someone grabbed his hand. He quickly looked over at Aria. She smiled but kept her hand on his. Cole was frozen in place, but now all of his focus was on Aria.

The soldiers were still looking around. One of them was walking over to where Cole and Aria were hiding. Cole knew they would be found. There was no way they could escape.

"I see him. He's running this way!" Sarge called out from the opposite end of the clearing. All of the men turned and took off after Sarge, who was running in the opposite direction from where Aria and Cole were hiding.

Cole was so surprised and confused by what had happened that he didn't move.

"Come on!" Aria whispered quickly, pulling Cole in the other direction. Cole's trance broke and he ran after Aria as quickly as he could.

They kept running until they were out of breath. Luckily, Aria still knew where they were going, so they were able to keep moving toward the Center Stones. Once Cole thought they were far enough away, they slowed to a walk.

"I'm starving," Aria finally complained. "Should we stop to eat yet?"

Cole looked behind them nervously. "We're still pretty close to the guards. We don't have much food left, and—"

"But if we don't eat soon, we're not going to have enough energy to keep going," Aria interrupted. Before Cole could argue any more, she stopped and started digging through her bag. "Here," she said as she handed him a bar. "We can eat while we walk if it makes you feel better."

Cole frowned, but he took the food Aria offered him. He knew Aria was right to make them eat—he was so hungry that he had developed a very bad headache.

"Who was that man—the one who saw us?" Aria asked. "You seemed to recognize him."

Cole nodded. "His name is Sarge. He's one of the general's soldiers. When I was first captured, he was the only soldier who talked to me. He said he wanted to help me, but I didn't believe him. I still don't."

"Well, at least he was nice enough to help us now."

Cole laughed. "Sure, he's nice," he said sarcastically. "Did I forget to mention he was the one who found the mark on my arm and told the general about it? He's the reason the general is after me in the first place."

"Oh." Aria was silent for a few seconds. Finally, she asked, "Why do you think he helped us?"

Cole shrugged. "No idea," he said. "Not that I'm complaining, though."

Cole looked at Aria, but she was lost in thought. After several minutes of silence, she said, "Back there, when we were hiding, what happened? You scared me. Your eyes got so angry, and you looked insane. I thought . . . I thought you were going to kill them."

Cole's attention focused on her, and he looked surprised. "What? I mean, yeah—I was thinking about it. Why not? They deserved it, and we were gonna be captured."

Aria looked at him in shock. "You could have done that? Killed someone?"

Cole shrugged. "They would've done it to me."

Aria frowned. "Yeah, but I thought you were different."

"You're not one to talk," Cole pointed out. "You said yourself that you don't feel sorry for people who get what they deserve—like your dad. So what's the difference?"

Aria looked at him. "Killing is wrong," she said decidedly, leaving no room for debate. "Whether or not they deserve it isn't the question. Anyway, you didn't do it. You put your sword down. So a part of you knew it was wrong. But if you had done it, you would've been no better than they are."

Cole scowled. "You don't know everything."

Aria stared at him for a long time. Cole stared back at her. He couldn't help thinking how beautiful Aria's eyes were.

Then he blinked and tried to remind himself to focus. Aria's eyes weren't what he was supposed to be focused on right now.

Cole was the first to break eye contact. When he looked away, she simply said, "I know you're better than that."

"We should keep going," he quickly replied as he put his sword back in its sheath and stood up.

Aria stood up, too, and without another word she grabbed her bag and continued walking. Cole knew she was upset, but he didn't know what to do or what to say.

A while later, Cole finally spoke. "Look, Aria—I'm sorry."

Aria sighed. "No. I am." She forced a laugh. "I guess I overreacted. I've just never thought about having to kill someone before—or that you'd be willing to."

Cole tried to ignore the horror in her voice. "Well, I haven't ever killed anyone," he clarified. "So you can relax—I'm not some crazy murderer. But what if Sarge hadn't helped us? Then we would have been captured, and I would've been taken back to the general—who knows what they would have done to you! It's not like they're innocent."

Aria clearly didn't agree with his reasoning. "Let's just finish this," she said, turning away and continuing to walk.

Cole tried not to let her silence bother him. He reminded himself that she was just living in her fairy-tale world again—if she bothered to see the world for what it truly was, he was certain she'd agree with him.

They walked for a few more hours and then finally stopped. Cole stared in front of them. The forest they'd been walking through ended less than a few feet away. In front of them was nothing but long, flat dirt with patches of grass and weeds.

"The Wasteland," Aria said, confirming Cole's suspicions. "This is all that exists outside of Rhomac and the forest—at least, as far as we know." She grinned. "No one's ever gone out there and returned to tell the tale."

Cole tried not to look worried. "You could have told me that before we decided to come all the way out here!"

Aria laughed. "We'll be fine," she promised. "And besides, this is the only way to the Center Stones—and the only way out of Lathinium. We have to go this way."

Cole looked out at the Wasteland again. "So what do you think's out there?"

"Not sure," Aria admitted. "But Ulrik did have a theory. Way back before Rhomac was created, the people deported from Nilrith were just dropped off in the middle of nowhere. He thinks they might be out there somewhere, in tiny villages spread out across the rest of the world."

Cole nodded. At least it didn't sound like there was anything dangerous out there.

As the sun set, Aria handed out some food. "Here," she said grimly. "After this, we've only got one more bar each."

After eating, they sat together silently and stared across the huge land in front of them.

Finally, Aria turned to the side and pointed. "See that canyon over there?"

Cole had to squint to see it in the fading light, but he could just barely make out the edges of the cliff side. He nodded. "Yeah."

"Rhomac's just on the other side of it. All we have to do now is to follow the canyon, and we'll eventually get to the Center Stones. It's not far now."

Cole sighed contentedly and laid down on his back. "Almost free," he mumbled to himself.

Aria laughed. "I'm so glad you're doing this," she admitted.

Cole hesitated. He knew Aria needed to know the truth, and he was tired of lying to her. "There's something I need to tell you," he started quietly.

Aria looked at him. "What's up?"

Cole looked away, refusing to make eye contact. He stood up and walked toward the edge of the forest. He thought about the general and what he would do to Cole if he ever caught him.

"I'm not going to release the magic, Aria," he finally admitted. "I can't give up my life for that—"

Aria interrupted him with exasperation. "You don't have to give your life. Ulrik told you it wouldn't kill you."

"And he also betrayed us," Cole added. "I can't trust anything he says! And there was this look in his eyes—like he wasn't telling me the whole story."

Aria shook her head. "You can't be serious." She walked over to him, but Cole continued to look out at the desert. "Ulrik looked at you funny, and now you think you're going to die? Do you realize how crazy you sound?" She laughed, but Cole didn't join her.

"I'm not going to release the magic," he repeated, more firmly. "I mean it, Aria. You can't change my mind."

Aria wasn't ready to give up convincing him yet. "You need to bring the magic back," she whispered. "Please!"

Cole shook his head. "No."

"But that's your destiny. You were going to be a hero—"

"I told you, Aria," Cole said, his voice rising in anger. "I'm not a hero. I tried to warn you. I never asked for this. I never wanted any of this. I don't want a destiny; I want a life!"

Aria was furious. "You're just being selfish! You know releasing the magic is the right thing to do. The world deserves to have it again, and all you're doing is hoarding it for yourself! All you have to do is return the magic, and everything will be fine."

Cole turned around and looked at Aria in disbelief. "It will kill me, Aria!" he shouted. Aria took a step back. Cole composed himself and repeated himself again, his voice barely above a whisper. "Whatever you say, I know what I saw in Ulrik's face. He knew it would kill me."

Aria wasn't even trying to understand. "I should have expected this." She glared at him angrily. "You're the one who can bring back the magic, and you won't!"

"Why should I?" Cole said, just as angry. "What if by releasing the magic we're doing just what the general wants? Why not just let the magic die? Maybe the world is better off without it!"

"You're just trying to justify your selfishness," Aria said through gritted teeth.

"And you're just trying to justify your hero complex," Cole countered. "You don't care about me or the magic—you care about getting noticed. You want the fame and glory."

Aria shook her head. "You don't understand. I don't care about being noticed; I'm just trying to help you make the right choice. You need to release the magic because it's the right thing to do—because you're the only one who can."

Cole looked down at the ground. "It's not that simple, Aria," he said, quietly but firmly. "What about me? I don't want to die."

"There's a reason the general's looking for you still—he's going to release the magic eventually. You know he'll just keep doing this until he succeeds. What if he does this to more kids?"

Cole shrugged. "Then that'll be someone else's problem—not mine."

"I thought you were better than that, Cole." Aria's voice was hard. "I believed in you. But you're just like Ulrik."

"I'm nothing like him," Cole argued.

"Yes, you are!" Aria was so angry that she was practically shouting. "You're both too afraid to do the right thing—too worried about yourselves to notice anyone else around you. You lied to me. You've been lying to me this whole time." She paused for a moment. When she spoke again, her voice was quiet. "I'm done, Cole."

"What?" Cole said, trying to understand.

"I'm done. I'm done helping you. You know the way now," she stated as she angrily marched toward their bags. She picked up Cole's pack and threw it at him. Then she started packing up her stuff.

"Aria—" Cole said. Even though he was angry, he wanted her to stay. He frantically tried to think of something to say, but he couldn't find the right words—so he said nothing.

Aria shook her head. "I'm not going to help you do the wrong thing."

Cole grew angry again. "It's my life, Aria. I want to live it. I want to make my own choices. I'm tired of other people deciding for me—the mine drivers, the general, Ulrik, and especially you. Leave me alone."

Aria was silent for a minute. Then she whispered, "Fine." Just like that, she turned and walked off into the woods, back the way they had come.

CHAPTER 27

Cole barely slept all night. Any time he heard a noise in the forest, he'd wake up quickly, hoping Aria had decided to return. But Aria was gone, and Cole was completely on his own.

When he woke up the next morning, he tiredly sat up and yawned. Out of habit, he looked over to see if Aria was awake yet, but then all the events of last night came rushing back to him. He groaned and fell back onto the ground.

He laid there for a while, recalling everything that had happened yesterday. He didn't want to get up and start the day. He knew a part of him was hoping that Aria would still come back, even after everything that had happened.

He spent a few more minutes trying to go back to sleep, but he eventually decided sleeping would be impossible—

and he needed to keep moving, anyway. Cole looked at the flat landscape in front of him and remembered the directions Aria had given him yesterday. He was almost free. As he sat up, his stomach growled loudly. He began rummaging through his backpack, which turned out to be pointless because Aria had taken the rest of the food with her yesterday.

He finished packing up his things and then looked at the sword. He didn't feel like carrying it today; besides, he was almost out of danger, anyway.

Almost free.

He tried to shove the sword in his backpack, but half of it still stuck out of the top. Cole didn't care, though—at least he wouldn't have to carry it in his hand. Then he took another look at the large desert in front of him. Aria had said to follow the canyon, so that was what he planned to do. Hopefully, he could get to the Stones before he was too hungry to keep going.

Just as he was about to begin walking, he heard a noise behind him. Cole turned around and saw Aria standing just a few feet away. At first, he just stared at her, certain it was too good to be true.

Aria smiled at him. "Cole?" she said hesitantly.

Suddenly, Cole came to his senses. He ran over to her excitedly with a big smile on his face. "I'm so glad you came back!" The words flew out of his mouth before he could stop himself. "I want you to come with me, Aria. I need you. We can travel together, and maybe there is something outside of Lathinium. If there is, we can find it together—it would be an adventure, like you wanted."

Aria didn't say anything and Cole waited, confused by her silence. "What's wrong?" he finally asked.

"Nothing," a cold, unfamiliar voice called out from behind Cole, causing him to start with surprise. "In fact, everything is perfect." Cole spun around. A soldier with a very triumphant look on his face moved from out of the cover of the trees and stood behind Aria. That soldier was quickly joined by a group of at least ten more soldiers who had followed him out of the forest. As Cole stood rooted to the spot in shock, the soldiers quickly surrounded Cole and Aria.

Cole looked at the soldiers with dawning realization. The timing of Aria's appearance right before the soldiers arrived couldn't be a coincidence. He turned to Aria in disbelief. "This was you," he said quietly. He watched her face, hoping that he was wrong. He didn't want to believe she could do something like this.

The guilty look on Aria's face confirmed his fear. "I'm sorry, Cole," Aria said gently, taking a step closer to him. "You need to understand. It'll be better this way."

"Better? For you, maybe—but not for me." Cole stepped away from her quickly, shaking his head. "No. Just stay away from me, Aria." His head was spinning as he tried to understand what was happening.

Aria had turned him in. She had betrayed him.

Cole wasn't thinking clearly. He needed to stop thinking about Aria; instead, he needed to think about escaping. He reached behind his back, trying to grab his sword. But it wasn't there. Cole could see the top of it was sticking out of the top of his backpack, which was lying next to one of the soldiers.

Left with no other choice, Cole tried to summon the magic without the sword. He focused on his anger and frustration and tried to use that to focus the magic.

Nothing happened.

Cole glanced at Aria. She stood behind the soldiers, watching him. Cole locked eyes with her for a second. He wanted to see her emotions—wanted to know if she felt guilty—but Aria's face was completely expressionless.

Cole wished he could mask his own emotions that well. Deliberately putting her from his mind, Cole took a deep breath and focused solely on summoning the magic. Suddenly, Cole could feel the magic coursing through his veins. He closed his eyes for a brief second and let the power wash over him.

When he opened his eyes, the magic exploded. An invisible wave of energy encompassed Cole and moved toward the soldiers. The second it hit them, they flew backward as if they had been hit. There was now an open path through the soldiers—it was Cole's one chance of escape.

Without thinking, Cole sprinted toward the opening. A soldier nearby grabbed his wrist, and Cole turned to punch him in the face. This time, the magic moved with his punch and sent the soldier flying away from Cole—he flew much farther away than what should have been possible. Then Cole turned and continued to run. He wasn't sure where he was going; the only thing he knew was that he needed to get back to the cover of the forest.

He was almost at the tree line when another soldier ran at Cole from the side, knocking Cole to the ground. Cole moaned as he hit the ground hard. The blow had knocked the wind out of him, and he struggled to catch his breath. He knew he needed to get up, but he couldn't. The soldier who had knocked him to the ground pinned him down, while another soldier chained Cole's wrists together.

Cole's head was spinning. He was dizzy, disoriented, and nauseated. He tried once again to summon the magic, but that was when he noticed it: the chains on his wrists were made of Anyrite. Cole suddenly remembered the metal band Ulrik had placed around Cole's wrists during a training session. It had left him feeling so weak. Ulrik had obviously taken note of how the band had affected Cole—and Cole was sure that Ulrik had passed the information on to the general. He'd trusted Ulrik enough to train with him, and now Ulrik was going to use the knowledge he'd uncovered to capture Cole. The irony was so terrible that Cole almost found it amusing.

Ulrik wasn't going to take any chance of Cole escaping this time.

Cole's heart sank. He could already feel the chains draining his magic, and within a few seconds he knew there would be no way to escape.

He stopped fighting. He didn't have enough strength to try another escape. He looked at the soldiers who had captured him. None of them looked familiar, and there was no sign of Sarge or his unit.

Aria took a few steps closer to him. Cole stared at her, barely able to comprehend what had happened. Now that he had been caught, he realized the finality of his situation. Once again, he felt like he couldn't breathe, but this time it wasn't from physical injuries.

One of the soldiers, who Cole guessed was the leader of the group, walked over to Aria. He was the same soldier who had talked to Cole earlier. The soldier nodded at Aria and said, "Thank you for your service to Lathinium. You have no idea what a help you have been. You have single-handedly stopped the most dangerous criminal in the world. You should be proud."

Aria blushed, which made Cole even more furious. "I'm happy to help," she said graciously. She looked at Cole and her eyes flashed with sadness. "Hopefully, the general will make the right decision and put the magic back where it belongs."

Cole felt numb. He couldn't believe what he was hearing. Aria had done this because she honestly believed that the general would be the solution she had been looking for.

The lead soldier finished his polite conversation with Aria. He walked back over to Cole and gave him a disgusted look. "I don't see why the general's looking for you," he said in disbelief. Grinning cruelly, he took a step closer to Cole, who looked down but refused to back away. The soldier spoke in a low voice that only Cole could hear. "Well, aren't you brave," he said mockingly.

Then in the same low voice, he added, "I hope you like suffering—because in a few hours you're going to wish we had just killed you now."

Cole continued to look down at his feet and refused to respond. At this point, it didn't matter, anyway. Without warning, he was then punched in the stomach by the soldier, who said angrily, "That will teach you to fear me." Cole doubled over and released a quiet groan. Aria gasped, but Cole refused to even look at her.

The soldier glanced over at Aria, and when he saw that he was upsetting her, he walked away from Cole. "Tie him down somewhere. He's harmless as long as we have those chains on him, but I'm not taking any chances."

Two of the soldiers nodded and led Cole over to a tree near the edge of the woods. They forced him to sit against the tree while they quickly tied him to the tree with thick cords of rope. Cole's shoulder blades dug into the bark of the tree. He tried to shift into a more comfortable position, but moving was difficult because he was tied so tightly.

"No moving," one of the soldiers yelled. Cole immediately froze and made himself sit still.

Eventually, the soldiers left to join the others, and Cole was left alone. He watched as some of the soldiers unpacked their bags of supplies. In a matter of minutes they had set up camp, and soon all of the soldiers were laughing and eating. Aria would occasionally join in on their conversation but spent most of her time with the soldiers' leader.

Cole tried not to pay attention to what she was doing. He told himself that he didn't care what she did, but he knew he was lying to himself.

He *did* care. And that was why her betrayal hurt so much.

With nothing else to do, he listened to Aria's conversation with the soldiers' leader. Soon he knew the leader's name was Bryant, and he was the commander of a small battalion. He was eighteen but had already been in the army for three years. He also seemed completely captivated by Aria.

Aria talked a lot about herself and her dreams to travel, but Cole noticed that she left out anything related to him or the magic.

Bryant asked how Aria had met Cole.

"I have a house in the woods a few days from here," Aria said offhandedly. "I met him there, and then when I found out he was dangerous, I turned him in. It had to be done. The magic is too important for one person to keep." She spoke so confidently that Bryant didn't ask her any more questions.

Watching Aria and Bryant made Cole's stomach turn. He wished they were sitting farther away, but Bryant picked the seat closest to Cole's tree and didn't seem interested in keeping his conversation quiet. Cole wondered if Bryant was purposely trying to get a reaction out of him. If that was his plan, then it was almost working.

Cole still couldn't believe that Aria had turned him in. He didn't want anything to do with her. But he still couldn't keep himself from watching her, waiting for her to look at him to see what she had done to him—and to look sorry.

She somehow managed to avoid looking at him the entire time. Finally, Cole just leaned his head down on his knees and closed his eyes, accepting his fate. It was obvious Aria wanted nothing to do with him. After an hour of being forced to listen to Bryant and Aria talk, one of the general's large airships flew overhead, halting further conversation.

Bryant called out orders. "Let's pack up quickly. Get the prisoner ready to move. I want two men with him at all times. Take him directly to the cell and make sure he's locked up. Everyone else, continue packing up camp as quickly as possible. The general's already on the airship, and he'll be throwing a celebration tonight." Bryant turned to Aria. "And since you helped us find him, you are formally invited as my guest," he told her with a smile.

For the first time all day, Aria looked uncertain. Bryant's smile turned into a frown. "You *are* coming, aren't you? You wouldn't dare refuse?"

The look on Bryant's face seemed too forceful. Without thinking, Cole angrily tried to move toward Bryant and Aria. Before he could finish his step, the soldiers pulled him back sharply.

Bryant laughed at Cole's attempt to interfere. "You're pathetic," he said to Cole with a sneer. "What were you even hoping to accomplish?" Cole only glanced at Aria for a second, but it was enough time for Bryant to follow his gaze back to Aria. Realization dawned on Bryant's face, and he smirked. "Well, this changes things," he said slowly.

He walked toward Cole and forced him to his knees. Aria looked away uncomfortably, but she didn't say anything. "Is it possible that you have feelings for her?" Bryant asked in disgust. Cole quickly glanced up at Aria but then looked away again. All he felt right now was anger. If Aria cared about what Bryant was saying, Cole couldn't tell. He tried to stand up, but Bryant pushed him down again.

"I can't even imagine how terrible you must feel right now," Bryant said as he looked down at Cole with a fake look of sympathy. "Being betrayed by the one person you trusted." Cole felt like he had been punched in the stomach.

Motioning for two soldiers to hold Cole in place, Bryant then walked over to Aria again. He moved a piece of her hair out of her face and tucked it behind her ear. Aria stiffened, but she didn't move away.

"You deserve better than him," Bryant told Aria, looking at Cole with a sneer on his face. "Someone like you shouldn't be hiding in the forest with a runaway. Come back to Ambroise with us. Let me show you the life you deserve."

Cole watched in horror as Aria nodded. A platform was lowered from the general's airship. Bryant offered Aria his arm, and she took it. Together they walked onto the platform and rose toward the ship's deck. Cole watched until they were out of sight.

Suddenly, a punch sent him reeling to the ground. The soldiers laughed as they stood over him. Cole didn't have the energy to get up again. He stayed on the ground where he had fallen until one of the guards jerked him to his feet and forced him onto the same platform Aria and Bryant had used.

With each passing second, Cole rose closer and closer to the airship. His fear grew until he was barely able to breathe. Cole knew the general wouldn't rest until he had forced every bit of the magic out of him, and Cole was certain the results would be worse than death. As they rose, Cole was able to see the forest line. For a small second, he even thought he could see the Center Stones.

He had been so close.

The platform rose to the same height as the airship, and one of the general's guards shoved Cole forward. Cole was barely able to keep his balance. He got one last look at Aria. Their eyes locked for a brief second. He thought she looked upset—he hoped she was. He wanted her to feel guilty.

Two soldiers led him down a few flights of stairs, finally stopping in front of a large door.

Cole was surprised. He was expecting the guards to take him down to the lowest level of the airship where the prison cells were. Instead, they took Cole into a large room which looked like a laboratory. Cole's stomach churned when he saw the variety of sharp tools laying on the stainless-steel utility tables.

The guards led him through the room and down an adjoining hallway. Cole passed a few more rooms, which he assumed held more supplies. At the end of the hallway, they arrived at an even larger metal door—without any windows.

It was Cole's cell.

The guards opened the door, pushed Cole inside, and shut the door behind him. The room was dimly lit, with a small bed in one corner and a toilet in the other. Other than that, the room was completely empty.

As soon as the guards slammed the door, Cole sat down on the bed in a daze. He barely registered the danger he was in. All he could think about was Aria. He wanted to scream, but he felt like he couldn't move—he could barely even breathe.

He remembered how she had stared at him in amazement every time he used the magic. He pictured how her eyes lit up whenever she talked about her dreams. Aria was both stubborn and idealistic, but she was also fun, brave, and amazing. Cole had trusted her with all his secrets—and she had betrayed him.

When the door opened again, Cole didn't even look up.

"I hope your little stunt last time we were together was worth it," General Sylvester said quietly. "Because I promise you, you're going to wish you had let me kill you then."

Cole didn't move. He just stared at the ground silently. He didn't think anything could be worse than the pain he was feeling right now.

The general laughed. "Clearly your manners haven't improved since the last time I saw you."

The general walked over to Cole's bed. "Get up and face me," he ordered angrily.

Cole slowly got to his feet, but he still refused to look at him.

"Your resilience amazes me," the general admitted. "You are audacious, I'll give you that. But don't worry—you will be terrified soon enough." The general then motioned with his hand and two more guards entered the room.

One guard stood on each side of Cole and forced him to follow the general back into the laboratory. This time, two men wearing lab coats were discussing some paperwork they had placed on a desk. They stopped what they were doing and faced the general when he entered.

One of the men was Ulrik, who Cole had expected. But he was stunned when he recognized the other scientist—someone Cole never thought he would see again.

"Allow me to introduce my newest assistant. Apparently he is quite a genius—top of his class when he lived in Nilrith. I'm sure you remember him. After all, you did save his life."

"Gale," Cole mumbled.

General Sylvester smiled. "Oh dear, I hope this isn't too awkward for you. After all," he said, looking at Cole, "you sacrificed your life to save his. And you—" He turned to Gale and smiled. "You are going to assist us in ending his life."

Gale looked at the floor. The general continued, "But we're getting ahead of ourselves." He pointed to Ulrik and introduced him to Cole. "This is my lead scientist, although I'm sure you already know him." For a second, Ulrik looked guilty, and then his expression became neutral—even cold. "He will be in charge of all the proceedings in this room."

The general turned to Ulrik. "I will leave you to your work, Professor. There will be a guard stationed outside of the labs at all times in order to help keep the boy in order. Additional assistance or supplies can be provided to you at a moment's notice. Just inform any one of my soldiers as to what you desire, and they will immediately make your request known to me."

Ulrik nodded. "Thank you, sir."

With that, General Sylvester and the soldiers left, leaving Cole, Ulrik, and Gale alone.

Ulrik was the first to speak. "I'm sorry it had to come to this, Cole. I had hoped you would have been able to make it to the Center Stones."

Cole snorted. "Really? Was that why you ratted me out to the general?"

Ulrik looked shocked, but before he could respond, Gale interrupted. "Wait—you know each other?"

Cole nodded. "After I escaped the first time, I found his house in the woods. I was nearly dead when his daughter Aria found me. She helped me get better, but when Ulrik saw the mark on my shoulder, he told me about the magic and tried to teach me to control it. Then the general showed up, and Ulrik tried to turn us in."

Ulrik looked surprised. "We heard you two talking," Cole explained. "While the general sent soldiers to the barn, we ran away and hid in the forest."

Ulrik frowned. "Speaking of Aria, where is she? She wasn't captured, too, was she?"

Cole face hardened, and he turned away. "Aria's fine," he said coldly. "She has everything she ever wanted. I don't want to talk about it, though. Let's just get this over with."

Ulrik nodded and led Cole up to a large metal chair with ankle and wrist restraints. Cole's chest tightened. Ulrik put his hand on Cole's shoulder, but it wasn't an attempt to comfort him. Cole knew he had no friends on this ship. Gale was over at a table, organizing supplies, and neither Gale nor Ulrik said anything.

Ulrik leaned down and whispered, "We have no choice. You can either do what I say willingly or I will have to use force. There's no way out this time. You know that, don't you? We've all run out of options. It's time for you to accept that."

Cole stared straight ahead, trying not to look as terrified as he felt. He knew he had no choice. He had no idea what Ulrik was about to do, but he knew it was going to be painful. Cole silently vowed not to give anyone the satisfaction of knowing how afraid he actually was.

Cole stepped up to the chair and sat down. After tightening the restraints around Cole's ankles, Ulrik pulled a key out of his coat pocket. He removed the chain from Cole's wrists and immediately put the chair's wrist restraints on him.

Ulrik called out to Gale, "I need you to watch him until I get back." He handed Gale a small black circle with Anyrite crystals lodged inside of it. "Put this on his chest, right above where his heart is. It will prevent him from being able to use the magic to escape."

Gale nodded, and Ulrik went down the hallway to one of the additional rooms.

When Ulrik was out of sight, Gale frowned and gently put the disk on Cole's chest. As soon as it touched Cole, an intense pain shot through his body. He clenched his jaw but was determined not to make a sound. He didn't want anyone to have the satisfaction of knowing how painful the disk was.

Gale looked at Cole apologetically. "I feel terrible about all this," he admitted. "If I had a choice . . . I wouldn't do this if the general wasn't forcing me. I'm sorry."

Another shock of pain moved through Cole's body, and this time he grimaced. Gale looked even more upset. "If things were reversed, you'd be doing anything to help me. You probably wouldn't hesitate, even if it meant risking your life."

That last comment almost made Cole snicker. He shook his head slightly. "You're wrong, Gale. I helped people, sure, but not because I was brave. I was just too scared to live with the guilt of being the one who survived." Cole's mind flashed back to the last person he had made that confession to. He tried to avoid thinking about her, but it was too late.

His mind flashed with memories of his time with Aria. He remembered her taking care of him and her reaction when she saw the scars on his back. He remembered how she was always playing with her necklace when she was thinking.

He thought about how bright her eyes looked when she was laughing and how nice she had looked that night in the hayloft—how honest she appeared staring up at the stars and sharing her dreams. But mostly, he thought about how stupid he'd been to trust her with all of his secrets.

Cole knew he needed to forget these memories—they were more painful than anything Ulrik or Gale could do to him. "It doesn't matter anymore," he said quickly, trying to convince himself.

Gale was about to respond, but at that moment Ulrik returned. Cole saw what Ulrik had gone to get: Rubilac, the sword the general had used on him when he had been captured the first time.

Ulrik frowned. "Sorry about this, Cole. We will do our best to make sure you don't suffer unnecessarily. I promise."

Cole was silent. He knew Ulrik's promises were just empty words—they meant nothing at all.

Ulrik removed the disk and gently touched the sword to Cole's chest. The intense pain began instantly.

Initially, Cole could feel all the magic being pulled away from him, leaving him feeling sick and extremely tired. Then he suddenly felt as if his heart was being pulled out of his chest. He screamed and tried to free himself, but the restraints prevented him from moving. Just before his vision went completely black, the pain instantly stopped. His head cleared and he found himself panting heavily.

Ulrik looked disappointed. "Well, experiment one failed. This isn't working." Gale nodded in agreement, walking over to a nearby desk and writing what Ulrik said in a thick lab notebook.

"The magic is too connected to his heart," Ulrik said. "I'm not sure how we can draw it out. Additionally, once I figure out how to draw it out, I will need to figure out how to store it. We'll need to run additional experiments to explore this further."

CHAPTER 28

Cole was completely exhausted as he walked back to his cell hours later. Gale followed behind him in complete silence. Once Cole was locked inside his room, he sat down on the bed and stared at the wall. He was hungry, thirsty, and every muscle in his body ached. With the Anyrite shackles back on his wrists, Cole couldn't feel the magic at all. He was helpless.

To make everything worse, Cole couldn't sleep no matter how hard he tried. A thousand thoughts were rushing through his mind, and they all ended with Aria.

Eventually, the door opened again, and Bryant entered the cell.

Bryant gave Cole a condescending look. "Not so tough now, are you? Stand up!" he demanded. When Cole didn't respond, Bryant repeated himself. "Stand up! Now!" This time, Cole obeyed. Not even standing straight up, Bryant was nearly a head taller than Cole. The height difference made Bryant smirk. "I just came to see how the general is treating you. Are you having a good time?"

Cole looked at the ground and refused to answer. Bryant continued, "I know Aria and I had a great time. I showed her all around the ship, and then afterward we went to the celebration dance. She looked absolutely radiant in the new dress I bought her. It's too bad you didn't get the chance to see how beautiful she looked."

Bryant paused and then said, "You know, she didn't mention you—not even once." He looked at Cole with mock sympathy. "It must feel terrible knowing she doesn't care about you. I just wanted you to know we danced together the whole night. She seems quite taken with me."

Cole tried not to show how much Bryant's comments hurt him. He chuckled and told Bryant, "Somehow I can't see Aria ever being interested in you."

Bryant angrily punched Cole in the jaw. Cole stumbled backward a little and felt his face gently. He wasn't bleeding, but the punch hurt, and Cole knew it would swell later.

"I wouldn't say anything like that again," Bryant warned. "General Sylvester has given me permission to do whatever I want to you. The only rule is that you remain alive." Bryant grinned. "And you'd be surprised how much a person can live through."

Bryant narrowed his eyes and pulled a whip from his coat pocket. Cole instinctively took a step back, which only made Bryant's grin widen.

"At least you have enough sense to be afraid of this." Bryant flicked his wrist and the whip snapped. Cole tried not to act bothered, but that just made Bryant angrier. He flicked his wrist again, but this time aiming for Cole's face. At the last second, Cole raised his arm to protect his face. The whip didn't break his skin, but it still stung horribly. Cole clenched his jaw, determined not to give Bryant the satisfaction of knowing he was in pain.

Bryant lowered the whip and looked at Cole condescendingly. "You have nothing. Aria doesn't care about you at all—she's made sure to tell me so. You're in here just waiting to die, while she's out there, getting everything she ever wanted. How does that feel?"

It felt terrible, but Cole wasn't about to admit that. "I don't care," he muttered. Unfortunately, the words didn't sound as convincing as he had hoped.

Bryant smirked and shook his head in mock sympathy. "I did some research on you, Cole. I know about all the kids you tried to help in Nilrith—how you helped them escape the patrols, even though you ended up getting captured. I know about the other miners you stood up for in Rhomac—but now one of the miners you tried to protect is here, experimenting on you. And now you've even lost Aria. You've lost everyone. No one cares about you." He laughed cruelly. "You have a horribly ironic history of sacrificing everything, only to be betrayed by all the people you tried to help."

Cole clenched his jaw tightly, refusing to say anything. For a moment, he thought of Rubert at the mines. He tried to remind himself that Bryant was the same type of horrible person and that Bryant's words didn't matter—but they did matter because Cole knew they were true.

"I'm so sorry," Bryant said mockingly. "Really—I wish someone cared about you." Then he pushed Cole up against the wall. "But no one will ever care about you, will they?"

Bryant turned toward the door but paused and looked back. "I wouldn't worry about it too much, though," he said offhandedly. "After all, you will likely be dead within the next month." Bryant turned and left the cell, locking the door behind him.

Cole gritted his teeth and sat down on his bed. He gently rubbed his face where Bryant had punched him, but he could barely feel the pain.

He barely felt anything.

The door opened and Cole struggled to wake up. He hadn't been sleeping long and felt very disoriented. Gale stood in the doorway, and Cole knew he was here to take him back to the lab. Gale must have noticed the new marks on Cole's face, but he didn't say anything about it; in fact, he didn't say anything at all. He simply opened the door and led Cole out of the cell.

The rest of the day was a blur for Cole. The Anyrite chains were only taken off of his wrists when he was locked to the chair, and even then Ulrik usually put the black disk on Cole's chest. They weren't going to give Cole any chance to use the magic.

Ulrik tried experiment after experiment, looking for a way to extract the magic, but nothing worked. All the experiments left Cole feeling like he was being torn apart. Soon Cole's wrists and ankles were raw from trying to get free of the restraints.

Sometime later that day, Cole was allowed a break to eat a small meal in the lab. The restraints were removed from his wrists, but his ankles remained securely fastened to the chair. They didn't bother putting the Anyrite chains back on him—not that it mattered because Cole was too weak to even think about using the magic. He was starving, but he forced himself to eat as slowly as possible. Cole hoped the longer he took to eat, the less time Ulrik had to experiment.

Cole was halfway through his meal when Ulrik complained, "We have nothing—nothing at all! We haven't made any progress. Every day, the subject gets weaker, and we have no results."

Cole stiffened when he heard Ulrik call him "the subject." A glance from Gale told Cole that Gale had similar thoughts about Ulrik's choice of words.

Gale walked over to Ulrik. "If the—" He cringed slightly at the term. "If the *subject* is so weak, why are we continuing the experiments? We can't afford to lose him, can we?"

"Because we are running out of time! The general is demanding results before we arrive in Ambroise." Ulrik's eyes looked wild with fear. "We need to press on, and we need to figure this out quickly." He sighed. "But perhaps you are right. Maybe he needs time to rest. We can forgo any more experiments for the day. Take him back to his cell. I will continue working. I'll have to draft up some more ideas for tomorrow. Try not to disturb me for the rest of the night."

Gale nodded his head. "Yes, sir."

He walked over to Cole and unlocked the ankle restraints, releasing him from the chair. Cole struggled to get to his feet and stumbled slightly. Gale frowned and waited to make sure Cole was able to walk. Then he put his hand on Cole's shoulder.

"Come on," Gale mumbled.

Gale picked up the Anyrite shackles and a lantern on his way out of the lab. Cole noticed Gale didn't put the chains back on him yet. Cole was grateful for any break he could get, so he didn't bother to say anything.

When they reached the cell, Cole stopped and waited for Gale to put the chains back on him. Gale just shook his head and sat down, leaning his back on one of the walls. Cole sat down across from him.

Gale turned on the lantern and shut the door behind him. "So you have magic, which is always running through your body, strengthening you, et cetera?" Gale asked.

Cole nodded, and Gale continued speaking. "And when I put these shackles on you, or when that black disk is touching you, they suppress the magic inside of you?"

Cole nodded again.

Gale frowned slightly, deep in thought. "Then why can't these same tools be used to remove the magic?"

"I don't really know—isn't that supposed to be your job?" Cole tried to reposition himself, but the movement was more painful than he had expected. He gritted his teeth.

Gale changed the subject. "I'm not going to put the chains back on you yet. I doubt you will get a significant amount of strength back, but it should help a little. In order to keep the chains off, though, I need to remain here with you to monitor you and make sure you don't regain too much strength."

Cole laughed. "Wouldn't want to risk me escaping, would you?" he said sarcastically.

Gale looked hurt. "I'm really sorry about this. When the general offered me this job, I had no idea what it was for—honestly. I had to take the job, Cole." Gale said, clearly begging Cole to understand. "Everyone knows there's no future in the mines."

"So now you're going to help kill me." It wasn't even a question in Cole's mind.

Gale shook his head. "I've spoken with Ulrik. We're trying to find a way to do this without causing you too much pain."

Cole stared at Gale in shock. "Without causing me too much pain?" he repeated slowly.

"Well, we're still researching new ideas," Gale protested. "I'm trying."

Cole laughed. "You don't get it, do you? You're turning into them. Just like Ulrik. You try to find any way to justify what you're doing. Doing wrong is wrong—no matter what." Cole froze. Those weren't his words. He remembered Aria telling him that at her house.

"What?" Gale's voice returned Cole to the present. "No. That's not it at all—"

"Then what is it?" Cole asked harshly. "What do you see it as?" Gale opened his mouth but didn't seem to have an answer. Cole just shook his head. "Just forget it. You should get back to your experiments, Gale." He held out his wrists, waiting for the shackles to be put back on.

Gale hesitated but finally began putting the shackles back on Cole's wrists. "I'm sorry, Cole. I'll try to help."

Cole shook his head. He was past the point of help. "No, Gale. Don't put your own life at risk. Even if you try to help me, the general is planning to kill me once he gets what he wants. I'm not going to survive this, and there's nothing you can do to change that."

Gale sighed. He looked like he wanted to say more but couldn't seem to find the right words. Finally, he picked up the lantern and walked out of the cell, shutting the door behind him.

Cole was alone, but he didn't mind. In fact, he welcomed the solitude.

The next few days were a blur. Cole had no idea how much time had passed. Gale would open the door and take Cole to the lab. He'd usually be given two meals between experiments. They would run the experiments until Cole thought he was going to pass out. They tried everything they could think of, but the magic refused to leave Cole.

Bryant always made sure to visit Cole to tell him about activities he and Aria were doing together. There always seemed to be a party or fancy dinner, and Cole tried not to give too much thought to what Bryant was telling him.

After Bryant left, Cole had a few hours to rest before Gale came back to get him—just a few hours before he had to go back to the lab and do the same thing all over again.

CHAPTER 29

After another round of experiments, Cole was led down the long hallway back to his cell. Gale walked in front of him, but he didn't say anything. They hadn't talked since the day Gale had ended the experiment early.

"How many days have I been here?" Cole asked quietly.

Gale didn't answer right away. Finally, he said, "You aren't supposed to know."

"Wow, thanks for your help," Cole said sarcastically.

"But it's only been three days so far," Gale added. "We'll get to Ambroise in another three."

Gale opened the door to the cell. "Try to sleep more if you can. I'll give the guards an order that you are not to be disturbed tonight. It should keep Bryant away for at least one night." He looked at Cole sadly before shutting the door.

All of the muscles in Cole's body burned as he sat down. The experiments were getting more and more painful, and Cole bleakly wondered how long it would be before Ulrik accidentally killed him in the process.

Just as he was about to fall asleep, he heard the door creak open. Cole looked up to see Gale standing by door. Cole groaned and tried to stand up, thinking it was already time to go back to the lab.

Gale shook his head. "No, you don't have to get up. It's not time to go to the lab yet. I just wanted to see if you were awake. There's a girl here who desperately wants to see you. She said if I didn't let her see you, she'd make a scene and get the guards' attention. She's in the lab now."

Cole stared at Gale. There was only one girl who would ever want to see him. "I don't want to see her," he said angrily.

"Well, I can't get her to leave, and if she's caught, we'll all be in trouble. She's going to be here whether you want to see her or not. I just wanted to give you a heads-up." He opened the door but then looked back and added, "She'll only have a few minutes to talk, though."

Before Cole could protest anymore, Gale left and returned with Aria. Cole backed into the far corner of the room, as far away from her as possible. He was still too angry with her to want to be anywhere near her. And he certainly didn't want her to see him right now and to have the satisfaction of knowing what she had done to him. Luckily, the lights were too dim in the corner for her to be able to see more than a shadow of him.

Aria looked like she was dressed for a party. She was wearing a midnight blue dress accented with elegant beads. Cole couldn't help noticing that the neckline was lower than anything she normally wore. Her hair and makeup were done, and Cole couldn't believe how different she looked. The only thing this girl shared with the girl he'd met in the forest was the sapphire necklace around her neck. She looked beautiful, but she didn't look anything like the person he remembered.

Cole gave her a disgusted look. If this was the real Aria, he didn't want anything to do with her.

"Will you come forward so I can see you?" Aria asked him in a low voice.

Cole didn't respond.

Aria, unaffected by his lack of response, just kept talking, her voice growing louder as she spoke. "Cole, I really am sorry it had to come to this, but I needed you to see the truth." Her voice was very matter-of-fact, and she spoke quickly. "That night, when you said you didn't care about bringing the magic back, I made a decision. Cole, you were wrong. Running away was wrong. This was the hardest decision I ever had to make, and I never wanted to hurt you—but we have to bring the magic back. Things will be better this way."

Cole voice was low. "Who is this better for, Aria? You? Now you get the life you always wanted—congratulations!" he replied angrily.

"It will be better for everyone," Aria countered. "One person isn't meant to keep all the magic to himself; it's meant to be shared. For the world."

"So you're helping the general steal it? And you honestly think the all-powerful General Sylvester is going to share the magic?" Cole said sarcastically.

"Yes," Aria said bluntly. "Bryant says the general isn't going to keep the magic for himself—he's trying to find a way to give it back."

"Oh, come on!" Cole said angrily. "You can't seriously believe anything Bryant says!"

"Why not? I believed you."

Cole was silent for a few seconds. "That was different," he mumbled. Aria was getting off track, so Cole tried to redirect the conversation. "Besides, that doesn't justify what you did." He started getting angry again. "You ruined my life—"

"That was your choice, too." Aria said calmly. "I encouraged you to do the right thing, but you chose not to. Someone had to make the hard choice."

"You still don't get it." Cole voice grew louder as he continued. "To you, this is still some fairy tale. You turned me in so you could be some hero in your made-up story!"

Aria looked at him with frustration. "I wasn't trying to help myself. Bringing the magic back will help everyone. But you—all you care about is yourself. You value your life more than the happiness of everyone else in the world! You had a mission, something greater than yourself, and you threw it all away because you were too afraid to do the right thing."

Cole froze. He was past the point of feeling angry. Now he just felt numb. "And that's why you turned me in?" He had to hear it from her even though he already knew the truth.

Aria nodded. "The magic has to be released," she repeated earnestly. "It's the right thing to do."

"But that should have been my choice to make!" Cole argued. "You can't decide all that for me!" He laughed and shook his head in disbelief. "I can't believe I actually ever liked you."

For the first time all night, Aria hesitated. "You liked me?"

Cole hadn't meant to say that. His face warmed. "I trusted you," he said, trying to recover. "I thought we were friends."

"And I trusted you," Aria said. "It looks like we were both wrong. You told me you'd release the magic, but you never had any intention of doing so. It was all a lie."

They were silent for a while. "I want the magic back," she finally said. "It's the right thing to do—you know that! It was your job to bring it back. When you decided you weren't going to help, I needed to find someone who would."

Cole had enough of this. "You don't even know what you've done, do you?" he said in disbelief.

Aria crossed her arms. "I'm doing the right thing! I'm helping bring the magic back to Lathinium—just like you should have done. At least I'm not being selfish!"

Cole still couldn't believe what he was hearing. Before he could stop himself, he stepped into the light. "Look at me, Aria," he said. Aria's eyes widened. She hadn't seen Cole since the day he'd been captured, and Cole knew his appearance would be shocking. The daily experiments and the recurring pain he was experiencing were taking a huge toll on his body—not to mention the fact that he had barely slept since his capture. In addition, Cole was covered in cuts and bruises from Bryant, he hadn't had a chance to clean up since he'd be on the general's airship, and his clothes were filthy.

Cole knew he was a mess, but now he didn't care. He wanted Aria to see what she'd done. "Tell me—why is it so selfish for me to try to avoid this?" Aria stared at him but didn't say anything.

Cole wasn't satisfied with her silence. He wanted her to care. He needed her to feel sorry for all of the pain she had caused him. "This is because of you, Aria. All of this—every single bruise and cut—is because of you. Every day they torture me, stopping right before they kill me so they can do it again the next day. All they want is to get the magic back.

They don't care how much they hurt me in the process—just like you!"

Cole walked to his bed and sat down. When he looked at Aria, Cole's voice was barely above a whisper. "Well, I hope you're happy."

Aria finally looked apologetic. She stepped toward him. "Cole, I didn't know. I—"

"No, Aria." Cole shook his head. "You *did* know. I tried to tell you. You just didn't listen. All you ever cared about was your fairy-tale story. You were determined to make me a hero. And when you found out the truth, you made me into the villain. Well, guess what? You ruined my life, and I let you do it. I was so stupid to ever think I could trust you."

Aria shook her head, but she didn't say anything. Cole could see the pain in her eyes, but he didn't care. Nothing mattered anymore.

"You don't get it," Cole said. "You never did, and you never will. You haven't ever had to worry about where your next meal was coming from or if you would even survive long enough to eat another meal. You've never had to worry about anything!"

"Why don't you just give the general the magic?" Aria asked feebly. "That's all he wants from you."

Cole looked at her in disbelief, and he shook his head. "No, Aria," he said coldly. "You're wrong again. I can't give him the magic even if I wanted to. I don't know how."

Cole moved to stand again, wincing slightly. Aria tried to step toward him, but Cole shook his head. "You've done enough. Just stay away from me."

"Cole, please," Aria begged him, looking stricken. Her voice wavered slightly. "Look, we can fix this somehow . . . maybe if I talk to Bryant or someone and explain that you can't give it back on your own. There has to be a way for you to survive this."

Cole turned away from her. "The only chance of me surviving was lost when you made a deal with those soldiers."

"Talk to me, Cole. Please."

Cole looked at her. He wanted to believe her, like he had before. But he reminded himself that he could never trust her again. "I can't," he told her, turning his back on her once again.

Aria wasn't giving up. "We'll figure out a way to fix this," she promised. She stepped forward and placed her hand on his shoulder.

Cole turned around quickly and pushed her hand off. "Just stay away!" he yelled at her. He swallowed hard and tried not to let his face betray his emotions. He was still angry and hurt—he hated what Aria had done—but being this close to her was bringing back all the pain he'd felt when she had betrayed him. He couldn't stand to be near her.

Aria took a step back. She looked shocked and sad, but Cole couldn't feel pity for her—not now. He watched as she moved toward the door, but she stopped in the doorway. "I'm sorry," Aria said. "If I'd known, I wouldn't have done it this way."

Cole shook his head. "I'm sorry, too." His voice was cold, and he didn't care how much he hurt her. "I'm sorry I ever thought I could trust you. I'm sorry I ever let myself believe you cared about me. But mostly, I'm sorry we ever met."

Aria still looked dazed and stayed silent for a long while. Then she looked Cole in the eye determinedly. "I'll fix this," she repeated earnestly. "You'll see."

Cole just shook his head. Even if he escaped, it suddenly didn't matter anymore. "Just leave me alone. Goodbye, Aria." He turned toward the wall and refused to look at her again. After a long silence, Aria left the room, shutting the door behind her.

CHAPTER 30

A few hours later, Gale opened the door to the cell. He nodded to Cole, signifying that it was time to continue the experiments. Cole stood and waited for Gale to take him to the lab.

Instead, Gale grabbed Cole's hand and put something in it. Before Cole could see what it was, Gale said, "She wanted you to have it." Then he walked out of the cell and toward the lab without waiting to see if Cole followed him.

Cole looked at what was in his hand. With a shock, he recognized Aria's necklace. Cole couldn't even look at it; instead, he angrily threw it into the corner of his prison cell. Then he walked up to where Gale was waiting for him. He could tell by Gale's expression that he had seen what Cole had done with the necklace, but Gale didn't mention it.

Cole walked up to the laboratory chair and waited while Gale strapped him in. When Gale finished, they waited for Ulrik to arrive. A few minutes later, the laboratory door opened and Ulrik walked in, accompanied by the general. Cole clenched his jaw. The general had never visited any of the experiments before. He wondered what his presence in the lab meant.

Ulrik was near the end of a conversation, and all Cole was able to hear was, "As the magic joined with him under a period of intense stress, it stands to reason that the only way to remove the magic is by similar means. But I think that there may be an additional element to this. The key is close, but just out of reach."

General Sylvester did not look pleased with Ulrik. "I asked you to bring me results, Professor. But all you seem to be giving me is excuses—and failure after failure."

Ulrik nodded. "Yes, sir. I know. But I really think we are close this time. My assistant has a theory." He motioned for Gale to step forward. "Would you listen to it?"

The general nodded slightly. Although he seemed hesitant, Gale began talking. "I did some further research into the magic from long ago, before it was destroyed. The differences between it and Anyrite struck me as interesting. The magic can do more than Anyrite, but it cannot be controlled as easily. It's almost as though the magic has a mind of its own, like it chooses who controls it. Now, I didn't believe that the magic has a mind of its own, so I researched further to see what makes some people better hosts than others."

The general waved his hand. "Go on."

"Well, it seemed to me as though the magic is enhanced by willpower. Before it was destroyed the first time, there were some people who believed that everyone had the magic inside of them, but the only way to use it was by acquiring a plethora of both the magic and willpower."

General Sylvester was paying attention but looked slightly irritated. "But how does this help us now?"

"My theory is that Cole's willpower, combined with the Anyrite heart, was what made Cole—I mean, *the subject*—the ideal host. If this is accurate, then it was not in fact the stress of his situation that caused the magic, but it was his reactions to the situations he encountered."

Ulrik cut in, saying, "So that means that more experiments will never be enough to extract the magic."

Gale nodded. "I also wondered why Cole acquired the magic after saving my life, and I think that is the key we were missing." He looked over at Cole. "When he challenged you, General, he must have known that his punishment would be death. I believe this courage might have triggered another part of his brain—the part that was later used to control the magic."

General Sylvester looked intrigued. "So this was what gave him the magic?"

Gale shook his head. "That is what made him an ideal host. Since the magic no longer existed, it had to be created. This was done by the reaction between his Anyrite heart and your sword, which initiated the reaction. However, I don't think we can extract the magic the way we created it."

"Then what is the point of this talk?" the general asked.

"I think it's important to understand the magic's past in order to affect its future." Gale paused, as if considering something. "But there is one more thing."

"What is it?" the general asked impatiently.

"I think the magic reacts to Cole's emotions. It seems to be activated to help him or people he cares about. It appears to respond directly to his feelings. If Cole is angry, the magic responds accordingly and destroys things. If his life is in danger or he is in pain, the magic will react accordingly and root itself even deeper. But my theory is that if Cole gives up the magic willingly, it will comply and give itself up. So far, we have been causing Cole pain by trying to extract the magic. But by hurting Cole, we make the magic defensive."

General Sylvester didn't look convinced. "So you're saying that we need to wait for him to offer the magic willingly?"

Gale nodded, but the general sighed. "I had hoped you had come up with a plausible solution. But this? This is madness.

We do not have the time nor the resources to wait for the subject to 'feel like' helping us. You will continue your work, but you must try even harder to pull the magic out. Force it out of him!"

Gale's face fell, but he nodded. "Yes, sir."

The general nodded. "Good. Now, back to work. You have already wasted valuable time today." With that, the general left, leaving Gale and Ulrik to their work.

After eight more lab visits, there was still no progress. Since the general's visit, Ulrik's urgency had only increased. Cole was in the labs longer, and the experiments they tried were more dangerous and painful.

Finally, Ulrik stopped and ordered Gale to lead Cole back to his cell for the night. Gale unlocked Cole's wrists and ankles, but Cole didn't stand up yet—he couldn't. He closed his eyes and took deep breaths, trying to find the strength to walk back to his cell.

Ulrik didn't have any patience. "Get up!" he ordered Cole irritably. "If you do not leave immediately, I will just lock you back in and continue the experiments."

Cole's voice was hoarse from screaming earlier, but he forced himself to talk. "I can't stand yet." The experiments were created to pull the magic out, but the pain affected every muscle in his body. Cole was certain he would fall over if he tried to stand at this moment.

Ulrik shook his head. "Get up," he repeated angrily. "Do you think you are the only one who is tired?"

Gale reached out his hand and helped Cole to his feet. Cole stumbled but quickly regained his balance. With the help of Gale, Cole made it back to the cell, collapsed on the bed, and closed his eyes.

Cole was nearly asleep when Gale said quietly, "She was asking about you again today." Cole didn't need to ask who he was talking about.

Without opening his eyes, Cole just said, "Stay out of it, Gale. I don't care about her or what she was doing today."

Gale laughed. "You might be telling yourself that, but there is no doubt she cares about you."

With that, Cole heard footsteps and then the sound of the door closing. He opened his eyes to be sure Gale was gone and then closed them again. But even though he was exhausted, he couldn't sleep. He couldn't stop thinking about Aria.

Cole finally gave up on sleeping. Even though every movement hurt, he got up and walked to the far corner of his room. Then he bent down and picked up the necklace Aria had given him. He clenched his jaw and tried to ignore the mixed emotions running through his mind. Seeing this necklace just reminded him of everything he had lost, but he still couldn't bring himself to let go of it.

He couldn't bring himself to let go of Aria—and that frustrated him more than anything. He made his way back to the bed. This time, he didn't even bother trying to sleep.

He reminded himself that he didn't want to see Aria ever again. He reminded himself that she had just been using him for the magic—she didn't care about him. But he also couldn't stop wondering why he secretly did want to see her again.

Even though he was still angry with Aria, Cole wrapped the necklace around his hand, closing his fist around the jewel heart. He thought about what Gale had said. He wanted to believe Aria cared about him, but he couldn't forget what she'd done.

Finally, he just closed his eyes and imagined a better future where Aria hadn't betrayed him and he had managed to escape the general forever.

CHAPTER 31

Cole heard footsteps coming down the hallway. He tried to prepare himself for another visit from Bryant, but to his surprise, this time Sarge opened the door.

"Hey, kid," he said with a smile. "I'll be honest—I was hoping I'd never have to see you again."

Cole nodded. "I was hoping the same thing." Then he looked at Sarge suspiciously. "Why are you here?"

"Just as friendly as I remember you being," Sarge said. "Relax—I'm just paying a visit. Bryant apparently took the day off, so it's my job to watch over you tonight, and I 'accidentally' took a stop by the kitchen on the way here." He threw Cole a sack, which had a bottle of water, an apple, and a few rolls of bread in it. The bread looked—and tasted—better than any of the meals Cole had been given here in the past.

Cole ate the food quietly, slowly savoring all the flavors. After a bit, Cole stopped eating long enough to ask, "Why are you being nice to me?"

Sarge laughed. "It's like I said before—I want to help you. Not everyone's out to kill you, you know."

Cole snorted. "You could have fooled me," he muttered, thinking about Gale, Ulrik, and Aria. "Thank you," he said to Sarge gratefully. "This food is delicious."

"Leftovers from the general's own table. Made by the best chefs in Lathinium."

Cole swallowed a bite quickly. "Won't someone notice the food's gone?"

"Not a chance," Sarge said, shaking his head. "Nobody on this ship eats leftovers, so whatever's not eaten is thrown out."

Cole wasn't convinced it was that easy. Gale had mentioned that the general was extremely strict over how much food Cole received—he was allowed just enough to keep him from starving to death. He could only imagine how difficult it must have been to sneak food down here. "Really—thanks for helping me."

Sarge shrugged. "It's just food," he said simply. "Figured you could use it more than the trash could."

Cole nodded and continued to eat. Finally, he asked, "So what are you doing back on the general's ship? And are we almost to Ambroise yet? How many days has it been?"

"One question at a time," Sarge said. "Your sense of time is all messed up. The general did it on purpose. We've been flying for about five days, but to you it probably feels like a lot more." Cole nodded.

"We'll probably arrive at Ambroise in two more days, but that's just because we aren't really in a hurry to get back. The general doesn't want to risk moving you, so you'll probably be staying on the airship until they're finished. I got here yesterday. Our group had gotten a message that a different patrol group had found you." He smirked. "Apparently you passed right by us, and we didn't even see you! Imagine that."

Cole laughed. In a more serious tone, he said, "Thanks for that. It's too bad we were still caught."

Sarge raised an eyebrow. "We?"

"Me and the girl I was traveling with. She grew up in a house in the middle of the woods and was showing me the way to the border of Lathinium so that I could escape." Cole paused and mumbled under his breath. "Before she turned me in."

Sarge nodded. "I've heard that story before: runaway finds a pretty girl who helps him escape. Although I've never heard of the girl handing over the runaway to the people who are going to kill him," he admitted.

Cole laughed and twisted Aria's necklace around in his hand. "Yeah, well, she was something else," he admitted.

"She wanted me to be a hero. She thought if we could free the magic . . . she thought that I would help a lot of people."

Sarge looked at Cole. "And what did you want?"

"Obviously, I wanted to just avoid all of this," Cole said, gesturing to the prison cell around him. "I wanted out—I wanted freedom."

"Sounds reasonable to me," Sarge said. "So why did she help you if she knew that?"

"She didn't know," Cole admitted.

Sarge's expression changed. "She didn't know? You lied to her?" he asked in surprise.

"No, I told her that I didn't want to free the magic," Cole argued. "At least, I told her that at first. I was just afraid that she wouldn't help me because she wanted me to be a hero."

"So you did lie to her," Sarge clarified.

"I had my reasons," Cole mumbled.

Sarge just laughed. "And how did that work out for you?" he asked.

Cole looked at the necklace in his hand and ran his fingers over it. He reminded himself of what Aria had done. "This isn't my fault," he said angrily. "She was just too naive and stubborn!"

"Okay." Sarge didn't sound convinced. "Whatever you say."

"Well, what was I supposed to do?" Cole said defensively. "If I'd told her, then she wouldn't have helped me."

Sarge didn't say anything for a minute. Then he asked, "So what now?"

"What do you mean?"

"I'll be honest with you. You look terrible. Frankly, I'm surprised you've survived as long as you have. With these conditions, you can't have much longer to live." Sarge stared Cole in the eyes. "The truth is that you are going to die. I know you wish there was another option, but there isn't. What's been done can't be undone. My question to you is this: Do you want her to live the rest of her life thinking this was all her fault?"

Cole glared at Sarge. "I'm the one who's going to die. She deserves to live with the guilt of that."

Sarge held up his hands defensively. "Okay."

Cole didn't think he sounded very convinced. "But this is all her fault," he repeated.

Sarge was silent for a few seconds before he asked Cole, "Are you sure?"

Cole thought for a while. At first, he was angry. Of course, it was Aria's fault! She had been the one to turn him in. She had found the guards and helped them capture him. But then he remembered how upset she had been just before she had turned him in—when she had found out he'd lied to her. And when Cole had talked to Aria in his cell, he could tell Aria was still hurt that he had lied to her.

"What's that in your hand?" Sarge asked suddenly, interrupting his thought process.

Cole handed the necklace to Sarge. Sarge looked at it, and then his eyes widened. "Where did you get this?" he asked, his voice barely above a whisper.

"It belongs to the girl I've been telling you about. Why?"

Sarge looked at Cole in disbelief. "Aria?" he asked intently. "Is the girl's name Aria?"

Cole looked at Sarge in confusion. "Yeah. How do you know her name?"

"Because . . . because she's my daughter." Sarge spoke as if he couldn't believe it himself. "Cole, this was the necklace we made for my daughter when she was born."

Cole shook his head. "You realize what you're saying sounds crazy, right? Anyone could have a necklace that looks like that—"

"The necklace was custom-made. It was completely one-of-a-kind," Sarge held up the necklace. "And it looked exactly like this."

"Well, Aria told me that she was abandoned on the streets in Rhomac—"

"Now I know it was her," Sarge interrupted.

Cole frowned. "I'm confused. You left her on the streets?" If that was true, then Sarge should not have been giving him life advice just a few minutes ago.

"It's complicated." Sarge looked devastated. "Do you know where I can find her?"

Cole shrugged. "I've been trapped down here, remember?" Sarge's face fell. Cole immediately regretted his apathetic tone and quickly added, "I know that she's on this ship and that she's been talking with a soldier named Bryant a lot. Maybe he would know more?"

"Thank you, Cole." Sarge looked so eager. Cole just hoped Aria would share his enthusiasm. "Really. If there's anything I can do for you, let me know." The irony of the comment irritated Cole slightly—there was a whole list of things Sarge could do for him— but he just nodded.

"Good luck!" Cole called out to him as Sarge left. Then Cole shook his head and laughed. If Aria got as mad at Sarge as she got at every other injustice in the world, Sarge was going to need a lot more than luck to survive.

Soon after Sarge had left, Gale entered. "Hey, Cole," he said. Cole groaned, and Gale quickly added. "Don't worry—I'm just visiting. You don't need to get up."

Cole laughed in relief. "You know, your visits are starting to become the thing I dread more than anything."

Gale laughed back and cringed slightly. "I'm really sorry about that."

There was a moment of awkward silence. "Have you seen Aria at all today?" Cole finally decided to ask him.

Gale looked a little confused. "Aria?"

Cole nodded his head. "You know—that girl you snuck in."

Gale grinned. "So that's her name. I was wondering. She never told me, and you never wanted to talk about it before." Gale paused for a moment and then said, "I saw her walking near the lab this morning, but I haven't seen her since."

Cole suddenly had a thought. "Wait—you saw her this morning? What time is it right now, and why aren't you running more experiments on me today?"

"Luckily for you, the professor is trying something new, and he won't be ready to test it until tomorrow. Until then, you can rest."

"There's a soldier up there. His name is Sarge, and he is looking for that girl. He said she is his daughter. Could you help him find her?"

Gale nodded. "I can try," he said as he walked out of the room, shutting the door behind him. He had only been gone for a few minutes before he returned. "Good news, Cole. They already found each other, but Aria isn't too happy about it. She wants to see you."

Cole shook his head. "No. Don't let her in here—"

Before he had finished speaking, Aria stormed in, barely containing her anger. She was practically shouting at Sarge, who followed her in. "No! I don't believe you!" She glared at Cole. "Is this some kind of mean trick?"

Sarge walked in after her and shot a glance at Cole, as if he was asking Cole for help.

Cole rolled his eyes and got up from where he was sitting. He wasn't exactly in the mood to talk to Aria, but he also knew she wouldn't leave until she'd calmed down. "Aria," he said calmly. "Aria, look at me."

Aria was shaking her head and pacing back and forth, refusing to cooperate. "What is he talking about?" she demanded. "And why did he say to talk to you?"

Cole glanced at Sarge questioningly. Sarge just shrugged. "When she got angry, I thought you might be able to calm her down," he said apologetically. "I'm not exactly good at this."

Cole turned his attention back to Aria. "Well, that answers that question. Aria, this is the man that let us escape in the woods, remember?"

Aria looked at Cole. "He can't be my father," she said resolutely. "My real father left me."

"That's how he knows he's your dad," Cole spoke calmly. "He might have a good excuse, but you'll never know if you refuse to talk to him. Besides, didn't you say you always wanted to know more about your parents?"

Aria still looked furious, but she had calmed down a little. Cole leaned against the wall, waiting for Sarge to explain.

Sarge began quietly, clearly upset. "What I did to you—leaving you—I have regretted it every day of my life."

He looked at Aria. "It was the hardest decision I ever made." He sighed. "I suppose I should start at the beginning. My wife—your mother—and I have been happily married for over eighteen years. We met when I was a new recruit for the army. Neither of us had any idea what we were getting into."

He paused, looking lost in thought. "We had heard warnings about joining the army, but I thought they were just people trying to justify their cowardice. We should have listened. The general . . . he does things to you—to your mind. He confuses right and wrong, and limits your options until you have no other choice but to do as he says."

Cole looked up and saw Gale nodding in agreement to that last part.

Sarge continued, "Well, Marylie and I married right before I was officially enlisted into the army. Almost two years later, we had a baby—a daughter. When she was born, we went to a jeweler to have a beautiful sapphire necklace made for her." Sarge held up a necklace—Aria's necklace.

"It was custom-made, and we had to save for months to afford it, but we wanted it to be a sign of how much she meant to us—of how much we loved her," Sarge went on. "The first three years were beautiful. Our baby daughter grew older, and every day we loved her more and more. But as time passed, I moved up in the army. Soon I was one of the best in my legion. The general began to notice me. He sent me on more covert missions. I was one of the people who would 'sweep things under the rug.' I helped make sure the general's secrets stayed secret."

Sarge sighed before continuing. "Things went downhill from there. The general called me into his office one day and gave me a mission: to buy young children from some of the poorer parents in Nilrith. I was told that they were to be used as part of an experiment, and the general was very specific about which children he wanted. He told me that I was to offer each parent a generous amount of money per child, and if they refused, then I was to take the child by force."

Everyone was silent. Cole knew exactly what those children were going to be used for. Finally, Aria asked, "Did you do it?"

Sarge laughed. "No. I couldn't do anything like that without thinking of you and your mother. I'd been in the army for years and sometimes had to cross 'gray areas,' but this was too much. I refused."

"Why didn't the general just kill you?" Cole asked.

Sarge shrugged. "By then, I was too high up. I did a lot of work for the general, and I was good at it—really good." His eyes darkened for a moment, and Cole couldn't help wondering what exactly Sarge had done. "At that point, I knew too much to be disbanded, and it wasn't cost effective to kill me and train someone to take my place. So the general resorted to the only power he had left: threats."

Sarge looked straight at Aria as he said, "I knew—at least, I feared—the general would take you. I couldn't imagine you in one of those horrible experiments, barely clinging to life. I went home, and Marylie and I talked all night. My enlistment was going to last for the next three years, and trying to leave sooner would have put us all in even more danger. So we came up with a plan. We knew it was risky, but we also believed it was our best chance of keeping you safe from the general. We took you to Rhomac. You were too little to understand what was going on, and leaving you there was the hardest thing we've ever done. But we knew you were safer there than with us."

Everyone remained quiet, captivated by Sarge's story. "Aria. That was our daughter's name—Aria Nasher, " Sarge continued. "Just before I left her, I made her promise to always keep her necklace with her so that she'd always be able to keep us close—"

"Keep you close?" Aria interrupted. She had remained very quiet during Sarge's story, but Cole could tell she was still upset. "How could I keep you close when you abandoned me? It's a little hard to love someone you don't remember."

Sarge looked at Aria. In the dim light, Cole was barely able to see the tears in his eyes. "I am so, so sorry for what I did. Leaving you was the most painful decision of my life, but I did it for you—because I loved you. I still do. I always will."

Cole couldn't help thinking of how awkward it was to be witnessing their reunion. A quick glance at Gale told him that Gale shared his thoughts. Cole wished Aria would leave, but she seemed more determined than ever to stay put.

On the bright side, Aria's anger appeared to be dissipating, and now she just looked very overwhelmed. She stared at Sarge in silence for a minute. Finally, she spoke. "This is so strange. I can't even process it right now." She shook her head, looking apologetic. "It's just a lot to take in. I need more time."

Sarge nodded, but still looked devastated. "I'm so, so sorry," he repeated. "If there had been any other way at all to keep you safe—"

Gale cleared his throat. "Sorry to interrupt, but I think we should leave now. The professor could return to the laboratory at any minute, and if he sees you in here, we could all get in trouble."

Sarge nodded and left, but Aria stopped in the doorway and ran back to Cole.

She looked nervous, and she made sure to stand a few feet away from him. "Thank you," she said cautiously. "If it hadn't been for you, I never would have known about any of this. Thank you. For everything—"

"I didn't do it for you," Cole clarified. "And I didn't do it on purpose, actually."

Aria looked hurt, but Cole tried not to care. "So you're still mad at me," she said quietly.

Cole laughed grimly. "Well, I'm still trapped here, aren't I?" he asked.

Aria was silent for a while. The tension between them was so strong that Cole thought he could cut it with a knife.

Aria took a deep breath and squared her shoulders. To Cole, it looked like she was preparing for war.

"I'm not going to force you to forgive me," she finally said. "And honestly, I don't know that I care anymore." She clenched her fist. "Which is why I have no problem saying this." She looked Cole in the eye and said, "I did care about you, and I still do. I never wanted to hurt you. You're my friend, and that's not gonna change—even if you keep deciding to hate me."

Cole watched her. He knew he should say something, but he couldn't find the right words to express all the emotions he felt. He needed more time, but Aria seemed to be tired of waiting. She looked at him once more and then walked toward the door.

"Goodbye, Cole," she whispered.

Then she was gone.

Immediately, Cole wanted her back. He stared at the closed door, hoping that Aria would come walking back through it.

A few minutes later, the door did open. Cole looked up eagerly, but it was just Gale. He held out Aria's necklace. "I'm really tired of playing mailman for you two," he muttered. "If you like her, why can't you just make up?"

Cole laughed. "Look around you," he said. "Look at where we are—where I am. I'm gonna *die*." The sentence was strange on his tongue. "I'm gonna die," he repeated. "You know that. I know that. Everyone on this airship knows that it's only a matter of time. Even if we did make up, we'll never see each other again."

Gale shook his head. "Maybe not. You could still survive—"

"I'm not an idiot," Cole said. He wasn't even going to allow himself to hope things could be different. He stared at Aria's necklace. "Just . . . tell her I'm sorry," he whispered. "I'm sorry I lied, and I'm sorry it came to this. Tell her I'll miss her. But whatever you do—" He stopped for a moment and swallowed hard. "Whatever you do, don't let her back here again."

CHAPTER 32

Gale had been right—Ulrik never did come to get Cole that day. Cole was glad for the break. He slept for most of the day and was only interrupted once, when Gale brought him some food.

Then the door opened, and Bryant entered the cell. Cole quickly grabbed Aria's necklace and tried to hide it in his fist, but he wasn't fast enough. Bryant saw the gem out of the corner of his eye.

"What was that?" Bryant asked. When Cole refused to answer, Bryant held up the whip. He asked again, "What was that?"

Cole reluctantly held up the necklace. Bryant clearly recognized the necklace and grinned. "I wondered where that had gone. She didn't seem the same without it." Bryant grabbed the necklace out of Cole's hand. "But how did she give it to you?" He raised his eyebrows in mock surprise. "She hasn't been visiting you, has she? She knows that's not allowed. And if she was, she'd be directly violating the general's orders. That would make her a criminal." He smiled. "And if I told her that you gave me the necklace out of anger—"

Cole knew Aria would think he'd tried to get her in trouble. "If you tell her that—" he threatened.

"What are you going to do?" Bryant asked. "You'll never be able to tell her the truth."

Bryant continued, "What I never understood about you is why you always try to help people, even the people who have ruined your life. You should be begging me to lock her up, but instead you threaten me."

When Cole didn't respond, Bryant shook his head. "You are weaker than I thought." He dangled the necklace out in front of Cole, just out of his reach.

Cole knew that Bryant was hoping that he would reach for it, but he denied Bryant that satisfaction.

Bryant leaned down and whispered to Cole, "I'll let you know a little secret. I overheard the general talking to Professor Ulrik today. Apparently, they are working on something huge. The rumor going around is that they are *planning* to kill you this time." He smiled cruelly. "I just wanted to give you some time to think about that before they come to get you tomorrow." He chuckled as he walked out of the cell and closed the door behind him.

Cole wasn't really surprised, but he still struggled to grasp what Bryant had just said. He felt like everything was moving in slow motion. His chest tightened, and he couldn't breathe.

He didn't want to die.

The door opened again later. This time, Gale entered the room. Cole's heart felt like it dropped to his feet as he slowly stood up. Gale's face was bleak, which only confirmed what Bryant had told him.

Cole walked forward, but Gale stopped him. "Whatever happens today... I want you to know that I didn't want this. I didn't think—"

Cole shook his head and tried to look brave. "Gale, I know what Ulrik has planned for today. It's okay. I'm ready." Without looking back, Cole left his cell for what he was sure would be the last time. When they arrived at the lab, Ulrik was already waiting patiently.

Ulrik nodded to Cole. "Thank you for your sacrifice. You will be remembered as a hero."

Cole shook his head. Ulrik's speech was comical, and they both knew it was a waste of time. "Just get this over with," Cole muttered, trying to act braver than he felt.

Ulrik nodded. He fastened Cole to the chair and then roughly held a cloth over Cole's mouth. Cole smelled something strange on the rag, and his eyes were already heavy. He knew breathing in the chemicals was going to make him lose consciousness, so he tried to hold his breath.

Ulrik turned toward the surgical table and picked up a large, thin knife. He looked at Cole sadly. "I'm sorry there wasn't any other way, but your Anyrite heart really belongs to me. And I'm afraid I need it back now." Cole couldn't hold his breath any longer—he had no choice but to breathe in the chemicals. A few seconds later, the world went dark.

"Wake up." Someone was talking, and they seemed angry. Cole attempted to ignore the voice and go back to sleep.

"Wake up!" the voice repeatedly demanded. Suddenly, cold water dumped all over Cole's face.

"What was that for?" Cole spluttered, wiping the water out of his eyes.

That was the first hint something was wrong. Cole could move his hands. They weren't restrained to the chair anymore. The voice spoke again. "Wake up! We don't have time for this."

Cole opened his eyes, and the world slowly came into focus. He was still in the laboratory, sitting in the chair. Aria was standing in front of him with a worried look on her face.

She was dressed for another party, but this time her clothing and makeup were much less extravagant.

Cole couldn't help smiling as soon as he saw her. He had thought he would never see her again. "You look really nice," he said without thinking.

Aria scowled at him. "How dare you scare us all like that!" she yelled at him.

Cole jumped and then smiled weakly. "Sorry," he said, although he wasn't exactly sure what he'd done wrong.

Then Cole recalled what had happened before he had passed out. Ulrik had intended to kill him. "Wait—what are you doing here? How am I still alive?"

Aria answered only the second question. "You almost weren't. Gale snuck us in here, but by the time we arrived, Ulrik had already given you the sleeping gas. At first, we thought—I thought—that we were too late." She looked away from him.

Cole tried to sit up, but he instantly fell back on the chair. A searing pain exploded from his chest. "Ouch!" He looked down at his chest in surprise.

"Don't look!" Aria said quickly, but it was too late. Cole closed his eyes, suddenly feeling very nauseated.

"Sorry," Aria said with a grimace. "Ulrik had already started the surgery before we got here. It's not too bad, though," she added optimistically.

Cole shook his head. His chest had a deep gash through the middle of it, and there was blood all around it.

"It's not fatal," Aria promised. "Just sit still until I can bandage you up, and then we'll get out of here." She grabbed some gauze and a roll of bandages. "Sit up and hold still," she ordered. Cole obeyed, and Aria quickly wrapped Cole's chest.

While she worked, Cole looked around at the rest of the room. Sarge was standing guard over Ulrik, who had been tied to a chair.

"You know the general will find out about this," Ulrik warned. "And when he does, you'll be sorry." He glanced at Cole and said, "Tell them to let me go."

Cole rolled his eyes and snorted. "So you can run and tell the general?" he asked.

"If you don't free me, I'll shout and alert the guards,"

Aria said to Ulrik, "Actually, Bryant told me that the laboratory is soundproof. Right now, we're the only people who can hear you." Ulrik's confident smile disappeared.

"Unfortunately for us," Sarge muttered.

Then Ulrik turned and looked at Aria. "Aria, please leave," he begged. "You shouldn't be here. If the general comes, you'll get in as much trouble as the rest of them."

Aria's eyes flashed with anger. "I don't care," she said as she finished tying Cole's bandages. "I'd rather die while doing the right thing than live like a coward—like you."

Ulrik looked like he was in pain. "I just want to protect you," he whispered. "I love you."

"I know." Aria's tone softened. "And I still love you, too. But I can't stay—you know that." She looked over at Cole and the others. "I have to go with them."

Ulrik looked devastated, but he nodded.

Cole tried to get out of the lab chair, but Aria shook her head. "Not yet," she warned. "You were out for a long time, and those chemicals were meant to kill you. It might not be safe for you to move around too much yet. Try to rest for a little while longer."

"What are you doing?" Cole mumbled. "Now you're all gonna get caught."

"No," Aria said impatiently. "Actually, we're all going to escape." Aria grinned triumphantly. "Just like I promised, remember?"

"Who's *we*?" Cole asked, but before he could answer, Gale came into the room with a middle-aged woman, who was pushing a cart. Cole vaguely remembered her from the last time he'd been captured and realized that it was Sarge's wife, Marylie. The cart was covered with a cloth, which Marylie soon removed. Underneath the cloth, she had stored a variety of supplies, including lots of food, water, and even some weapons. Cole was glad to see his sword in the pile.

"How did you get the sword back?" he asked.

"She insisted on finding it," Marylie said, nodded at Aria.

Aria shrugged. "It might come in handy," she argued. "In case you need to use the magic."

Cole nodded and grabbed the sword. "So, how are we getting out of here?" The idea of escaping seemed impossible.

"Don't worry about it," Aria said quickly. "We've got everything ready."

"Almost everything," Marylie corrected. She glanced at Cole and frowned. "This boy needs some clean clothes." Then she pulled out a pile of clothes she had stored at the bottom of the cart and handed them to Cole—a shirt, pants, and socks. "I also brought these. I think they will fit nicely." She handed Cole a pair of sturdy hiking boots.

"It's about time you cleaned up," Marylie said with a smile. "There's a bathroom down that hallway—the second door on the left, I think. You go wash up and try on those clothes while we figure out what to do next."

Cole nodded and walked down the hallway. Marylie had been right about the bathroom, and he found it easily. He immediately put his whole head under the sink faucet, trying to scrub all the grime off his face. Afterward he cleaned as much of his hands and arms as he could.

Eventually, Cole forced himself to turn off the water. He found a towel nearby and dried off. He quickly rubbed his hand through his hair, glad for it to finally feel clean again.

Then Cole changed into the new t-shirt and jeans Marylie had given him. He was glad to finally have something clean to wear.

Cole examined himself in the mirror. He still looked pretty terrible. He had a large bruise under his eye and his face looked sunken in from lack of food and sleep, but at least he had hope.

He was going to escape.

When he went back to the laboratory, everyone was deep in a discussion with the exception of Ulrik, who was waiting patiently in his chair.

Cole looked at Gale. "How long before the general comes down here to check on the progress?"

"He said he was preoccupied most of the night, so he would be checking in sometime tomorrow."

"Okay, then we have a while," Marylie said.

"But how can we get off the ship?" Cole asked, looking around at the group. "Please tell me someone has a plan?"

"Glad you asked," Gale said with a grin. "There are some small airships onboard. They'll move faster than this huge thing, and they're unguarded. Sarge will fly it."

"That'll never work," Ulrik imputed. "The general will catch you all and make you miserable." He struggled wildly against the bonds that held him to the chair. For a moment, Cole almost felt sorry for him.

Aria shook her head. "No, it will actually work perfectly. There's another party tonight," she said, blushing slightly and fumbling with her elegant dress. "I'm going to go first and make sure there aren't any guards stationed along the way." She looked at Sarge. "Meanwhile, it shouldn't be too hard for you to get into a ship, right?" Sarge nodded in agreement.

Gale looked at Marylie. "You can go with Sarge and take all our supplies in the food cart. Then I'll come with Cole, since he'll attract the most attention. Once we're all in the airship, we need to be ready to leave immediately."

Cole pointed at Ulrik. "What do you want to do with him? Should we take him with us?" Cole had never really liked Ulrik, but it still didn't seem right to leave him here.

Ulrik's eyes went wild with fear. He shook his head, looking at them as if they were insane. "Don't take me with you," he begged. "When the general finds you, you'll all be punished. I want to live."

Cole nodded. "Okay, that takes care of him then. We'll leave him tied up so that the general will know he didn't help us escape."

Gale looked at Cole. "But we're still forgetting the most important part—you."

"I'm not completely helpless." Cole grinned. "Without those chains, I can already feel the magic returning. It'll take a while to get it all back, but by now I have enough to use if we get into trouble. Hopefully it won't come to that, though," he added. Cole looked around at the small group. "Gale and I will come as fast as we can," he promised. He didn't mention that they would have to take a quick detour.

Cole looked around at everyone. They were all putting their lives at risk for him, and Cole didn't take their sacrifice lightly. "Thank you," he finally said, feeling a little choked up. "For everything. I thought I was alone, but I now realize how many friends I have."

Marylie smiled at him. "It's the least we could do, dear. I just wish we had done something earlier."

There was a moment of silence, and then Aria asked, "Now what do we do?"

Cole grinned. "We escape."

CHAPTER 33

Sarge and Marylie left first, and then Aria followed. Cole was starting to feel both nervous and excited.

Gale looked at Cole. "Are you ready?" Gale asked.

Cole nodded. He put the sword in its sheath, and they walked out the door. Aria had already distracted the one guard that had been in their path. Since almost all of the soldiers were already at the party, most of the corridors were empty.

Cole followed Gale up flight after flight of stairs until they were finally on the deck of the ship. Cole looked over the railing. They were so high up that he couldn't see anything below him but clouds. Gale motioned to him and then whispered, "The ship Sarge was talking about is down those stairs." He pointed to another flight of stairs across from where they were standing.

Cole nodded. "Okay," he said. "Would you happen to know where the party is, by any chance?"

Gale stopped and turned to stare at Cole. "You cannot be serious." When Cole didn't answer, Gale shook his head. "Why do you want to go to the place where every soldier on the ship is? Are you trying to get captured again?"

"No," Cole said quickly. He couldn't help laughing at how stupid this was. Every part of him was screaming to escape, but he couldn't leave yet. "There's something I need to do first."

"Is it worth more than your life?"

"Probably not," Cole admitted. But he knew he needed to do it, anyway.

When Gale looked uncertain, Cole said, "I promise I won't get caught. Now, where's the party?"

Gale didn't look happy, but he pointed to the left. "Is there any way I can help?" he asked.

"Actually, yes," Cole nodded. "Could you go in there and find Bryant and tell him to come here? Then you can head to the airship, and I'll meet you there." From the look on Gale's face, Cole knew Gale was about to refuse. "Or I'll go and find Bryant myself," he threatened.

Gale groaned in frustration. "This is a terrible idea," he warned. Cole just smiled—Gale was already walking toward the party.

A few minutes later, Cole heard a soldier's boots clicking down the hallway in his direction. He hid behind a corner and pulled out his sword. Then he waited, trying not to panic. Bryant was only a few feet away.

The clicking stopped. Cole took a deep breath and stepped around the corner.

When Bryant saw Cole, he looked shocked, then furious. "What are you doing here?" he asked furiously. "We were told you would be killed tonight."

"Sorry to disappoint," Cole muttered sarcastically.

Bryant looked at Cole suspiciously. "So you're free. Now what? You know you can't hope to escape."

Cole's grip on his sword tightened. He tried to sound menacing. "You took something from me, and I promised I would get it back. Give me Aria's necklace, and you won't get hurt."

Bryant smirked. He pulled the necklace from his pocket and dangled it in front of himself. "Hurt *me*? I doubt you will be able to. Besides, it's too late. I've already shown it to Aria. She actually believes you gave it to me." Bryant laughed. "I'll give it back to her after you're dead."

Cole clenched his teeth. "Unfortunately, I'm not dying. So why don't you just give me the necklace?"

"Make me," Bryant taunted.

"Gladly." Cole held the sword up and pointed it straight at Bryant's chest. Even though they were several feet apart, a blast of energy shot out of the sword, throwing Bryant up against the wall. Bryant's head hit the wall hard, and then he went unconscious.

Knowing the noise would attract the guards' attention, Cole moved as quickly as possible. He grabbed the necklace from Bryant's limp hands and then sprinted down the stairs Gale had pointed to earlier. Soon he was in a large aircraft hangar full of smaller airships. Aria was standing near one of the airships waving to get Cole's attention.

Cole ran over to the airship, jumped in, and shouted, "Go! Now!" Sarge nodded and began flying the smaller airship out of the hangar.

Amazingly enough, no one had even noticed their escape.

Soon their airship was in the air, and before Cole could process what had happened, the general's airship was already out of sight. Sarge had been right—this smaller airship was much faster than the general's, and with the cloud coverage to help hide them, they were nearly impossible to find.

Cole sat down, breathing heavily. Everyone sat quietly for a while, smiling at their success. Finally, Gale asked the question no one else wanted to ask. "So . . . now what?"

No one had an answer. All Cole wanted was freedom, to be able to live his life how he wanted, but he knew General Sylvester. The general would never stop looking for him. Not as long as there was a chance the general could recover the magic. It wasn't hard to imagine what the general would do with that power.

There was only one course of action. Cole took a deep breath and said, "We do the right thing."

Everyone else looked confused, but Aria instantly understood what Cole meant. "No," she said stubbornly, shaking her head. "I was wrong to force you to do that, and I'm sorry—okay? You don't have to do this."

Cole shook his head. "No, Aria. For the first time, I actually want to do this. Think about it: the magic's too powerful. Someone will always be searching for it—for me—trying to find it and control it. I'd always be looking over my shoulder. What kind of a life is that?"

Cole looked over at Sarge. "Can you fly us to the Center Stones? Follow the canyon surrounding Rhomac until we get to the corner where two canyons meet."

Aria was furious. Cole knew he should be taking the situation seriously, but all he could do was laugh. He found it very funny that suddenly Aria didn't want him to release the magic anymore.

"It's not funny," Aria said with irritation. "This is serious."

"Would someone like to fill the rest of us in on what's going on?" Gale finally asked. Aria looked at Gale, and he shriveled under her intense glare. "Or not," he added hastily, "since you two are obviously very busy right now."

"No," Aria said, calming down. "It's not you, Gale." She glared at Cole again. "He's just trying to do the one thing we finally agreed *not* to do—the thing that he says will kill him!"

"Um, that makes no sense," Gale stated.

Cole shook his head. "She's just upset because this was what we argued about—right before she turned me in," he said, trying to explain. "I have no idea how to do it or if it will even work, but Ulrik had a theory. He said if we traveled to a certain place—he called it the Center Stones—then I would be able to release the magic."

"And Cole thinks it will kill him," Aria repeated.

"So . . . we just risked our lives to free you, and now you want to do something that could kill you," Gale summarized.

"See?" Aria said triumphantly. "This is a terrible idea."

Cole shrugged. "I want to do this," he said bravely, trying to convince himself. He looked at Aria. "You might be crazy," he teased, "But you were right when you said the magic wasn't meant to belong to just one person. As long as I have the magic, the general will always be after it—after me. I'll never really be free from him unless I give it up."

Aria was still shaking her head, but Gale nodded in agreement. "All right."

Now the full force of Aria's anger turned on Gale. "What?" she asked in confusion. "No, you're supposed to stop him—"

"We can't stop him," Gale said. "And he has some good points. It's a shot in the dark, but it's also the only plan anyone has right now."

Cole nodded. "He's right, you know," he said, trying to suppress a yawn. "You're not going to be able to stop me."

Aria's glare darkened, but Cole looked out the window and tried to ignore her. "I'm exhausted." He was barely able to keep his eyes open. "If you don't mind, I'm going to try to get some sleep. Wake me up when we get there."

He spread across several seats that were in the back of the airship, and he was asleep almost as soon as he had closed his eyes.

CHAPTER 34

Cole was still sleeping when Sarge landed the airship. When Cole woke up, he opened his eyes to find Aria giving him a furious look. She had traded her dress for jeans and a t-shirt, but she still looked beautiful. Cole smiled at her, but that only made her even angrier.

"We're here," she said furiously. "I still wish you wouldn't do this."

Cole laughed. "You spent all that time earlier trying to convince me to do this—telling me you wanted this more than anything. Why the change of heart now?"

"I might have changed my mind about the whole 'hero' thing," she admitted. "I want you to do what you want. I don't want you to do it because of me. If something happens to you . . ." She faded off, but the sentiment was clear.

Cole looked at her, trying to act braver than he felt. "If something happens, then it will have been my choice, not yours." He paused for a moment, trying to decide what to say next. He wanted so much for her to understand. "The general will always be searching for us—for me. He wants the magic, Aria. And if he gets it, who knows how much pain he will cause. I need to do everything I can to prevent him from ever being able to control it."

Aria nodded. "I know," she said softly, turning away from him. She walked out of the airship, calling back over her shoulder, "Come on. Everyone else is waiting."

Cole hesitated. Even though he had told Aria that he wanted to do this, he hadn't been entirely honest. He was absolutely terrified. He looked up at the ceiling of the airship, trying to calm his frantic heart. Ulrik's warning came rushing back to him, reminding him that he may not survive.

Either way, Cole knew he needed to do this. If the general ever captured Cole again and discovered a way to control the magic . . . Cole shook his head. He couldn't let that happen. Taking a deep breath, he gathered his courage and climbed out of the ship.

After Cole's feet hit the ground, he turned and looked at his surroundings. The ground was still the same—flat plains full of tall grass and weeds. Towering over the otherwise flat landscape were seven tall, black rocks, forming a circle. In the very center was a huge, black rock shaped like an anvil—just like in the story Aria had told Cole.

In that instant, Cole realized what he had to do to release the magic. His sword didn't look like the one from Aria's story, but he hoped it would still work. Ulrik had said that he needed to release the magic into the Center Stones, and he had a feeling the anvil was the key.

He walked toward the giant anvil.

Then he stopped and turned around, remembering something. He walked over to Aria, who had been standing a few feet behind him, and he held out her necklace. She looked at Cole in surprise. "But . . . Bryant had it. He showed it to me last night at the party. He said you *gave* it to him."

Cole laughed. "Well, Bryant lied. What a surprise," he added sarcastically. "Bryant saw it in my hands and took it from me. I promised him I would get it back and return it to you."

Aria suddenly realized what Cole had done. "That's what you had to do before we left, wasn't it?" she said as she took the necklace and held it tightly in her hand.

Cole nodded. "I couldn't let Bryant keep it."

"Well, that wasn't very smart of you," Aria said. "You could have been captured or killed."

Cole smirked, which just earned him another glare from Aria. He turned and began to walk away.

"Wait!" Aria suddenly called out to him. "I have something to tell you."

He turned around to look at her, but she didn't say anything. "What?" he finally asked.

She hesitated and then shook her head. "I can't tell you—not unless you survive this. Promise me you'll make it through this."

Cole smiled, but he didn't say anything. They both knew there was no way he could promise that. He walked over to Gale, who was standing nearby.

"You sure you want to do this?" Gale asked quietly. "No one will blame you if you back out now."

"Actually, I'm sure I *don't* want to do this," Cole admitted. He wanted to back out. He was terrified of what might happen. He didn't want to die, especially now.

Cole shook his head. "No, I don't *want* to do this, but I *need* to do this," he said resolutely.

Gale nodded in agreement with Cole's decision before saying, "Then I have to ask, what is 'this' exactly? Have you figured out what you are supposed to do yet?"

Cole frowned. "Maybe," he said unconvincingly. "I have an idea, at least."

Then he took the sword over to the giant anvil. The surface of the anvil was smooth, without even a scratch. There was no slot for the sword, but Cole knew the magic would create one. With the sword's tip pointing toward the anvil, he raised the sword high above his head.

Cole took a deep breath and then plunged the sword into the anvil.

The sword easily pierced the anvil. Cole could feel the magic coursing through him. It was working. The anvil was accepting the magic. It reminded Cole of the time the general used his sword to extract the magic from Cole.

Then, just like in the laboratory, the magic fought back. Cole clenched his teeth. The magic resisted and tried to hide deeper inside of him, fighting against the pull of the anvil. It was as if the magic didn't want to leave him, but the anvil was forcing it out. The pain was excruciating, and Cole struggled to keep hold of his sword.

But he wasn't going to give up this time. He held on to the sword with all of his strength, refusing to let go.

Cole tried to remain focused on his reasons to keep fighting. He reminded himself of all the pain he would endure if the general ever captured him again, and this was the only way to prevent the general from ever getting his hands on the magic.

Despite the pain, Cole looked over at Aria and smiled. He was willing to let the magic go. Suddenly, the magic stopped resisting. The pain stopped. Cole could feel the magic's willingness to go. He continued to feel it leaving his body until there was nothing left.

All of the sudden, a giant light filled the circle of black rocks. Cole wasn't sure where it came from, but it was blinding. When the light disappeared, Cole looked at Aria again and grinned. He'd done it. The magic was gone. He took a step toward Aria, but then next thing he knew, he was falling toward the ground. He heard someone call his name, and then his world went dark.

CHAPTER 35

✵ ARIA ✵

Aria looked down at the necklace—her necklace. A million thoughts rushed through her head: surprise, sadness, anger, frustration. She didn't know exactly what to say. "But . . . Bryant had it. He showed it to me last night at the party." She didn't want to mention how much it had hurt to see Bryant with it. "He said you *gave* it to him."

"Well, Bryant lied. What a surprise," Cole said sarcastically. Aria was relieved Cole hadn't actually given it to Bryant. "Bryant saw it in my hands and took it from me. I promised I would get it back and return it to you." He held the necklace out to her.

As Aria took the necklace and held it tightly in her hand, she suddenly realized how Cole must have gotten it back. "That's what you had to do before we left, wasn't it?"

Cole nodded, "I couldn't let Bryant keep it."

Aria reminded herself that she was still angry with him. She narrowed her eyes. "Well, that wasn't very smart of you." She crossed her arms. "You could have been captured or killed."

Cole just gave that annoying smirk that made her want to punch him in the face, but at the same time she couldn't help wanting to smile back at him. Instead, she just settled for another glare.

Cole turned toward the Stones. Aria knew what was going to happen. She recognized the anvil from her stories. She remembered the story she had told Cole—the one about the girl. She also remembered what happened to the girl at the end of the story.

She wanted to stop Cole. She wanted to tell him he couldn't do this, that he couldn't die for this. But she saw the determination in his eyes.

She looked at her parents—she still wasn't used to calling them that. They were standing nearby and silently observing. She thought about everything that had happened since she found Cole. She knew he was willing to do this, and she also knew he needed to do it. He was right; there was no other way to escape the general.

But she wasn't willing to let Cole go.

"Wait!" she shouted all of the sudden. "I have something to tell you."

Cole looked back at her. He raised his eyebrow and waited. But for the first time in her life, she didn't know what to say.

"What?" Cole finally asked.

Aria opened her mouth, but what was she going to say? There were too many things that needed to be said. She knew none of it would matter—if he died. She looked at him and shook her head. "I can't tell you—not unless you survive this. Promise me you'll make it through this," she begged.

Cole smile, but he didn't promise anything. With mounting dread, Aria realized that neither of them knew what was going to happen. He couldn't promise to survive. Just like that, he walked away. She couldn't hear any of his conversation with Gale, but it was over soon. Aria watched Cole move toward the giant anvil in the center. She didn't want to watch, but she couldn't tear her eyes away from him.

With a determined look on his face, Cole lifted his sword above his head. Aria couldn't help smiling as she realized how much Cole had changed since the first time she met him. Then Cole quickly plunged the sword into the rock.

Aria could see the pain in his eyes.

She wanted to help him. She tried to step forward, but Sarge put a hand on her shoulder and kept her back. She watched silently, but every part of her wanted to help him. She held her necklace close and rubbed it nervously.

Even though none of them could see what was actually happening, the pain on Cole's face was evident. Suddenly, he looked up, right at Aria. She looked back at him, hoping it was finally over. Cole looked at her and smiled. She smiled back at him. He was okay. She knew everything was going to be fine now.

Then a blinding light exploded from the anvil. Aria's heart leapt out of her chest. She knew that the light was the magic. It spread out toward the black rocks until the whole circle was covered in the blinding light. She closed her eyes to shield them from the light.

Cole had done it! He had released the magic.

Just as quickly as the light had come, it disappeared. Cole grinned and took a step toward her. Aria allowed herself to breathe again. He was fine. Everything was fine now.

Then Cole stumbled and fell toward the ground. Aria called his name, but he didn't stand up again. She immediately ran toward him but stopped suddenly, unable to make herself move again, barely able to breathe. "No," she whispered to herself.

Cole was lying there beside the anvil. Aria didn't have to move any closer to know she was too late.

He was gone.

Aria couldn't move. She couldn't cry. Everything moved in slow motion. She felt the wind blowing across her face, and for a brief second, she smelled the wild flowers around her. She watched everyone else run up to Cole. Sarge checked Cole's heart rate. Gale spoke quietly, but Aria couldn't hear what he said. She stared at the scene as if she were watching a play.

This wasn't real. It couldn't be real.

Marylie stepped toward Aria. "Are you all right?"

Suddenly, the spell was broken. Aria looked at Cole again, but this time she knew the truth. "No," she whispered. She stared at Cole for another second. Then she stepped backward and began to run.

Aria ran as far and as fast as she could. With every individual beat from her heart, she was reminded that Cole's heart was silent. With each gasping breath she took, she remembered his face. She saw him laughing, teasing her. She tried to run harder, hoping that the wind rushing past her face would also take the memories with it. No matter how hard she tried, she couldn't erase the image of Cole lying on the ground.

Dead.

Finally, she couldn't run any further. Aria suddenly stopped and fell to the ground, barely able to breathe. She could feel the warm tears falling down her face, and that only made her cry harder. She remembered the adorable face Cole made every time he was irritated with her. Despite the tears, she couldn't help smiling as she remembered when he had admitted to liking her. And she remembered how embarrassed he had gotten every time she had teased him.

The long, dry grass blew in the wind and rubbed against her arms. She heard someone in the distance calling her name. But all she could see was Cole's face.

She thought back to every time she had imagined this event. She had wanted Cole to be the hero so badly, but this wasn't how it was supposed to end. This wasn't the fairy-tale ending she had envisioned.

Everything was all wrong.

Aria opened her hands and looked at the necklace she was still holding—her necklace. She wrapped the necklace chain around her fingers, imagining the risks Cole had taken to give it to her. Even after everything she had done to him, he risked being captured again just to get her necklace back.

She slowly traced the metal trimmings that decorated the sapphire heart. This heart had meant everything to her.

Now she couldn't even stand to look at it.

Cole had been right. He had warned her that this could happen, but she had never really believed him. And now it was too late.

He was gone.

She dug a small hole in the ground. The cool dirt crumbled easily under her fingers, like pieces of sand. She looked at her necklace one more time and then clutched it in her fist.

With tears running down her face, she whispered. "I loved you." The wind carried her secret confession away, but with that one phrase, Aria knew she had finally grown up. She had unveiled the deepest secret in her heart—the one she had never had the courage to tell Cole.

And now, it was a secret no one would ever know.

Tears dripped onto the dirt ground like tiny raindrops. Then Aria took a deep breath and gently placed her necklace in the hole. With shaky hands, she picked up a small handful of dirt and buried it forever.

"There you are!" someone called out. Aria lifted her head off the ground and looked around. Marylie was running toward her. "Your dad and I were so afraid that we had lost you again."

Aria looked at this woman—her mother—silently. Aria was a little hesitant to share too much because they still barely knew each other. But right now, more than anything, she needed someone to comfort her. Without thinking, she stood up and hugged her. If her mother was surprised, Aria couldn't tell. Aria wanted to cry, but she had no more tears left. All she said was, "I couldn't stay and watch that, to watch him—" Her voice caught again.

Her mother's arms wrapped around her tightly. "I know," she whispered.

Aria nodded, but she was barely paying attention. She swallowed hard. She couldn't breathe. "It hurts so bad," she moaned softly.

Marylie smiled gently. "That's why they call it heartbreak," she said. "You can pick up the pieces and put yourself back together, but nothing will ever be the same as it was before. For better or worse, you'll carry a fragment of him around with you forever."

Aria choked on another sob. "I didn't want this." All of her fears came flying out of her mouth. "This is all of my fault. I'm the one who convinced him to do this, and I told him nothing would happen."

Marylie wrapped her in another big hug. "This was his choice, and he stood by it. Cole was many things, but he wasn't stupid. He knew what he was getting into, and he accepted those risks. Now we just need to accept his decision."

Aria didn't answer. Marylie hugged her tightly. Aria stayed in her embrace for as long as she could, letting the comfort wash over her heavy heart. She would have stayed there forever if it meant she could forget Cole. Unfortunately, she couldn't—and she'd never be able to.

"Let's get back to the others," Marylie suggested.

Aria nodded, and they walked back together.

When they got back to the ship, Sarge was digging a hole. Not just a hole—it was a grave.

Gale was standing beside Cole's lifeless body. Reality hit Aria afresh—Cole was really gone.

When Gale saw Aria, he walked over to her quickly. "I'm sorry, Aria. I tried everything, but it was no use. His heart was made of metal, infused with Anyrite to make it work. When he released the magic, he unfortunately also released his heart's lifeforce. Without it, he just has a piece of hard metal where his heart should have been."

Aria nodded and stood back as they prepared to bury him. Gale and Sarge bent down to carry Cole's body. They were about to put him in the ground.

"Wait," Aria said suddenly. She walked over to the sword and pulled it out. It came out of the anvil easily. Aria carried it over to Cole. Then she grabbed his cold, lifeless hands and gently wrapped them around the sword. Even though he was dead, she didn't shudder or back away. Instead, she stared at his face. More than anything, she wanted him to be alive again. But nothing happened.

He was gone.

Another tear rolled down Aria's face, and she stood up. "There. He's a hero. He should be buried with his sword." She smiled through her tears—if Cole were still alive, he would be cringing at the thought of being called a hero. She knew it was a bit dramatic to be buried with a sword, but she couldn't think of any other way to honor his death.

Gale again leaned down to help Sarge pick up Cole's body, but he stopped suddenly. He quickly looked at Aria, then back at Cole. He put his head to Cole's chest and looked up in disbelief.

"I think he's . . . breathing!"

CHAPTER 36

"Shh. Try to stay still and rest." Aria's voice was the first thing Cole heard. He turned his head toward the noise, and Aria's face slowly came into focus. He was back in the ship, and he was lying down on the seats in the back. His head felt like it was about to explode, and he felt too weak to even move.

Aria smiled, but there were tears in her eyes. "You're awake," she said, as though she couldn't believe it.

Cole grimaced. "What happened? I feel like I just died," he joked.

"You did," Aria said. Now tears were actually running down her face. "You did just die." She was crying even harder now. "I was so scared. I thought you were gone forever—" She broke off suddenly and rubbed her eyes.

Cole wanted to comfort her. "It's okay." He tried to sit up, but then he felt a sharp pain in his chest and fell back down with a groan.

Aria laughed. "You never listen, do you? I already told you: stay still!"

Cole glared at her, but he wasn't really mad. "I'll stay still if you stay here and talk to me," he offered.

Aria nodded and sat down nearby. "Deal."

They talked for almost an hour straight about every little thing they could think of. Aria told Cole all about what she had been doing while they were on the general's ship.

"It drove Bryant crazy knowing I had given you the necklace," she said after a while. "When he showed it to me, he was furious. He told me that he was going to have the general kill you."

Cole laughed. "I still can't see how he ever thought you liked him."

Aria blushed slightly. "I talked with him at the parties, mostly because—" She sighed. "Well, it was mostly because I wanted to teach you a lesson." She cringed and laughed uncomfortably, saying, "It sounds so stupid now."

Cole laughed. "Well, consider that mission successful," he said, only half-joking. "Bryant definitely made sure I heard about every dinner and dance you two went to."

Aria winced. "I really am sorry," she said.

"Me, too," Cole said. "I shouldn't have lied to you, either." He grinned and put a hand over his chest. "Trust me—I learned my lesson."

Aria didn't look convinced, but she changed the subject. "What did you do to Bryant, anyway? How did you get the necklace back?"

Cole told her the whole story, assuring Aria that he hadn't killed Bryant.

Aria sighed. "Good. As annoying as he was, I've had enough death lately to last me a lifetime."

Cole laughed. "Can you tell me what happened? After I..." He paused. The words felt strange to say. "After I died."

Aria's face clouded with grief, and she shook her head. "I can't. I can't even describe how terrible it felt. It was the worst thing I have ever experienced in my life." She paused for a moment. Then she smiled. "Besides, it really doesn't matter now."

Cole was able to walk around later that night. He left the ship with Aria and went into the circle of rocks to join everyone else. Sarge and Gale were busy setting up tents for everyone to sleep, and Marylie was busily cooking over a large fire. When they saw Cole, everyone stopped what they were doing and came over to talk.

After Sarge and Marylie had expressed how glad they were to see him up and moving, they took Aria over to the fire and began talking to her. They had barely had a moment alone with their daughter, and Cole knew they deserved it. Aria seemed to be more and more accepting of their relationship.

Gale stood near Cole, watching the reunion.

"That's got to be hard," Gale said sympathetically. "And very awkward."

Cole nodded. "I can't imagine," he agreed. "Maybe we should give them a little more privacy?"

They began walking slowly out of the circle of rocks. At first, neither one of them spoke. "Well, you sure scared all of us," Gale said.

"Aria said I died?" Cole still couldn't believe it.

Gale nodded. "When you released the magic, it also took the Anyrite from your heart. The Anyrite enabled your metal heart to pump blood through your body. The actual metal heart wasn't lost; however, the life force that made it work was no longer in you. Without it, your heart couldn't work, and you died."

Cole stood still, deep in thought. "It's strange to think about." He was silent for a while, and then asked, "How am I alive now?"

Gale shrugged. "I'm not entirely sure. My theory is that when you released the magic, a part of it stayed inside the sword. When we were going to bury you—" Cole looked at Gale in shock, and Gale added defensively, "You were dead!"

Gale continued, "Anyway, when we were going to bury you, Aria thought it would be more fitting to bury you with your sword. She pulled your sword out of the rock and put it in your hands. After she did that, you started breathing."

Cole stared out at the wasteland in front of them. Nothing looked any more different than it had before. "Did it work?" he finally asked. "Did I release the magic—or whatever I was supposed to do?"

Gale shrugged. "It's impossible to tell for sure, but I think you did. When you thrust the sword into the anvil, there was a bright flash of light that seemed to spread out across the sky—like a wave."

Cole frowned. "Do you think it's gone for good?"

Gale shrugged. "I have no idea," he admitted. "But I'm sure people will find out soon. If the magic is back, then there's going to be plenty of people with questions."

"Well, at least the general won't be able to get to it now, right?" Cole said, trying to be positive.

Gale hesitated. "Hopefully. The magic is so spread out now that it would be nearly impossible. Besides, there's no way to harness it from people—like we saw with you."

Cole nodded, and they began walking back toward the others. When Aria saw them, she walked up to Cole.

"I never told you what I was going to tell you before you released the magic," she said teasingly.

Cole smiled and looked at her. "I have something to tell you, too. But it can wait," he said, looking around him. "Right now, this is perfect."

Aria laughed. "I'm so glad you're still here," she whispered to him quietly.

"Me, too," Cole agreed.

ACKNOWLEDGMENTS

You would think that the Acknowledgments would be the easiest part to write, especially since I just wrote a book! Truthfully, though, there are so many people that deserve to be thanked for the time and encouragement they have given me throughout this long process. There aren't enough words to describe how grateful I am.

First, I'd like to thank my parents for their endless support. I'm sure they thought I was crazy when I first announced my plan to write a book, but they still encouraged and helped me every step of the way. They listened to me and supported me through the many highs and lows of the writing process. I could never have done this without their faith in me.

Next, I'd like to thank my sister Carissa for reading and rereading the many versions of my book. From the very beginning, she was there, listening to me go on and on—and on. She spent many late nights reassuring me that everything would work out. She's the greatest little sister in the world!

Also, thank you to my younger brothers, Brayden and Derek. They often seemed more excited about the release of my book than I was, and I love them both so much.

I would also love to thank my Aunt Maribeth for all of the amazing suggestions she brought to the editing and formatting process—and not just because she is editing this page. Seriously, though, she was a lifesaver. She spent countless hours reading, editing, and formatting my book. Her insight and experience with publishing has helped strengthen not only *Magic Made* but also my writing as a whole.

In addition, I would like to acknowledge my two other excellent beta readers, Sarah Gillenwater and Beth Cofer. Their detailed analysis of my book helped me see and overcome the weaknesses in my original story and transform it into the book it is now. Because of them, I have a much stronger story.

Thank you to all of my other family members as well. So many of them provided feedback, offered proofreading skills, and showered me with encouragement along the way. It is very reassuring to have so many people supporting me and my book. I wish I had enough room to mention everyone by name, but I want them to know how much I really do appreciate each of them! They helped make this dream possible.

Lastly, I would like to thank all of my friends, teachers, and classmates for sharing my excitement throughout this long process. Their help was invaluable—they offered to beta read, gave me feedback on my cover, and even just provided me with an encouraging smile when I needed it. Their incredible and amazing support really helped me to persevere to the end. I would especially like to thank my entire Creative Writing class. Throughout the year, their excitement for writing encouraged me and gave me the confidence to believe in my book.

Once again, thank you to everyone who shared in my writing adventure. All of the support I received is more appreciated than I could ever fully express.

ABOUT THE AUTHOR

Ashley Hayes is an adventurer, with a love for anything magical, mysterious, or exciting. While she would have loved to have wings, super-super speed, or the ability to shape-shift, she has no significant superpowers (yet). Even more unfortunately, she never received her Hogwarts acceptance letter, and she still hasn't found a way into Narnia. Left with no other choice, she decided to create her own adventures.

Ashley currently lives at home with her mom, dad, sister, and two very loud brothers. Once she graduates high school, she will be attending college to begin her next life adventure. When she isn't writing, Ashley enjoys reading, singing, or exploring the great outdoors.

For more information about Ashley Hayes:
ashleyhayesbooks.com

Book 2—Coming Soon!

An excerpt from

MAGIC TAKEN

Cole stood still and stared out at the wasteland in front of him. He could feel the tall grass moving around him. Other than the sound of the wind rushing past his face, it was completely silent. Everything was so calm that it almost felt magical. Then Cole remembered why he was here. He took a deep breath, closed his eyes, and waited patiently to feel something—anything.

It had been a week since Cole had released the magic and set it free across Lathinium. He hadn't seen any difference, but he had definitely felt the change inside of him. He could feel where the magic had been, and he could also feel that it was now gone.

Before, it had been like a storm inside of him that he had barely been able to control. Now, though, he was empty.

The magic had left him.

Cole finally gave up. He knew he wasn't going to feel the magic anymore. He opened his eyes again and watched the grass bending in the wind. Cole knew he shouldn't be upset about losing the magic. He had never wanted it to begin with, and compared to everything else that could have happened, losing the magic seemed like such a small price to pay.

But Cole missed the magic. He missed the strength it had given him—the feeling of raw power running through his body. Without it, Cole was powerless.

He looked behind him, just to make sure no one was nearby. Then he pulled out the sword that was strapped to his back and swung it around in the air slowly. He always felt a little ridiculous when he had his sword out. It was old—pretty much useless against the guns used by General Sylvester and his soldiers—but it had allowed Cole to control the magic. He remembered training with Ulrik, feeling the power coursing through his body. He had been so strong.

Then the general had found him again and reminded him of how weak he really was. Even with the magic, Cole had barely been able to escape alive. Now that the magic was gone, Cole was completely unprepared. He looked down at the sword in his hands. If anything happened, all he would have is this rusty old relic from the past to defend himself.

Cole dropped the sword to the ground in frustration. It was powerless.

He was powerless.

"Good morning."

Cole jumped and then relaxed when he realized it was Aria. She grinned. "Wow, you're tense today. What's wrong?"

"Nothing," Cole said quickly.

"Oh, sure," Aria said sarcastically. "That's why you're up early, standing in the middle of nowhere—by yourself." She picked the sword up and examined it. "Were you trying to attack the grass?"

Cole laughed. "Give that back." He reached for the sword, but Aria kept it out of his reach.

"Tell me what's wrong first."

"Nothing," Cole repeated. "I mean, everything's perfect now, right? We escaped, released the magic, stopped General Sylvester and Ulrik from controlling it—"

"Kept you from dying," Aria added.

"Right," Cole agreed. "Everything's great."

Aria nodded and handed Cole his sword back. "So why don't you sound convinced?"

Cole hesitated. He hadn't told anyone the truth yet. "The magic's gone."

"Isn't that obvious? You released it, remember?"

"No, that's not what I meant," Cole corrected. "I meant that it's all gone inside of me. I can't feel it anywhere—not even a little."

"And that's a bad thing?" Aria looked surprised. "I thought you didn't even want it in the first place."

"I didn't. I still don't—" He broke off suddenly because that was a lie. He did want the magic.

"Then I'm confused. What's the problem?"

Cole struggled to find the right words to describe how he was feeling. "The problem is that I need the magic. It was an energy boost—it made me stronger, braver, and more powerful. It protected me. What if something happens now? I can't do anything to help." He looked at his sword again. "I can't even use this piece of junk in a fight," he muttered.

Aria laughed. "The magic didn't make you anything different; it just helped you show off who you were. Just because you have a weapon, it doesn't mean you're a warrior. The magic works the same way. Sure, it was powerful, but you were only able to use it because you were already strong and brave. Nothing's changed." She thought for a moment and then added, "Except I think all the heroics should be saved for the fairy tales—no more dying, okay?"

That made Cole grin. "Really?" he said sarcastically. "It's funny. I feel like I've told you that before."

"Okay," Aria said. "You were right about the fairy-tale thing. Don't let it go to your head, though." They were silent for a minute. Then Aria added, "But I was right, too. You were right to release the magic."

Cole tried to hide his smile. Even after everything, Aria still suffered from a severely strong case of moral obligation.

"So . . . did you get any magic?" he asked, remembering how badly Aria had wanted it before.

Aria's face fell. "No," she admitted. "It's too bad—I would have been great with the magic." Her eyes lit up. "Can you imagine me being able to move objects or freeze water or explode things?"

Cole just stared at her. For some reason, the thought of Aria having the magic absolutely terrified him. "I think you would do a little too much exploding if you had the magic," he said. But he still couldn't help grinning as he imagined Aria charging into Ambroise, fighting all the injustice in the world.

Aria glared at him. "I would have used the magic responsibly," she argued. "Probably better than you did."

"Well, I guess we'll never know," Cole said. "Since you didn't get any of the magic."

That comment earned him another glare.

Then someone cleared their throat, and they both quickly turned around. Gale was standing a few feet behind them. "Sorry to interrupt." Cole didn't think he looked too sorry.

Aria smiled. "Good morning! How did you sleep?"

"Yeah, good morning," Cole repeated, with slightly less enthusiasm than Aria had shown.

"I slept fine." He looked at Aria. "Your parents are awake. They asked me to get you two for breakfast. Marylie's cooking this morning."

Cole grinned. Aria's mom made the best food. "Then what are we still doing here? Let's go eat."

Aria grinned mischievously. "Race you back," she said. Before Cole could even process what she had said, she was already sprinting toward their camp.

"Hey, no fair!" Cole shouted. He and Gale both took off after her.

When they raced into the campsite, Marylie was bent over a small fire, stirring something in a pot. She looked up when she heard them. "Good morning, dears. Breakfast will be ready in a little while."

"Great," Cole said enthusiastically.

"But first, we need to discuss something," she added.

Cole's good mood instantly vanished. The tone in her voice didn't sound good. "Discuss what?" he asked hesitantly.

Marylie didn't answer him.

"What's going on?" Cole repeated.

Marylie glanced at Sarge and coughed slightly.

Finally, Sarge took a deep breath and shifted his gaze as he looked at Cole, Aria, and Gale in turn. "Marylie and I have made a decision, and we expect all of you to follow it. Do you all understand?"

Aria and Gale nodded. Cole wasn't sure where this was headed, but he also nodded in agreement. "Fine. What is it?" he asked impatiently.

Sarge hesitated for a moment longer. "Remember that we have your best interest at heart—all three of you." He looked at Cole. "We're going to look out for you guys—"

"Dad," Aria interrupted impatiently. Cole noticed that she still made a slight face whenever she used that word, but at least she seemed to be making an effort to create a relationship with her parents. "Just tell us what's going on."

Cole held his breath. Whatever Sarge was planning, it didn't sound good.

Sarge met Cole's eyes. In a low, quiet voice, he finally said, "We've decided to go back to Rhomac."

Made in the USA
San Bernardino, CA
13 May 2019